My Hipster Santa

My Hipster Santa

MAG MAURY

WARM PUBLISHING

Translated from the French by Rafaela Reece

WARM PUBLISHING
El Paso, Texas
www.warmpublishing.com

Original title: *My Hipster Christmas*
published by Éditions Addictives
Paris, France

Copyright ©2020 Edisource
Interior design by Rafaela Reece

ISBN: 978-1-7345961-7-5

*But if you tame me, then we shall
need each other. To me, you will
be unique in all the world. To you,
I shall be unique in all the world.*

Antoine de Saint-Exupéry,
Le Petit Prince

To my father, gone too soon.
Every snowflake is a tear that
I shed upon your absence.

one

*Be the change you want
to see in the world.*

Ghandi

Line[1]

As I stand among the boxes cluttering my apartment, my eyes rest on the rooftops of Liverpool where the low clouds seem to caress each tile. I hope to see the snow fall, to catch winter's first snowflake swirling in front of the window. Even though my childhood spirit usually resurfaces at this time of the year and fills me with wonder, this year, I'm having a hard time getting in the mood.

I'm petrified.

But this fear is only temporary. It's nothing but the reflection of our ignorance about certain things. And quite often, it's the fear of the unknown that paralyzes us. Once we take that first step, it flies away, and we can breathe again. My grandpa would always say: "Time heals almost everything, so give yourself a little bit of time." And I think that it is now time for me to turn the page and start fresh. This new life that I'm about to undertake, I will undertake alone. Choices will be mine and I will own my decisions. Up until now, I was a model employee, always following orders. My actions weren't my own, I was just mindlessly doing as I was

---

[1] "Line" is short for "Pauline" and is pronounced accordingly.

told. The rare times I tried to show initiative, I was immediately put back in my place. And reminded that my duties as a waitress were limited to serving and cleaning. Working in the restaurant industry isn't easy. Crazy schedules making it impossible to have a social life, having to deal with bitter comments from disrespectful customers, and let's not even get into the number of thankless tasks that are assigned to us. Don't get me wrong, I'm not biting the hand that fed me. Those jobs helped me become financially stable, independent, and they forged my character. It took me six months to get my act together, to give notice to leave my two jobs and my apartment, and to complete my business management training. As I turn twenty-six, I will take my life into my own hands. And that, I owe to my grandpa. What a shock when he left us! It's as if my entire life was disappearing. He, the one who took me in when my parents died in a car crash when I was just a child. He raised me, gave me advice, comforted me, but also lectured me. He always encouraged me in my art studies, a passion he passed on to me very early on. I really thought I would find a job in that field after I graduated but I had to come to terms with the harsh and cruel reality of the job market, which left me completely disillusioned. Up until now, my future seemed bleak, insipid. I felt like I was tilting against windmills. What a shock when I learned that he had left a will! I wasn't ready to say goodbye, I refused to think or talk about those kinds of morbid details with him. But he had taken care of everything. It took me quite some time to build up the courage to go see the executor. I was somehow avoiding reality by pushing our appointments further and further down the road. But in the face of Mr. Brown's insistence, I eventually gave in. And after a bout of crying that I didn't even try to control, he read me my grandfather's will. I was to inherit the Magic Cave, his antique shop, a place that marked my childhood. I used to love to root around in there and thought of it as Ali Baba's treasure cave. What Grandpa Joe left behind for me is priceless, without a doubt. A whole life's work. Done with the cashier's jobs, done with the moonlighting. I will take the reins of the shop, hoping to find a little bit of him in those walls. There are so many memories here in this place. So many moments of shared bliss.

Oh, of course, I'm not leaving my little apartment to go very far. I'm just changing neighborhoods, which will make my job much easier. Living near the store seems much more pragmatic. And the small savings that I have will allow me to take some time off to get adjusted. Now I'm leaving for the Cavern Quarter, home to Mathew Street, and the Cavern Club, one of the most famous clubs in the world. It's a lively neighborhood that is an unrivaled hub for music and a focal point in the history of The Beatles. That is the neighborhood where my grandfather opened his shop, The Magic Cave, many years ago. His passion for flea markets and antiques was limitless and his knowledge exceptional. I just hope to live up to the task with which I have been entrusted. His brutal departure six months ago was a real shock. There were no signs that would suggest health issues. At 74, he was still lively, spirited, and mischievous. And his vitality never ceased to amaze me. Then, during our last meal together, when he was struck down by a heart attack, my whole world fell apart. My heart was shattered into a thousand pieces, leaving behind immense sorrow and unbearable suffering as my only companion. For the second time, I lost my family.

He was both a father and a grandfather to me, but above all he was my rock.

Now I'm all alone. But I made a silent promise to him: to take over The Magic Cave, to make my dreams come true, to believe in the future and, above all, to pursue my lost dreams.

"Line, are you there?"

A lonely tear rolls down my cheek when Victor's voice pulls me out of my melancholy. Victor is quite a character and is one of my best friends along with Capucine. Yes, I know, it's not much, but quality is more important than quantity, right? A year ago, I decided to get closer to them and Grandpa Joe. So I settled in the Ropewalks district which is the most bohemian place in Liverpool, with its large, 19th-century buildings converted into shops, chic hotels, and cultural institutions. This district is a haven for music and the arts. And today, again, I'm moving. "Yes, I'm up here, almost done packing the last boxes!"

The lively steps on the stairs tell me that he is taking them four by four. Very athletic, Victor is impressive in stature, which contrasts with the kindness for which he is known. Extremely fit, and golden brown thanks to his Mexican origins, he always sports a short, very masculine haircut. Dressed in his trademark baggy jeans and a hoodie, he turns to me with a devastating smile revealing his two dimples. "Hola beautiful, so how's the move coming along?"

He comes up and hugs me, kissing me loudly on the cheek before scanning the room. The living room stripped of all my personal belongings is now strangely cold, occupied only by empty furniture and piles of cardboard boxes spread out across the floor. His amused brown eyes linger on me as I finish taping one of them. "This is the last one! All that's left is to wait for Capucine, who should be here soon with the moving truck."

"OK! And that?" he says, handing me a cap that I forgot to pack.

"Oh, gimme!"

I take the headgear that displays the emblem of the University of Manchester from his hands and immediately put it on my head. "Problem solved!"

Victor's warm laughter echoes between the walls, easing the pain in my heart.

Lo and behold, all of my stuff is packed and ready to be moved to my new home. When my grandfather bought the shop, it came with an apartment overlooking it. According to him, he did not live there but rather used it as storage. I only saw the place once when I was a teenager, but I remember it as being beautiful. He told me that he had done some remodeling, but due to lack of time juggling my two previous jobs, I never got to see the changes he made.

Since Victor detects anxiety in my eyes, he approaches, his hands buried in the bottom of his pockets. As he is much taller than me, I have to raise my head to meet his eyes, which are filled with kindness.

"Ready for a fresh start, Line?"

"As ready as I'll ever be. Even though the doubts and the uncertainties are still there."

"You're going to do great, no question. You are a strong, professional, and courageous woman. I believe in you and so does Capucine. And you know we will always have your back," he says with deep conviction.

These words touch my heart and I feel my eyes begin to sting. "Oh, no! No tears, beautiful! Today is a big day! Today we smile."

"Thank you, Victor! I love you, you know that?"

He gives me one of those brotherly smiles, one of those that mean everything without having to say a word. I run the back of my hand over the tears that bead at the corner o f my eyelashes and display a huge smile for my friend, when the deafening sound of a horn worthy of a wedding procession interrupts us.

"Ah! I think Capucine is making her entrance," he says laughing out loud.

Indeed, no less than five minutes later, Capucine the tornado barges into the room. Naturally playful and spontaneous, she is a bold, brassy girl. Her long red hair is held in place by a clip, which clears her face, showing off her porcelain complexion. Her large sparkling green eyes bordered by long eyelashes are, without a doubt, her major asset. Seeing her today in denim overalls and a red T-shirt, she looks more like a rebellious teenager than the young woman she has become over the years.

"Hey, Gremlins! Well, is everything ready?"

She has been calling us that since... forever, I think, due to our ability to get up in the middle of the night to eat, our shared hatred of the rain, and our preference for dim lighting rather than blinding neon lights. I look at Victor and I can tell he is still amused by her commanding attitude. Capucine could easily be an army officer in that she has the natural capacity to lead. It is also this personality trait that allowed her to land a job as team leader in an import-export company. Perfectly bilingual, which is a key asset on her resume, she was able to establish herself and earn the guys' respect in this very macho environment where dockers and transporters rub shoulders. It was thanks to her that I was able to save on the cost of a moving van. Her job lets her borrow one for personal use once a year. She used that perk for the occasion and even brings two movers with her, who will be of great help. One glance at Victor to coordinate our movements and we happily mimic a military salute. "Ready to move boss!"

Laughter spreads through the room and it is in this spirit that we give instructions to the movers as to what needs to be loaded onto the truck, namely the furniture and all of the boxes. Two hours later, the truck is full and my apartment is empty.

Capucine and Victor are going to wait for me in front of my new building with the movers while I take my car to go and drop the keys to the old apartment off at the rental agency. After that, I can finally join them and settle into my new home. Once I'm done with this, I enter my new address, Mathew Street, which is located between North John Street and Rainford Square, into my GPS. I drive through this new neighborhood with a certain curiosity while trying as best I can get my bearings. My memories are distant and so much has changed! This bustling portion of Liverpool is now teeming with shops, cafes, restaurants, pubs, and nightclubs. Some stores are even starting to put lights on their windows, preparing for the upcoming holiday season. Grandpa Joe and I used to love walking the streets during this season, discovering the unfolding wonders in the shop windows. I was only a child the last time I came here and I hardly recognize the place. However, I am pleased to note that the traditional red brick facades have lost none of their charm. Suddenly, a violent bitterness takes over. Since I moved back to Liverpool, I have never been able to find time to go see my grandfather at the store. Juggling two jobs while putting in countless hours of overtime, he was usually the one who came to visit me. Lost in thought, I don't pay attention to the car that is right in front of me. But it's too late: I am unable to avoid it and end up ramming right into it.

This should have been a good day! But karma decided to ruin it for me.

When I see the driver furiously getting out of his vehicle and taking a determined step towards me, I curl up in the back of my seat, completely distraught, hands clenched on the steering wheel. My door opens suddenly, and this furious man starts shouting a plethora of insults far surpassing what any South Park character could conceive while holding the door to my car.

His deep and powerful voice penetrates every fiber of my body and I feel even worse when my eyes meet his. Through long strands of brown hair, his old-fashioned amber malt whiskey colored eyes strike me with their intensity. Massive and manly, this man is most impressive, and I can't stop panicking. My hands so far clutched on the wheel start to tremble and I'm getting short of breath as if the air in the car had been sucked out by his mere presence. His hard face freezes as he stares at me. A sculpted beard reveals his full and fleshy mouth on which my gaze lingers involuntarily. Dressed in scruffy old jeans and a plaid shirt with the sleeves rolled up, he simply looks gorgeous.

Yes... a breathtaking barbarian! With revolting sex appeal, but a scandalously sultry barbarian nonetheless.

Wait! What the hell am I thinking? The accident made me lose my mind, that has to be it.

His forearms feature many expertly crafted patterns, reinforcing the impression of brute force emanating from him. When he reaches out to me with his hand adorned with steel rings, I immediately jump back, which seems to irritate him even more.

"Hey! Calm down! Is everything alright?"

Words are stuck in the back of my throat. My hands can't stop trembling and I feel some tingling in my extremities as if I were about to faint. I'm usually not prone to panic attacks. But this is also my very first car accident and this abrupt-looking guy is staring at me insistently. So yes, a severe anxiety takes over and I start feeling dizzy. My vision is getting blurry. A warm hand comes to rest on my neck and words reach me through the fog in which I float. "Hey, Cupcake, stay with me!"

He pats my cheek to help me regain my senses. But his close presence doesn't really help me. His body odor creeps into me and the spicy scent is far too intoxicating. The touch of his rough, warm hand against my cheekbone catches me off guard, reminding me how long it's been since I have been with a man.

"Stay with me, OK? I'm going to call for help."

"No! No, it's okay, I'll be fine. I..."

I sit up as best I can, hoping to make this animal and its scent retreat.

"You don't look good, it would be better."

Better? Is he serious? Panic fades away, now turning into anger, I'm like a ticking time bomb ready to explode. It was his bad-mouthed asshole attitude that made me freak out and now he wants to be the savior? Who does he think he is, lecturing me after yelling at me like that? "What are you? A risk ranger? If you hadn't yelled at me like a dirtbag, I wouldn't have been afraid."

His brows wrinkle and I hear him hiss between his lips as I go off on him. Well, maybe pissing him off again isn't the answer.

"And if you had not crashed into my car, it wouldn't have happened! I took you for a guy with that cap! Damn, when are women going to learn how to drive?"

"Is that all you can think about in that big brain of yours? You filthy macho!"

He nods and stares at me for a long time, no longer showing any signs of anger, he just seems amused. Once again, his behavior throws me off guard and I don't know what to think anymore.

"You're a real piece of work," he says with a smirk.

He stands back up and heads to his vehicle, then returns with a bottle of water. "Here, drink, it will do you good."

"I'm fine, thank you. And no way am I going to drink from your bottle. Who knows where your mouth has been, considering the profanities that were flying out of it a while ago!"

His hand clenches the bottle tightly, causing it to emit an agonizing crunch. *Oh God. What has that poor bottle ever done to you?* Despite this obvious sign of exasperation on his part, I can't help but feel proud. Well yeah, I can stand up for myself as well and this small victory is quite satisfying. I'm not going to let myself be pushed around.

"Drink. This. Fucking. Water!"

"No!"

He lets out a groan then reaches out to me with his hand. "Get out of your vehicle!"

"What for?"

"I want to make sure you're okay!"

I drag myself out of the car, deliberately ignoring his help, then plant my fists on my hips in front of him. "There! Happy? Well, are we going to make a report? I'm in the middle of moving."

Ignoring my request, he lingers to inspect our vehicles and assess the damages. "It seems to me that there are only a few dents in the rear bumper, nothing too bad but I'm still going to have to take it to the garage."

Even though I don't know anything about it, I'm immediately reassured by what he said. My phone starts to ring, I turn away from this guy to grab my phone from my bag sitting on the passenger seat. When I turn around, that jackass is staring at my ass, then slowly looks me up and down, checking me out in detail until I catch him in the act. Troubled and blushing uncontrollably like a schoolgirl, I fiercely snap back at him, nonetheless. "Hey, don't be shy, you perv!"

"I don't intend to," he replies sarcastically with a provocative grin.

Exasperated by so much confidence, I refuse to play into his little game and turn my attention back to my phone which I picked up while looking away.

"Yes, Victor... I had a little hang-up... No, it's not worth it, I'm fine... Yes... I'm coming, don't worry."

When I hang up, the big brute is still posted behind me, arms crossed. I suddenly realize he's really tall. I raise my head towards him, intimidated by his stature, but as they say, to cover up a weakness, offense is the best defense. I refuse to let him see me sweat! "Well, are we going to do this report or what? As I said before, I'm in the middle of moving. I don't have time for this!"

"Was he your guy? This Victor? Are you moving in with him?"

"What the...!? Mind your own business!"

"OK, wow, no need to get excited. Do you have your insurance papers in the car?"

Suddenly, reality hits me in the face. Shit! I turn pale, ready to face *His Majesty*'s sarcasm because of my mistake.

"Uh, no. I forgot to put the documents back where they belong after cleaning my car."

Looking victorious, he looks up to the sky as if he had to thank God for this turn of events.

"In that case, we are at a dead end. I don't have one either."

Without letting go of his arrogance, he grabs the phone in his back pocket while biting his lower lip.

"Looks like I'm not done with you," he says, with a devastating smile. "Give me your your address and phone number. We will do the damage assessment separately, after which we will meet again to fill out the report."

"How do I know you're not a psycho? I'm not giving my

address and my number to a stranger."

"If I were crazy, I would have already taken it out on you, and it's not as if you have a choice. You are at fault!"

I hate to admit it, but he isn't wrong. So, I just give up and give him my information as he's typing on his phone with an enigmatic smile. This guy is really obnoxious.

"Line Thomas, 15 Mathew Street. Here! Duly noted!"

He smiles confidently, looking more than satisfied, and waves at me while walking back to his vehicle. "See you later, Nutsie!"

In shock, I watch him walk away without being able to think of a witty comeback to send him off and so I get back into my vehicle.

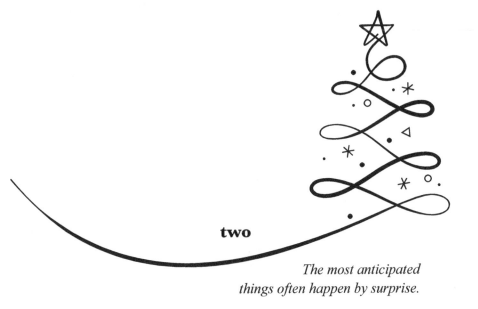

two

The most anticipated
things often happen by surprise.

Pierre Lemaître,
The Great Swindle

Line

When I meet up with my friends, I am still upset. To have stamped
a car, to have met an asshole, and to have been flustered by said
asshole. I'm not one of those who succumbs with two well-placed
words or a seductive smile. But he… he has this kind of magnetic
aura that makes you feel all kinds of things. And that makes me
crazy!

Capucine and Victor come running towards my car, all
atwitter, wanting to know everything about this mishap.

"Damn, your car! How did that happen?" says Capucine,
eyes wide open at the damage my Fiat 500 has suffered.

I look at my car in despair, and sigh at the sad looking
hood and underbody. "I was trying to find my way in this new
neighborhood when the guy in front of me slammed on his brakes
and I couldn't avoid the impact."

"But are you alright?" insists Victor.

I do my best to reassure him right away. Indeed, only the
car was damaged, which is a big relief. "Apart from some damage
to my car, it's okay, if we disregard my encounter with that
lumbersexual beast."

A shiver runs through me and although we are still on the sidewalk at the foot of the building, I know that it's not due to the cold. As I think about him, my heart throbs, reminding me of the impression this guy left on me, which is positively cringeworthy.

"What? Tell me!" my friends exclaim in perfect sync.

These two are as gossipy as ever! In turn, I look at both of them hanging on to my every word with amusement and give them the details they require. "The dude in the vehicle is a big bearded asshole in a plaid shirt. This guy is an open sore! Never seen such arrogance!"

"Have you made the report?"

"No. Neither of us had the papers with us. But we agreed to have the repairs evaluated and to meet again to make the report. He took my contact details and will be in touch."

Victor takes on a dubious air before going into overprotective mode. "Your name? Your address? Come on! What were you thinking? You don't know where this guy came from! If you want my opinion Line, you shouldn't have given it to him. I hope at least you took his!"

"Oh, give me a break! I know! But I was too disturbed to think properly. And then, honestly, I would prefer never to hear from him. He's downright obnoxious! Can we move on? I can't wait to check out my little nest, and I won't let this caveman spoil my day. Shall we go up?

I push the heavy door of the building, and we climb the wooden stairs to my new apartment. The building has only one floor on the landing, which will make our job easier, and has only two apartments. Without saying that it is old, the construction is not the most recent but that is also what makes it charming. On the doorstep, I pause while taking out the keys. I take a deep breath and open the door, excited and nervous at the same time. We check out the place together, and what will be my *Home Sweet Home* is just beyond my expectations.

In my memory, it seemed smaller but the way my grandpa arranged the apartment is magnificent and gives the impression of quite an incredible space.

The kitchen opens to a living room, a large and bright bedroom, and a bathroom whose shower cabin has massage jets that already fill me with anticipation. The picture window in the living room gives an unobstructed view of the district and its lively streets. The exposed beams add a very cozy cachet to the sober and delicate atmosphere, with nuances of pearl gray and white perfectly matching the weathered wooden floor.

"Holy crap!" cries Capucine enthusiastically. "It's great here!"

I smile at my two friends, letting the previous anger evaporate to take full advantage of this beautiful discovery. Yes, I will be fine here.

We go back to the movers who are waiting for us outside and tell them in which rooms to put the boxes, then start to assemble the furniture. All without exception, we set to work in a very relaxed atmosphere. We laugh a lot, talking about our memories from back when we were in school. We met at the University of Manchester where we lived on campus. After my studies, I found odd jobs there and stayed, while Victor and Capucine returned to live in Liverpool. It takes us no less than six hours to put everything together and position my furniture to my liking. We are scarfing down pizzas that Victor ordered down the street, and it is almost ten when I advise my friends to go back home to rest after this very intense day. I will continue to unpack the boxes and put away my personal belongings by myself. They have been invaluable and incredibly efficient today and I only want one thing now, to enjoy the jets in the shower stall.

Once alone in my new apartment that looks like a construction site, I go look for my bath towels. I finally find them at the bottom of a box and go into the bathroom. It feels so good! The power of the jets melts the tension accumulated along my neck and the hot water finishes the job of relaxing my stiff body. Wrapped in my towel, I finally go out and easily find in the boxes placed in my room a large sweatshirt and a lace boxer. I put them on quickly and continue my unpacking while listening to music.

I pick "Home" by Daughtry, a song that captures my current situation. The feeling, upon taking ownership of the place, of coming home. Strange, knowing that I never lived here. But it's as if Grandpa Joe's presence still floats between these walls and his simple memory makes me feel right where I am supposed to be, at home.

I lose track of time, lost in organizing the place, when I hear strange noises. First muffled then more intense. And when I say intense, that's an understatement, she is screaming. *Oh, my God, doesn't she have any sense of decorum?* However, I don't try to figure out where it is coming from and turn up the music in order to cover the vocal prowess of this girl expecting it to stop quickly. But after half an hour, the intensity of the moaning increases.

What the hell is he doing to her? It's not possible to scream like an animal for so long!

Finally, an hour later, the sex hungry seem to have finished their acrobatics. As long as it's not like this every night! Coming here, I counted on some peace and quiet. I decide it's time for me to go to bed and to see a little more clearly, I fold the empty boxes and put them in the hallway. I'll take them down tomorrow morning.

As I put the boxes against the wall in the hallway, a hairy thing scurries across my feet, and I can't help but shriek while covering my eyes. "Hiiiiiiiiiiiiiiiiiiiiiiiiiiiii!"

I jump around like crazy, my hands still on my eyes.

A door opens and a voice calls out to me.

"Hey, what's going on?"

"A rat, a rat, a huge raaaat!!!"

The person I'm talking to laughs frantically. OK, right now, for sure, he's making fun of me. I open my eyes and find myself face to face with my bearded barbarian. He is dressed in simple unbuttoned jeans falling on his hips, and my eyes immediately focus on the colorful patterns that cover all of his arms and massive chest. Virility in the rough. More sensual, more intense and more attractive than in my memory. A real call to sin.

Oh no, damn it! Not him!

"You! What are you doing here?"

"I live here!" he answers.

My jaw almost falls off at this news, which seems to please him as he doubles down on his laughter.

"Nothing funny! Stop kidding around and help me."

"Hello again, Nutsie! First of all, it is very funny! And seeing you bouncing around in that skimpy outfit in the middle of the hall is quite a show. Second, it isn't a rat but a ferret. I present to you Stringer. He is mine. He must have escaped when Elise left earlier."

As I take in this information, I realize that it was him and his girlfriend going at it with such ardor just now. And to make things even more uncomfortable, I realize that he guessed that I heard them. The provocative smile he displays is more than meaningful. Of course, to top it all, let's not forget that I'm wearing a skimpy sweatshirt barely masking my lingerie, and he's staring at it without any shame. I blush immediately as I realize what I'm wearing, desperately tugging on that damn sweatshirt that refuses to comply. "You're really a big jerk, you know that, huh?"

"Wow, such an ugly word in that pretty mouth. Very tempting by the way."

OK! He takes pleasure in provoking me openly.

Furious, I raise my middle finger in front of him, locking my eyes onto his. Before I even lower it, he grabs me by the wrist and draws me against him, making light of his habitual audacity. His mouth is only a few inches from mine, and I can feel his warm breath caress my neck. This sudden proximity makes me dizzy, and I'm angry at letting my body experience pleasure from this contact. Pressed against his muscular chest, I gasp for air in shock when he breathes in my ear: "Nice finger! But that... that is *my* area of expertise. And who knows? Maybe one day, you will have the pleasure of tasting it."

A wave of chills runs through my skin and suddenly makes me react. In the darkness of the corridor, this situation would easily be open to misinterpretation if anyone walked in on us. Me half-naked and him bent over me, almost brushing against my skin. No, he will not win the battle this time. I emerge quickly and push him away with both hands. "As if that would ever happen! And in the future, try to fuck quietly! And come get your shabby rat!"

I turn my back on him and hurry back to my apartment where I lock myself in twice. Leaning against my closed door, I struggle to catch my breath. This guy is a traveling nightmare for my nerves. And incidentally for my hormones too. And damn if he isn't my neighbor!

I hear his door slam and no less than five minutes later I receive a text from an unknown number.

[We didn't do the introductions.
I'm Jordan Miller. Your neighbor!]

[Go to hell, Jordan Miller,
you and your rat.]

[Welcome home, Nutsie!]

In a rage, I throw my phone on my bed and myself along with it. I hate him! I bury my head in my pillow and scream at the top of my lungs. I was really hoping not to see this guy again. He is too obtuse, annoying and provocative. But he's also terribly sexy and desirable, I must say. Some people meet people by chance, I meet them because I have bad luck. Jordan is obviously dangerous, yet there is something attractive in him that I can't put my finger on, as if I'm only seeing the tip of the iceberg. I no longer know what to think and tired, I decide to go rest from this long, very long day.

***

I wake up the next morning, as little rested as if I hadn't slept all night. The result of a day that was too trying both for the move and for my encounter with my neighbor. I pour myself a large coffee and sit on the windowsill of the living room to enjoy it, also enjoying this view of the city that emerges slowly on this November day. Today I'm going to take care of the currently closed shop. I will no doubt have some work to do but above all I want to study the books to find out how the business was doing before the death of my grandfather. Then, I'll take inventory. The coming weeks will be busy, but I am far from displeased, on the contrary. I'm excited to take over the store. It's a big challenge, but I'm determined to take it on.

I dress in a hurry, eager to rediscover the very special atmosphere of the Magic Cave. I put on a long bohemian skirt, my brown leather boots and a little coffee-colored mohair sweater whose neckline highlights my chest respectably. I take my scarf and my bag and lock the door behind me. I note in passing that the boxes that I took out yesterday are no longer there. Was it Jordan Miller who did it? Strange. Why would he have taken the trouble?

I don't dwell on the question any more than that and run down the stairs. The door of the shop is right next to it, I take out the key ring and look for the one that will open the doors to my cave of hidden treasures. After ten minutes, I finally hear the click of the lock.

"Are you taking back the Magic?"

Jumping at the sound of this voice, I drop my keys. I crouch down to pick them up when Jordan follows suit. I am thrown off guard because I did not expect to meet him again so soon. In his stonewashed jeans and his V-neck sweater, he seems to come straight out of a fashion magazine. The smell of his spicy scent tickles my nostrils, and again I find myself under the spell of an exhilarating sensation. If I had to describe it, I think dizzying would be the most suitable term. When he's there, it's like the world around me is on pause. This man has such magnetism that it should be punishable by law. Annoyed at not being able to control myself in his presence, I only want one thing: to go and snap out of it, safe in the shop. Our hands brush against each other and his gaze slips towards my cleavage. He grabs the keychain quickly and helps me up. His captivating smile and provocative gaze at least have the merit of being clear. The sight seems to please him, and I blush once more before his audacity. "Yes. Now give me my keys. And what are you still doing there? Don't you have a job?"

He smiles boldly as he points to the sign across the door from our building. I bend down to read the inscription:

"Hipster Maniac Liverpool"
Barbershop

The completely new and trendy facade features gray colors, on which the red and black logo stands out with class. The image of a retro vinyl record is plastered on the facade. In the center a red man with a beard seems to be looking right at me. I must admit that the contemporary style makes this re-emerging profession seem hip. On the edges of the LP, it reads "Hipster Maniac" written in the same color on both sides of the horizontal axis. Then, in white, the word "Liverpool." So he's a barber. I must say he doesn't look the part. Rock music comes from inside and a customer is already pushing the door open.

"Do you work here? We are also… work neighbors?"

He reaches out to give me my keys and nods.

Great! Twice as much Jordan, twice as many problems.

"You're going to have to get used to it, Nutsie!"

"Or not! I have no time to waste. Stop calling me that and stop staring at my cleavage."

I grumble between my teeth, turn around and rush quickly into my shop.

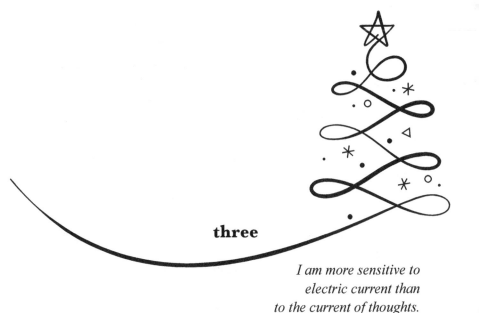

three

*I am more sensitive to
electric current than
to the current of thoughts.*

Philippe Bouvard

Jordan

Damn! What a character!

I push open the door of my barbershop and send a quick greeting to Timothy and Sonny, already busy with today's work. It's been three years since we started this business. Three years during which none of us counted their hours. We play good rock songs, in a setting halfway between vintage and modern. The red bricks associated with metal and wood make it a very masculine place where each man who enters can relax, have his beard trimmed, have a drink, or have a haircut. Yes, the barbershop "Hipster Maniac Liverpool" has a bar. We made this a hip place in Liverpool for the hipster community.

We quickly gained notoriety and there is no shortage of customers. But we also worked very hard to achieve this result and we are proud of it. Besides which, Sonny is an excellent barber, creating glorious designs on short cuts with impressive dexterity. Timothy and I specialize in beard trimming. And all together, we are a hell of a team. The idea came to us as each of us wondered about our professional future. We all worked in the same industry, but the urge to assert ourselves became more and more pressing.

So, we decided to team up and go for it. Tim is a childhood friend; as for Sonny, we met him during an evening at the Cavern Club ten years ago. Since then we have become inseparable.

A little later, as we wait for the next customer, I notice that my two friends keep glancing over at me. My tense mood has certainly not gone unnoticed and they leave their restocking activities to join me at the bar.

"What's going on, Jordan? Are your pants too tight?" teases Sonny casually.

"Unless Elise didn't come to see you last night?" adds Timothy.

I stare at my two friends and their idiotic airs, smirking at their terrible jokes.

"The girl from yesterday. The one who stomped my car. She's the new owner of the Magic Cave!"

"Oh shit! What a damn coincidence. Did you see her again this morning?" Sonny wonders.

"Rather late last night. She's also my new neighbor. She appreciated neither Elise's vocalizations, nor her meeting with Stringer. And even less the fact that I caught her half-naked in the hallway. Besides, she really has a bad temper. This chick is hysterical and more than a little aggressive!"

Timothy leans on the bar, joining his hands, suddenly looking very interested. "Well, I must say that Elise is very expressive. I can understand that she can be a pain for the neighbors. As, for your ferret, not everyone appreciates stretched rat-looking things. On the other hand, you will have to expand on the 'half-naked'…"

So I explain in more detail last night's skit in the hallway and how I came to surprise Line in that outfit. Suspicious, Sonny can't help but point out, "What are you not telling us? That she felt, embarrassed, that's understandable, but the anger, you must have said or done something stupid knowing you!"

OK. These are friends who know me all too well. Yes, I can play the part of the arrogant giant asshole, especially when I lose control. And at the sight of Line's little ass in my hallway, it's not just my mind that derailed. My dick did too. The simple fact of surprising her like that got me as hard as steel. Damn it! To lose control to this extent is totally insane and I hate it! The more she fights back, the more she drives me crazy.

"Yes, well OK, it was a little my fault, but don't forget that she demolished part of my car, guys!"

"Yeah. Just say that you want to fuck her, it would be more believable!" shouts Sonny.

"Besides, you haven't told us what she looks like. If she's able to throw you off your game like that, I guess she must be pretty hot," adds Timothy.

And they don't know the half of it. "Well, you will soon get to see her, she will be difficult to miss given the proximity of our two shops. Okay, guys, let's get back to work, shall we?" I say as I notice people coming.

We then resume our work, handling appointments back-to-back. Sonny made a few arabesque cuts with incredible precision to a group of young people wishing to assert their personality. Trimmers hold no secrets to him and his experience in handling them never ceases to amaze us. Timothy, after closely shaving a man with a straight razor, which is the ultimate tool, strives to clean and maintain the beard. This characteristic looking utensil has a foldable blade in the socket (or handle) that identifies it immediately. It's an essential tool for any barber worthy of his salt. Very careful and in order to protect his blade which is subject to oxidation, he then undertakes drying it carefully and oiling it over its entire length, from nose to hook.

As for me, I apply myself to grooming fairly dense beards, giving the clients advice on the different maintenance methods. There are many supplies on the market, and we select the best, ranging from the wooden comb, care oils to polishing waxes. We have even set up various displays where we offer popular products for sale.

* * *

A few days later, we are busy in the shop with the guys and the discussion drifts towards my dear neighbor. When it comes to her, things are at a standstill. Both of us are sticking to our guns and since our last discussion in front of her shop, neither of us has taken a single step towards reconciliation. We just greet each other when we meet, but I have to admit that things are rather tense between us. That's not working very well for me, and it's affecting my mood. My two friends won't stop teasing me about the situation, and maybe I deserve it. Both agree that it's up to me to call a truce for the benefit of everyone. I dwell on it for most of the day, wondering how to make peace with that nutjob when, around 4 PM, I have an idea.

I let the guys run the store and walk around the neighborhood. When I come across the store I'm looking for, I quickly grab a bag and return to the shop. I brew some coffee and go out to bring it to Line. I push the door to the antique store open, setting off the copper chime. "Line? You here? Hey, it's Jordan!"

Suddenly I hear a loud noise followed by a whole lot of cursing. I walk cautiously to the back room, finding her flat on the floor, rubbing her hands vigorously. I put my gift on the table cluttered with a pile of documents and kneel in front of her.

"Uh… Are you okay?"

She looks up at me skeptically still rubbing her hands vigorously against each other. My gaze then lingers on her outfit which, without being particularly sophisticated, is quite delightful. Her side braided hair reveals her thin and delicate neck, bringing out the shape of her perfectly oval face. She is molded in blue slim jeans topped with riding boots and wears a small turquoise mohair sweater: all of her sensuality is exacerbated by how her graceful curves are highlighted. Her beauty is striking and gives me a delicious shiver that runs down my spine.

"No, it's not okay, I just got electrocuted with that damn lamp!"

"Well, now you have a good reason for those goosebumps I guess."

She immediately squints and glares at me. *OK, I deserved it.*

"I'm joking! I swear. I was wrong. I came to call a truce."

She scrutinizes me intensely and gets up carefully. "A truce? Are you serious or is it another one of your bad jokes?"

"No, I'm serious. Look, I even brought you some coffee and that," I say, pointing to the bag on the table.

She approaches and opens it suspiciously, then exclaims, "An éclair from the Electric Bakery down the street? Are you serious? Decidedly a bad joke, Jordan"

"Uh, how was I to know that you were going to pull a Claude François[2]!?"

She smiles and grabs the steaming cup of coffee to bring it to her lips. I watch her delicate gestures which immediately stir up trouble in my jeans. *Damn it! She has no idea how charming she is.*

"Thank you, this coffee is so unexpected. I was totally freezing. The heating has been turned off in here. I called a technician but he's not coming for another couple of days."

"You can also come and warm up at the shop, Line. I'll take the opportunity to introduce you to the team. There are three of us working there."

I can't believe the words coming out of my mouth. Instead of getting out of here and leaving it at that, here I'm trying to drag her into my shop! This girl really has a way of making me do the inexplicable. I try making excuses by telling myself that I'm only following the advice of my friends by establishing a truce. However, this chick is drop dead gorgeous. And I made the choice not to let any of them into my life. Just one night stands here and there. Girls that I don't really care about, just for fun. I doubt Line is that kind of woman.

Her cheeks start to turn pink, and I can feel her discomfort.

"Oh, no! I... You have to work, I don't want to impose."

"If I suggest it, it's not a problem. Let's go, Nutsie! Follow me."

"Will you please stop calling me 'Nutsie'?"

OK, she has a point there. If the goal is reconciliation, it won't do any good to keep calling her that. Let's try to do better.

"Okay, Line. I'll drop it."

Satisfied, she finally gives in and follows me out. *It's a good start, isn't it?*

When we pass through the door of the shop, Sonny and Timothy keep looking at her, which is really annoying. Right now, I'm thinking that bringing her here was not such a good idea

---

2   Famous French disco star who died by electrocution when changing a light bulb while he was in the shower.

after all! Luckily, there are no customers, which is a relief. No need for other guys to undress her with their eyes. But what the fuck is wrong with me?! I slap myself inwardly and let her take in my shop, admiring every detail. Unlike the more traditional barbershops, the walls are not decorated with posters of beauty products or hair models. No, we chose to reinforce the modern vibe by hanging vinyl record covers from groups of bearded rock bands. The biggest names of pogonophiles on the music scene are there. ZZ Top, Eric Clapton, Jim Morrison, Ozzy Osbourne... Line seems to appreciate this touch of originality, which in turn stokes my pride.

"Can I get you another coffee?"

"Please, yes."

Sonny approaches and quickly calls me out. "Are you going to introduce us, Jordan?"

I roll my eyes. These two are worse than kids. As we head towards the counter where we settle in, I make the introductions. "Line, this is Sonny and Timothy. The three of us are business partners in this shop."

Timothy then intervenes by sitting down near Line. "So, are you taking over the Magic Cave? Did you know Grandpa Joe?"

"Yes, he was my grandfather."

I watch Line carefully. The veil of pain that passes before her eyes is deep, and I'm sincerely sorry to see her suffer from the loss of a loved one. With a sober tone, I reply, "All our condolences, Line. We knew Grandpa Joe well and he liked to hang out here too sometimes. He will be missed in the neighborhood. We really thought highly of him."

"Thanks, I appreciate it. I loved him so much. Well, I'll leave you, I still have a lot of work at the store. I'll return the cup before I go home."

She leaves her stool and walks out discreetly.

The guys can't even wait ten seconds before making fun of me. "Damn, did you forget to tell us that this girl is adorable, besides being a real beauty?"

"Worse than that, she is divine!" Timothy says, throwing a sugar cube at me.

I must admit that it deeply irritates me to see them succumb to Line's charm and I try to calm their ardor as best I can. "She's got a shitty attitude. *That* you haven't seen!"

"Or… it's just you who unleashes her bad temper. I'm sure she would be sweet with me!"

"Shut up, Tim! You don't go near her, understand? I don't want any drama here, it would quickly go to hell. Find chicks to fuck elsewhere than in the neighborhood."

And saying that is proof that my hypocrisy knows no bounds.

I run my hand through my hair and start putting in orders to suppliers.

It's almost 5 PM when my phone rings. My mechanic informs me that, if I'm available, I can bring the car in so he can examine the damage and give us a quote. I told him of my clash with the nutjob and asked him to kindly take a look at hers too while he was at it. I doubt Line would know of a mechanic nearby. Who knows, maybe this will help ease the tensions between us a little? I ask Timothy and Sonny to close the shop, take my jacket, and go to the store to inform Line.

She welcomes the news with some relief, and I'm glad I got it right.

"Where are you parked?"

"Up the street but I have to go to my apartment to collect my jacket and my keys."

"OK. My car is parked right outside but I guess you noticed it already."

She nods and then we leave the Magic Cave. Hands buried in the bottom of my pockets, I go to my car and sit down to wait. Strangely, I experience some kind of sudden melancholy. Is it due to Line's presence? No, I've had more than my fair share of female presence in my entourage. Starting with Elise. Even if we can't really call it a relationship, she is still at my place very often. Well, at least part of the night. Elise is a very practical way to let off steam.

A ho? Me? No… Pragmatic!

She too gets what she wants and knows what to expect. I'm made of shadows, and I chose my solitude.

My fingers tighten on the leather steering wheel, and I expel the air stuck in my chest. Ghosts from the past haunt me without warning. Insidious, they seep into my mind and leave that deep bitterness in the back of my throat. My thoughts drift back to ancient days when the light was still part of me. But it went out, leaving only an icy envelope. Images hit me violently. This is not the time to let go. In any case, I don't want to be caught in this moment of weakness. I swallow my pain, silence it momentarily.

"More bitter are the tears that don't flow," says an ancient Gaelic proverb. This is all too true. They permeate your body like a poison that eats away everything in its path.

When Line reappears at the door of the building, I can't help but look at her. She has the natural elegance of a woman who chooses to dress simply. Her long golden hair floats freely on her shoulders and her cheeks, rosy from the winter freshness, give her that irresistible candid air. When I caught her with her ass on the floor in her shop, her jade-colored eyes were brightly lit. She has that captivating look that grabs you, as if it contained a thousand treasures. Yes, her eyes are sublime. But to see them shine with desire and feel her lose herself in my hands is too risky of a challenge! For her, as for me. No way.

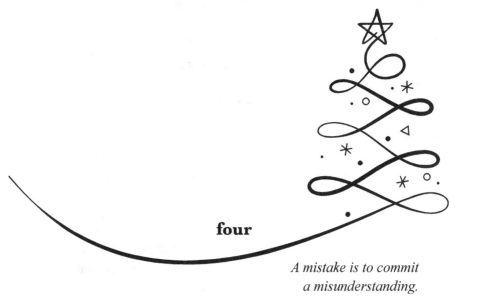

four

A mistake is to commit
a misunderstanding.

Bob Dylan

Line

I walk past Jordan's car and signal to him that I'm going to get mine. Mist rises from my lips as I walk up Mathew Street. In the past few days, temperatures have started to drop, and winter has settled in slowly. Jackets and down jackets are out on the streets. Even boutiques are starting to display Christmas-colored sweaters. Some are decked out with reindeer, fir and others sprinkled with snowflakes. Let's not forget that a special day is dedicated to them: "Christmas ugly sweater day" takes place every third Friday of December and the stores that lend themselves to the game make it their flagship item. I smile at the idea of this strange tradition we used to celebrate with Grandpa Joe. All that laughter.

The scarf wrapped around my neck doesn't prevent a shiver from running through me. But I doubt the cold is the cause. No, it's the insistent look Jordan gives me that makes me feel like that. I felt him envelop me as soon as I crossed the threshold of our building. A long, focused, inquisitive look. How not to feel troubled when faced with a man like him? He is loaded with licentious intensity, blowing hot and cold, playing daringly. This behavior troubles me and attracts me, upsetting my natural attitude which usually remains detached from any form of flirting. He easily gets me confused, like that disturbing grain of sand breaking down the most solid machines.

I get to my car and settle in, placing my purse as usual in the passenger seat. I turn on the ignition and the radio. This immediately lightens my mood, and the dynamic beat of Thomas Rhett with "Crash and Burn" quickly fills the car. I'm about to leave the parking lot when my phone beeps. I grab it before I start driving to see if it's an emergency or not. It's a message from Jordan.

[You coming?]

I answer him that I am, and start releasing the handbrake when a new beep rings out. *What now?* Obviously, I'm going to follow him, I don't know where his famous garage is!

[I knew you would, love!

Told you I was good at this…]

What the hell is he talking about?

I scroll back up the thread and… Fucking autocorrect, son of a bitch! Obviously, Jordan was going to react to such a text!

[Yes, I'm cumming!]

I'm totally mortified and red with shame that Jordan received this. Damn it!!! And on top of it, he doubles down. I decide not to answer and to clarify once we get there.

On the way to the garage, I'm so upset. Not to mention that at each red light, I meet Jordan's gaze in his rear-view mirror, and the expression of total satisfaction and extreme amusement that he sports adds to my discomfort.

It undermined all my confidence and I'm mad at myself for being so receptive to this barbarian. When we turn into an alley covered with gravel, I understand that we have arrived at our destination. I get out of the car, and I don't even have time to turn around when he's behind me. His arm comes to rest on the roof of my car, and he looks at me with confidence. The air is getting scarce in my lungs like every time Jordan enters my space. His charisma taking precedence over my hormones, I inhale in spite of myself this sensual perfume that he drags with him, like a formidable weapon. *Take control, old lady*, says a little voice in me, *he's going to knock you down.* "Forget your prepubescent asshole ideas immediately, autocorrect obviously twisted my words. Do you really believe that I would send you such a message?"

"I think your phone simply translates what you dare not say!"

"Yeah right! Your ego all right? You're really just a pi—"

We are interrupted by a man with a large gut and greasy hands. Jordan steps back, which allows me to breathe again. The guy walks in, outlines a smile and raises an eyebrow. He turns to Jordan smiling. "Is that the nutjob?"

What? Seriously, who the hell does he think he is?

"Hey! Don't bother! I'm standing right here, mind you!" I say, waving my hands.

"Calm down, Line! He's joking. Devon is the best mechanic in all of Liverpool."

I scowl and let them get busy with the cars. After an hour of observation after observation, the mechanic closes the hood of my Fiat and addresses Jordan. "Well, in itself, nothing very serious, just crumpled sheet metal. I'll take care of it for you quick. A week at most. However, it will need MECACYL CR. Can you handle it?" he says with a mocking expression.

Jordan gives me a carnivorous look and replies without waiting, "Oh, well you can count on me to take care of it! You know I'm always ready to help."

They exchange an intimate look as an apprentice arrives and hands over the keys to a rental car. And fuck this, I don't care! I'm just looking forward to someone giving me mine so I can go home. After a manly handshake, Jordan turns to me. "Let's go! Devon will contact me about the estimate, and I will pass along the info to you."

"And where is my rental car?"

The mechanic then casually addresses me. "Sorry my little lady, we only have one loaner vehicle available. You'll have to get along with Jordan for now."

Great! Couldn't get any better than that. I wanted to take off, but I find myself having to rely on Jordan for all my rides! Fuck! Worse than that, I will have to deal with him on my way home. Here we go for an episode of "Living Life with a Barbarian!"

I get into the black SUV, deliberately dodging Jordan's gaze. I sit in the passenger seat and remain silent.

"Oh, Cupcake, are you pouting?"

"Leave me alone, Jordan."

I sink deeper into the seat and keep my face turned towards the window.

"Come on, stop making that face! Cheer up a little bit. I sometimes find it difficult to channel my provocative side."

"Difficult to channel? But if you have plumbing issues, go buy some Draino! I've never met anyone as arrogant as you. One thing is certain, no one will ever accuse you of being modest."

He bursts into laughter.

"What do you want, apologies? So, all right, I'm sorry. I knew that this was a mistake from the start. I couldn't help but tease you. But you have to admit that your text was funny."

Despite my anger, he manages to snatch a smile from me. His frank and spontaneous character is the reason for my bad mood and I reluctantly decide to accept his apologies. He turns on the radio which, as if to taunt us, broadcasts "I Want Your Sex" by George Michael. A huge mischievous smile lights up the features of his face, and he starts to laugh. While driving, he turns up the volume, going so far as to sing over it, loudly. This is quite a surprising new facet of the bearded man and I must say that his warm, rocky tone of voice makes for very pleasant listening.

After a while, he turns his head towards me, suddenly looking more serious. "Where did you live before coming here? Well, it's none of my business, but we never saw you at your grandpa's store. You don't have to answer if you don't want to."

My eyes get lost on the horizon, and I decide to answer him honestly. Surprisingly, confiding in him comes easily. I have no trouble talking to him about my life and telling him about my journey. "In Manchester. I went to college there. When I was a child, my parents died in a car accident, Grandpa Joe took over. He was my paternal grandfather. I was only 8 years old. He was already a widower and not being able to provide the education he wanted for me, he sent me to boarding school. He had his shop to run and he never had a daughter. So, he thought that the best thing for me was to go to boarding school where I would have the opportunity to benefit from the presence of women to answer all my questions."

"Oh, it must not have been easy for you."

"It allowed me to learn to be independent. I have great memories of it and he came to see me very often. Every weekend, every vacation. I also came to his house, of course. But, in general, for the holidays, we often went on trips. He took me to Italy, France, Portugal, Sweden... He was very present for me and did his best to give me a good foundation in life."

"He was a good man! And after boarding school?"

"I moved to the University of Manchester campus. At the end of my studies, I stayed there. I only came back to Liverpool a few months ago. I lived in the Ropewalks neighborhood."

"This neighborhood is going to be a big change for you. It's different, but it's very pleasant."

"My life took quite a turn here, so a little more, a little less... And then the change is good. This is what he told me frequently. It opens up new horizons."

"Or not." he answers softly, more for himself than for me to hear.

Curious about this rather ambiguous answer, I try to learn a little more about this very peculiar man. "And you? What is your background?"

Immediately, the change in his facial expression sends a chill through my spine. He shuts down, bites his lips, pivots his gaze onto the traffic. Dry and without any appeal he answers, "There is nothing to say."

I gulp, uncomfortable in the face of this sudden metamorphosis. We were having a nice chat, it was even very pleasant and now he's clamming up right when we were getting to know each other. In the blink of an eye, his state of mind completely changed. Disillusioned, I don't even dare look at him any longer and fix my gaze on the landscape that scrolls by outside my window. What an oaf! I'm greatly disappointed. I thought we were getting somewhere. We ride the rest of the trip in silence and when we park in front of the building, I can't help but ask him the question that was burning my lips. "By the way, what exactly is the META thing the mechanic talked about?"

Jordan cuts the ignition, applies the handbrake and releases his seatbelt to put an arm behind my neck. I stand still, my mind confused by these mood swings, no longer knowing how to react. Leaning towards me like this, I can feel his warm, minty breath sliding in the hollow of my ear as he whispers suavely, "Lubricant."

Surely, there, he's not talking about car stuff right now! My cheeks flare up violently at the insolence that Jordan plays off so well. Seducing and provoking are his thing. He plays with me according to his own rules. I am frustrated that I have no control over it. Far too enigmatic, he is as complex as a Chinese puzzle. But what annoys me the most is the fact that he so easily manages to arouse desires in me even though he never stops behaving like a motherfucker. My whole body quivered when he brushed against mine. And Jordan knows it, I see it in his eyes. I immediately pull myself together and rush out of the vehicle under the amused eye of this wild animal.

Once on the sidewalk, I see Capucine pacing in front of the store. But what is she doing here? I don't remember her saying she was coming over. I go to meet her and, when she sees me, her face lights up. "Just to be sure Capu, did we have something planned?"

"No, don't worry, your memory has not betrayed you, I just wanted to pay you a surprise visit and see how you were doing with moving in here."

I'm about to reply when Timothy and Sonny step out to close the barbershop, joined by Jordan. Capucine's eyes instantly drift towards the three bearded men a few yards away from us.

I turn around and meet Jordan's gaze riveted on me, while he ignores the words of his two partners in crime.

"Line, who's that lumbersexual man who seems to want to eat you raw?"

"The guy from the accident."

My friend then looks Jordan up and down and scrutinizes him without the slightest bit of embarrassment.

"Are you serious?"

"More than ever, and guess what? He's also my neighbor, directly across the hall, and that's not all, he owns this shop with these two guys."

"You're kidding!"

"I wish! He's a jer—"

Before I can finish my sentence, she cuts me off in a burst of spontaneity that amazes me. "Adopt me!"

"Capucine!"

"I'll make myself very small, you'll put me in a corner. I'll even do the housework. Adopt me!"

I laugh out loud at my friend's mischievous behavior. "But you're being ridiculous, Capu. Stop! Jordan is not Prince Charming, far from it, I assure you. He is a real neanderthal."

"But, he's bearded," she whines, hopping up and down like a kid having a tantrum.

"Capucine! Stop!"

Three pairs of eyes are now targeting us, which doesn't seem to be reason enough for my friend to stop her little act.

"You say that because you never liked bearded men."

"That's totally not true!"

"Very well then, give it up! WHO?"

"Well... Santa Claus!"

Capucine looks disillusioned and can't help but respond, "I assure you Line. Bearded one day, bearded always! You should try it!"

I'm about to retort when I feel a presence right behind me. Jordan steps forward, accompanied by the other two dudes. I turn around, destabilized by his proximity but he displays an impassive air. His amber look seems to pierce right through me. It burns with a flame where you can see desire, excitement, and danger dancing. My stomach contracts while my mouth becomes as dry as the desert. "Capucine, I present to you the owners of the Hipster Maniac Liverpool shop. Here are Sonny, Timothy, and Jordan."

As she greets them and starts a discussion with Jordan's friends, the latter bends over and whispers in my ear, "I agree with Capucine. You should give it a try!"

Mortified that he heard this part of the conversation, my cheeks ignite, and a new shiver runs down my spine. The way he continually teases me bothers me more than it should. I feel my heart beating frantically in my chest when images of Jordan naked in a bed violently surge into my mind. I blush even more at the overly efficient imagination of my depraved brain, but nonetheless try to display a completely detached attitude.

OK, 0 credibility.

Timothy joins us, displaying a mischievous expression. "We're going to check out the Cavern Club tonight. Would you like to join us?

"The Cavern Club?"

"Yes, over there," he says, pointing to the storefront. "Don't tell me you've never heard of it. That place is legendary!"

"Of course, I know of that legendary place, but unfortunately I never found the time to set foot in there."

Seeing that I seem interested, Sonny steps forward and gives me the rundown on this well-known place in the neighborhood. "The Cavern Club is THE concert hall to see. This is where the Beatles' manager first discovered them. This room welcomed the biggest: the Rolling Stones, Arctic Monkeys, The Who, Pink Floyd, Oasis, Aretha Franklin, John Lee Hooker... It's a must! Everything you need to have a good time: great music and great atmosphere."

"Come on, join us, girls. You'll see, it's great!" insists Timothy.

Capucine turns to me, her eyes pleading for us to join them. "Oh come on, Line. Come on, let's go. We'll have fun."

Suddenly I realize that Jordan's attitude has changed. Again. Although he doesn't say a word, he stays there, his eyes fixed on me without being distracted by the exhortations of his companions. He remains silent, his face closed as if my presence was absolutely undesirable. He almost seems to dare me to accept. I immediately understand the meaning of his silence, without him needing to open his lips. "At your own risk."

I suddenly feel tiny under the intensity of his gaze and respond laconically. "Not tonight, maybe another time."

Capucine stares at me with those big eyes, annoyed that I refused the invitation.

"Up to you! But if you change your mind, don't hesitate to join us," insists Timothy.

I watch them walk away towards the building, noting in passing that the trio of hipsters monopolize all the attention of the girls walking down the streets. No doubt these three must've had their fair share of women. Which leads me to believe that

I've made the right choice. Caution is advised with a man like him, and I'm glad I didn't give in. Indeed, Jordan is to die for. But how many others before me have been ensnared in his web? How many others have been heartbroken by this man? Yes, that was the right call. I'm just going to spend a nice, quiet evening with Capucine, like we are used to doing.

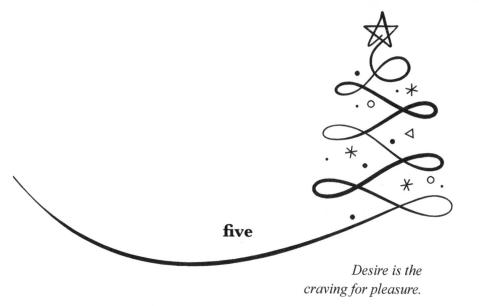

five

Desire is the
craving for pleasure.

Aristotle

Jordan

Settled comfortably on the club benches, I lend a distracted ear to the group performing on the stage. My thoughts are quickly invaded by the image of a piece of work with electric eyes. No matter how much I try to distract myself by mentally undressing several groups of girls, none of them make me want it as much as the troubling Line. I know that my attitude towards her was frankly not very delicate, but I couldn't help it. I don't do political correctness.

I have to manage to keep her away from me but damn, it's not that simple. Clearly, I want her, you don't have to be a genius to figure that out. I really feel on edge and my crankiness doesn't go unnoticed by Timothy and Sonny.

"Jordan, do you plan to stay in your shell all evening?"

I look up at them, blasé, and grumble into my beard while bringing to my lips the bourbon that has kept me company for a while. My eyes linger on the ice cubes bathing in the amber liquid. They collide, just like my thoughts in the back of my brain. Damn her with her big doe eyes!

I run my hand mechanically over my beard when I notice that a group of chicks keeps sneaking around our table, eyeing us openly. Tempting and uninhibited, one of them walks towards me swaying on her dizzying heels. "You dance?"

I watch her carefully but, for some inexplicable reason, I have no desire to rub myself against this bimbo. Normally, I would get super excited and it would mark the start of a decadent night. "Not in the mood," I mutter. "Go try your luck elsewhere!"

The stranger gives me a look full of animosity and returns to her friends, with a lot less confidence than a few moments earlier.

Sonny comes to sit in front of me, beer in hand.

"Jordan, what's the problem?"

"Piss off, Sonny, I'm not in the mood to be chasing after pussy."

"That's what worries me. You're usually always up for it!"

He swallows a mouthful of his drink and sighs, distraught at my attitude. "In any case, I know one who did not appreciate being rejected."

I look up at the bimbo complaining to her group of friends, all of them giving me nasty looks.

"I don't give a fuck, I'm not the Mother Teresa of hot pussy. If she gets bored, she'll just have to try stuffing some envelopes herself tonight!"

Timothy joins us and steps into the conversation with a bantering look. "Who's stuffing what? Where?"

We all look at each other before we finally burst out laughing. There is something irresistible about these two idiots. Obviously, I'm not immune to the pseudo-moralizing intervention from my two friends, aimed at making me aware of my lack of tact towards Line. They tease me so that I don't escalate the situation, and they even encourage me to calm down when I'm around her in order to maintain the truce that we had put in place. This idea makes its way into my mind. Should I take a step towards her? If so, will I resist my urge to play with her?

Later in the evening, my ass is still glued to my seat. I'm playing around with my phone, and the little demon within gets impatient. It itches. I try in vain to resist, but the desire keeps getting stronger. I quickly tap a message and press the send key. [Why didn't you want to come?]

After about ten minutes, my phone vibrates and when I see

Line's name appear on the screen, I smile.
[It seemed obvious to me that you
didn't want me to. Don't count on
me to act like a groupie.]
Her incisive tone, far from calming me down, only fuels my
desire to play with her. Under her soft and discreet attitude hides a
small impetuous nugget. I love the way she reacts when I push her
buttons. It may not be not commendable on my part, but stirring up
passion excites mine.
[How do you know what I want, Line?]
[You didn't look
very enthusiastic.]
A draft of a smile arises on my lips, strumming my answer,
savoring the ambiguous turn of the discussion.
[You really want me to
prove my enthusiasm towards you, Line?
Are you sure?]
[Oh! Stop this little game and lick me
Alone, Jordan]
That's it. I'm euphoric at the sight of the ravages of autocorrect
from this nutjob's phone.
[Will an hour from now work for you?]
I rejoice like a little idiot. Finally, this evening is becoming
much more interesting.
[I hate you!]
[Are you sure?]
I order another drink and let myself slip into my thoughts.
Fighting against my attraction to her is more difficult than expected.
Especially since I realized that a tenuous bond comes to life as soon
as we are in each other's presence. I saw the goosebumps on her
skin. I myself felt an electric current by grazing it. Despite our tense
exchanges, we are drawn to each other. Maybe this adorable little
nutjob would be up for more. No commitments, no obligations.
Just for fun. Maybe that would help me get her out of my head.
At this simple idea, I feel my jeans stretching. Exquisite
images tinged with eroticism are coming at me, further intensifying
my desire for her. I feel the palpitations of my heart racing as I
imagine myself slipping into it roughly. A vision of Line sighing

in pleasure, naked, languid between my arms, makes me choke on my whiskey. Shit! I'm really losing it. I know in advance that nothing will be simple with Line. She's not like those girls who keep quiet and accept the little I have to give. No, she faces things head on and responds fiercely. She is real, whole, and so adorable. Even if that worries me, it's also what makes her so attractive.

Timothy's voice startles me. "You were far away, weren't you?"

"You can't even imagine, my friend."

"Let me guess. Looking at your face, you must've made a trip to 'Sweet Line Land.'"

Denying it is totally useless. We exchange a long look charged with complicity when Sonny joins us with more drinks for the evening.

Once at home, lying in my bed, I go over the events of the past few days. Line came into my life like a hurricane when a storm has been brewing there for six years. I fall asleep accompanied by images of my delicious neighbor.

* * *

Blue lights tear through the night. The alarming sirens cover the conversations of the people who gather. Slamming car doors. Footsteps in the snow. The smell of iodine turns my stomach and makes me nauseous. The whirling snow seems insensitive to all this commotion and taunts me while dancing before my eyes. I blink. I try to keep in touch with my surroundings. The man in front of me puts his hand on my chest and prevents me from moving forward. I struggle, I scream, push him away, but strong arms surround me. My chest is burning, and I feel like my heart is about to explode.

I bounce up in the middle of my crumpled sheets. My vision is blurred and I'm having trouble catching my breath. Again. Always.

I get up and stumble to the window partially covered with frost. I open it wide and the icy air rushes in immediately, hitting me hard. My skin seems to react to this biting contact and little by little, I come back to my senses.

It's half past five.

A new day is about to break while I remain a prisoner of my past. Will it ever stop? I writhe in this inescapable hell.

I am so tired.

I close the window and go take a shower. Weariness starts overwhelming me. It grips me tight as the jets of hot water trickle over me. Hands pressed against the earthenware of the shower, I tirelessly hit this wall that resists my pain. Tears flood my face mixing with the water, exorcising the torture that harasses my heart. Time is running out and when I finally get out of the shower, steam has invaded the room, plunging the bathroom in a strange decor reminiscent of the London fog.

I tie a towel around my waist and wipe the mist that covers the mirror with my hand. The reflection it sends back to me is the direct projection of the field of ruins within me. Red eyes accompanied by deep blue rings mark my face. With laser precision, I try to trim my beard. This ritual soothes me every morning and helps me find my mask to face the day ahead. I put on rinse wash jeans as well as a thick heather blue turtleneck and I grab a cup of coffee which I drink surrounded by the velvety voice of Ella Henderson as she sings "Yours." As usual, as soon as I sit in the kitchen, Stringer points the tip of his nose, asking for his little piece of cookie. I have fun with him with the tip of my finger, easily recognizing that I have become attached to this unusual little companion. Stringer is a gift from Sonny and Timothy. Finding myself too lonely, they thought that this little companion might ease my loneliness. And they were right. The ferret is an animal that can live freely in an apartment. Endowed with a playful and curious character, he is also a heavy sleeper, which makes him an ideal pet for people absent during the day. But why a ferret? According to Timothy and Sonny's theory, we were made to get along because of certain similarities. What similarities, you ask? Well, mating in ferrets is quite wild and lasts from one to three hours. This kind of humor is typical of my two friends.

I leave my apartment around eight o'clock and can't help stopping by Line's door and looking over. Is she awake? Is she still asleep? Or is she taking a shower? Each of these possibilities arouses an undeniable interest in me and I quickly find myself forced to readjust my jeans with a wave of the hand. The contradictory feelings that my neighbor conveys exasperate me because they throw me off kilter. I won't give an inch and yet I am dying to see her. I slip my key into my lock, give it a turn and resign myself to go straight to the shop. I don't see Line until late afternoon, passing in front of the shop window. With a wave of her hand, she greets us, but doesn't stop and continues on her way. A touch of disappointment embraces me and, as a result, I lose my concentration. Fortunately for me, today most of our appointments are with regular customers so my blunders are easier to sweep under the rug. However, after two bottles of spilled oil, Timothy laughs at me and openly taunts me. "Is something troubling you, Jordan?"

My client Faruk, who has become a friend over time, bursts into laughter at the sight of my sheepish face. "I've never seen you so upset, Jordan. What's going on?"

"I didn't really sleep well. I'm a little bit out of it after staying up late night with the guys."

"Either that," continues Timothy mockingly, "or you have discovered a passion for antiques that clutters your thoughts."

Son of a bitch!

He knows me too well and can see right through me. Even though I'm not the effusive type, Sonny and Timothy can detect, with disconcerting ease, exactly what's going on inside of me. After that many years of knowing each other, this relationship that I have with them is more fraternal than friendly. I grumble at his comment full of truth and he smiles, proud to have called me out.

"If I can just give you some advice, man, be careful with her. She's not Elise."

"I realize that, Timothy."

"Then it's perfect! I don't want to see you kill each other. I like her. She looks like a good girl."

Faruk in turn intervenes wisely. "Jordan is an intelligent person, he will know how to make the right choice."

I nod to confirm that I get the message and welcome our last customer of the day. Finally, closing time is here and I have to admit that a little rest would be nice. However, I can't help but notice that Line hasn't passed by the store. And so, still hasn't returned home. It annoys me. Not that I'm worried, but not knowing who she's with irritates me, even when I have no right to feel jealous.

We close the shop and I leave Timothy on the sidewalk. He tries to convince me to join him and Sonny for a bite to eat, but I choose to go run instead. Jogging can hopefully clear my head. I run up the stairs and come out a few moments later from my apartment in sportswear. I run regularly to keep fit and clear my head.

My circuit is my neighborhood. I jog up Mathew Street to reach Rainford Square. I keep my pace, trying to clear my thoughts. I find my rhythm and fork on Harrington Street. Christmas lights are beginning to fill the windows. Two road technicians are decorating the lampposts that line the road. Red, green, white, they flash on all sides. I cringe. I breathe in, I breathe out. A white veil escapes through my lips. The evening's biting cold just got here and while I keep going at the same pace, I fold the hood of my black sweatshirt over my head. Fine drops begin to fall when I take North John Street. I pass by Victoria Street and stop at Shiraz, Faruk's restaurant.

As usual, I place a takeout order that he prepares efficiently by adding additional specialties for dessert. "This one is on the house, Jordan."

"Thank you very much, Faruk. With you, I won't starve any time soon!"

"If you found yourself a good wife, you would never starve, whatever your appetite may be!" he adds with the smile of someone who knows.

I let out a frank laugh in front of this man, always ready to give good advice.

"I'll think about it, Faruk. See you soon, my friend."

I push the heavy door at the entrance of my building and pause in front of the inscription on Line's mailbox. "Pauline Thomas."

Ah, shit! That's a good one!

When I climb the stairs to the apartment, I hear the sound

of keys in the hallway. Line is there, struggling with her lock. The white sweater she wears over her jeans accentuates her long, drawn out face. She seems to be tired from her day and that observation moves me. "Is there a problem, Line?"

She jumps, and without turning to continue her task, answers me in a detached voice. "Oh, good evening, Jordan. The lock seems to be a little loose, I'm going to have to change it for sure."

"Let me try."

I lean over her to grab her key ring, my chest touching her back. My eyes linger on her delicate neck, revealed by her hair rolled up in a wild bun, a few strands of which escape. I perceive the thrill that covers her delicate skin as the sweet aromas of her perfume seep into me. The desire to press her against this damn door crosses my mind, but I reject the idea. Our hands brush against each other for a moment and with a dry and quick movement I turn the lock which clicks open. I lean forward and with confidence I whisper in her ear, "It's all in the fingering…"

Her body reacts immediately but she rushes to open the door, ignoring my remark.

Finally, she turns around and her eyes latch onto mine.

"Thank you, Jordan."

"Don't worry, I wasn't going to leave you in the hallway. Despite what you may think, I'm not an animal. You…? Did you eat?" I surprise myself asking her.

A flash of stress came over me and yet the words came out on their own. Just an overwhelming urge to have her by my side. A moment after being taken aback by my question, her gaze settles on the bag I hold in my hand.

"No, not yet, I haven't had time."

"So should we eat together?"

"Uh… I…"

"Why are you hesitating, Line? You are hungry, aren't you?"

Her stomach takes the initiative by answering for her with a growling noise, and I can't help but smile.

"Okay, Jordan, let's do a meal."

"I'm going to go take a shower. Join me when you're ready."

Her eyes immediately widen, and I can't repress an intense feeling of satisfaction at seeing her blush like that. "To eat, Line. Just to eat."

I turn back and go home wondering what I just got myself into.

six

*You never go as far
as when you don't know
where you are headed.*

Christopher Columbus

Line

This is how an evening can suddenly and unexpectedly go off-course. Coming back from St Paul's Eye Hospital, I was thinking of making a TV dinner and going to bed. Never could I have anticipated that I would end my day in the company of my unusual neighbor. Although surprised by this unexpected proposal, refusing did not occur to me. My desire to learn more about him is too strong. I don't know what makes him so attractive. Even though our relationship was tense in the beginning, I remain convinced that Jordan is not what he claims to be. After a quick shower, I put on leggings and a sweatshirt and cross the hallway to knock on Jordan's door. I'm uncomfortable and shift from one foot to the other when it opens. Long strands of damp hair fall across his forehead, through which his amber eyes appear even deeper. Dressed in black tracksuit bottoms and a gray long sleeved T-shirt with a flared collar, he looks stunning. The fabric highlights the shape of his muscular torso where my eyes linger at length when he gallantly steps back to let me enter his home.

The complex nature of Jordan hits me again. Sometimes arrogant, sometimes courteous and helpful, he is a clever mix of genres all by himself. A particularly intriguing combination that totally undermines my confidence. Why bother lying to myself anymore? Jordan's beauty is raw. So manly, so intense.

Difficult to pin down a man like him. I suddenly realize that, immersed in my thoughts, I remained standing at his doorstep to observe him.

He smirks and tilts his head to question me. "You can come in, Line, I'm not going to eat you. It would be more comfortable to have dinner inside, don't you think?"

I enter his home and discover an intimate place that is just like him. Manly and natural. The wooden furniture meets that of wrought iron and gives off a raw, masculine vibe. The earth tones of the red brick walls highlight the large massive beams standing out from the ceiling. A chimney-stove, located in a corner of the living room, is lit and the dancing flames mesmerize me for a moment. The interior matches him perfectly, confirming his taste for the rustic and wild.

The wooden counter that separates the kitchen from the living room is cut from a thick trunk, revealing the knots of different sizes that adorn the surface. Whoever achieved this wonder has an undeniable talent. He knew how to keep the very essence of this noble material without distorting its appearance. I run my hand over the smooth surface, touching the shaped wood, admiring the result.

Leaning casually on a bar stool, Jordan watches me in my contemplation. "It's Timothy."

"What Timothy?"

"This is Timothy's work. It's one of his passions. He likes to work with wood."

"It's absolutely splendid!"

"Yeah, that guy has magic hands. A real artist."

He gets up, grabs the bag and begins to take out dishes in which he has all kinds of exotic cuisine. I raise an eyebrow and approach to examine these specialties. Aromas spread quickly in the apartment. The scents of curry and turmeric make my mouth water and I look at each dish with delight.

Jordan keeps glancing at me, gauging each of my reactions. He watches me, studies me, and the attention he gives me stirs up a spark in my stomach. I feel wanted.

"You like?"

"Uh... I really don't know. Is it Indian?"

"No, Turkish! It comes from Shiraz, a restaurant located two blocks up the street."

He answers me as he finishes placing the food on the plates and licks his finger innocently. I swallowed, unable to look away from this sensual gesture. Our eyes meet and I blush violently for being so indiscreet. To hide my embarrassment, I grab a plate and ask with feigned confidence, "Where do you want to sit to eat?"

A smile appears on his face as he takes the other bowls. "We're going to sit in the living room, near the coffee table if that suits you."

We sit on the floor, side by side on the huge brown carpet. As for background music, Jordan chose an album by Kris Allen whose melody "Lost" resonates softly across the room. We attack the food together and each time I discover a new flavor, I can't help but utter little cries of joy, which makes Jordan laugh. "Will you give me the address of this restaurant?" I ask. "These little things are a delight!"

"I promise, I'll bring you a flyer, I go there often when I'm jogging."

"Oh, were you coming back just now?"

"Right. What about you? You came home late, and you weren't at the store."

He noticed? A delicious feeling comes over me. I didn't think he cared about my whereabouts. Briefly taken aback by this realization, I answer without letting any signs of surprise show. "Once a week, I go to the hospital. I volunteer with hospitalized children. I read stories to them."

"You... you read stories to them?"

"Yes, fairy tales, that kind of stuff. You see, they endure a lot, sometimes they are alone because the parents work and the nurses are overwhelmed. Then there is the association of volunteers. We are there to allow them to dream a little bit through books."

"Whoa! What made you want to volunteer there? Have you been doing this for a long time?"

"When I was still in Manchester, one of the girls who worked with me had a little boy who got sick. He was in the hospital a lot. She wished she could spend more time with him. She was a single mother, and working was an absolute necessity to pay for his care. I suggested that we take turns hanging out with him according to our respective shifts. One thing led to another, and one day I started reading stories to her son."

Jordan looks at me strangely and tries to learn a little more. "And here in Liverpool?"

"Well, when I came to Ropewalks, I told Victor about it. I learned that the association he was a member of was looking for new ideas to help the children of St Paul's Eye Hospital smile a little. We drafted a proposal that we submitted to them and I joined the association. Since then, every Thursday evening, I meet my little patients."

"It must be hard..."

"Even more so for them!"

Jordan's face can't hide his surprise, and in a drawling voice, he doesn't fail to let me know about it. "It's all to your credit. The Amazing Line Thomas. Or should I say, 'Pauline Thomas?'"

"Oh no, please! I forbid you to call me that! Everyone calls me Line."

"What do you have against that first name? Pauline, it's adorable."

I mumble between my teeth and try to explain a little more. "It's my father's fault: He was a sworn French translator."

"What is that exactly?"

"They are ministerial officers authorized by the Ministry of Foreign Affairs. We call on them for translations or interpreting needs: police custody, interrogations, investigations, hearings, telephone tapping, document translation, etc."

"Whoa, that's impressive! But how does that connect with your first name?"

"Having a daughter was the greatest gift my mother gave him. He decided to celebrate by naming me after Pauline de Beaumont, the muse of Chateaubriand. He was a writer and one of the forerunners of French romanticism. My father read all of his writings. But in the end, even they called me Line. Today Pauline is a bit outdated."

"It's a muse's first name. Your father couldn't have chosen better."

Did Jordan really just give me a veiled compliment right now?

I don't have time to delve deeper into that subject as he is already following up with another question. "Were you able to get to the hospital without a car?"

"Yes, Victor came to pick me up."

Immediately, Jordan's face shuts down and I could swear I hear his teeth cringe. He rolls up his sleeves and runs his hand through his beard, scowling. Surprising him in this surge of jealousy sincerely troubles me and I come to experience a certain form of pleasure in telling myself that, ultimately, I do mean a little to him. "Victor is my friend, just like Capucine. We've known each other since college. And since then, they have been part of my life just like how Timothy and Sonny are a part of yours."

He seems to relax, and we continue to chat, honoring the Shiraz's specialties. My eyes regularly go to the tattoos that adorn his forearms. Most are black, mixed with some more colorful. I can distinguish dice, a checkered flag, some shading, a face, all skillfully made. These intertwining patterns undeniably reinforce Jordan's complex nature but also all the virility emanating from him.

I have been here for more than three hours and I must admit that Jordan's company surprises me. I have not seen the time go by and I am getting to know him from a new perspective. While chatting about Grandpa Joe, I discreetly observe him caressing the inscriptions inked on the skin of his forearm with the tips of his fingers.

Curiosity prevails, I lean over to read these words: "My memory is my purgatory."

His gaze intercepts mine and plunges into me, making me shudder. This expression of pain that I see in him makes my blood curl.

"Whatever you're thinking, don't you dare ask questions," he blurts out in a clear and irrevocable tone.

He spreads his legs and gets up to go to his kitchen where he takes away our leftovers. How to interpret this? Maybe it's time for me to leave? I'm uncomfortable with his terse reaction. I get up as well and move forward, hesitant, when he suddenly turns to face me. Before I have had time to make the slightest movement, I find myself in the crook of his arms, his hand plunged into my hair and the other hugging my waist forcefully. The heat of his body seems to envelop me entirely. Our eyes cling to each other, his piercing me with desire. His mouth then takes hold of mine. Harsh, hungry, as if carried away by an impulse that he is struggling to contain. My lips part before this assault and his tongue caresses mine with amazing softness. His kiss then becomes deep, intense and terribly sensual. I feel myself flare up under his expert intrusion. He tastes every furrow of my lips, relentlessly caressing my tongue which wraps around his. I surrender to this embrace that overwhelms me and feel each beat of his heart that pulsates against my chest. My hands venture to caress his chest and then slide slowly into his thick hair. Suddenly, he freezes, presses his forehead on mine and lets out a serious sigh. "You should go home, Line. I'm sorry," he says, stepping back. "It shouldn't have happened."

I'm mortified by such an about-face. I try to articulate but the words get stuck in my throat. "I…"

Fleeing my gaze, he turns his back on me, adopting a cold and distant attitude, almost insensitive to what we just shared.

"Go home, Line! Now!" he repeats more firmly.

I feel the tears coming. I turn away and run away from his home without looking back.

I feel humiliated and ashamed to have responded to that kiss. Everything went so fast that I come to wonder if I haven't dreamt of all this. But no, everything was very real.

I can still feel the taste of his mouth on my lips and my sweatshirt is imbued with his woody odor. The lump in my throat hurts. How can someone behave like that? Claim a kiss and dismiss the person right afterwards! Who does that? I am shocked and hurt. I collapse in my bed, the only refuge I can find to let go of my tears.

In the middle of the night, I get up and pace up and down my apartment, unable to sleep. I can see Jordan kissing me over and over as soon as I close my eyes. And each time my heart skips a beat. In order to push those images out of my head, I decide to sort out my Christmas decorations. It has always calmed me down and since I plan to decorate my apartment for the holidays, it will save me time. I unpack a first box containing my treasures. As I sit on my floor, surrounded by Christmas lights and snow globes, the silence is disturbed by a loud, repetitive noise. I hear muffled blows followed by an almost imperceptible plaintive moan. I listen to try to figure out where it's coming from but then I can't hear anything anymore. I resume my activities until daybreak, punctuated by tears of bitterness.

Shortly after seven o'clock and after having watched dawn spread slowly out over the city, I get ready to go down to the store. Mentally, I'm elsewhere, but I force myself to go over the tasks I want to accomplish today.

- Find the store's Christmas decorations. Mine are way too modern for the Magic Cave universe.
- Thoroughly clean the shop where the dust has collected. During the months following Grandpa's death, the store remained closed and a good cleaning is absolutely essential.
- Get Jordan out of my head.

I immerse myself in the mountains of boxes stored in the back room and finally find my groove. Once I'm done cleaning, the Magic Cave will once again be the most beautiful storefront in the whole neighborhood. And for Christmas, it will shine with a thousand lights! Just like when Grandpa was still there. Happy memories come back to me. Cinnamon hot chocolates that we savored while watching snowflakes fall, the smell of freshly baked gingerbread, and the sparkly gleam of countless lights.

It takes me no less than five hours to get rid of all the dirt accumulated in every nook and cranny. But once my work is done, I finally recapture my childhood memory. That of a place with a hushed and mysterious atmosphere. My phone rings and with a quick gesture, I grab it while putting back an old book illustrated with Grimm's fairy tales. The cheerful voice of Capucine resounds in the loudspeaker and this little break feels absolutely great. Sensing at the sound of my voice that something was clearly wrong, my friend rushes to inquire about what's going on but, rather than chatting over the phone, she offers to join me with salads for lunch.

An hour later, we are sitting cross-legged on the shop floor, blinds down, discussing the episode from the day before.

"I can't believe he did that!" she exclaims, amazed.

"I don't understand either. I feel really bad, you know… he's my next-door neighbor and business neighbor. Suffice it to say that avoiding him will be almost impossible. I should have been more careful and especially should not have responded to his kiss."

"He's devilishly sexy, so don't be too hard on yourself either."

"But meanwhile he was just messing with me. How does that make me look?"

"Like a woman who has the power to attract such a man! Many would die for him to deign to glance at them. However, that doesn't excuse his behavior. It's ugly on his part! He will regret it when he realizes what he has lost. You have everything you need to make a man happy, Line, and if it isn't him, well, it will be someone else. Even though this is quite a waste."

I get up, resolve to erase Jordan from my mind and continue the conversation while placing various trinkets on a shelf. "Well, you know what? She can have my spot! Are you going to help me install the Christmas decorations?"

"Oh, yes," she replies enthusiastically, clapping her hands.

The afternoon flies by at full speed and we get our hands on stocks of magnificent light garlands which we take care to untangle carefully. I rub my cold hands on my jeans and realize that the repair man hasn't come yet. Even Capu's nose is reddened by the cold. Calling the company didn't help. They are overworked and will not be able to come for at least ten days. Just my luck! I hang up, complaining under the amused look of Capucine. "What are you laughing at?"

"Oh, just the fact that you now have a good excuse to go visit the bearded spies next door and have something warm to drink."

"Bearded spies?"

"Yeah. You know, from that French movie *"The Great Spy Chase"* starring Lino Ventura with dialogues by Michel Audiard."

"Capucine, you forget that I don't have dual citizenship like you. I don't know anything about French cinema."

"Ah, yes. True. I'll have to show it to you then. It will be an opportunity to have a hot chocolate and marshmallow evening."

"Right! Except that, for the time being, I've had it up to here with bearded men!"

She gives me a mischievous look and heads for the door. "In that case, I'm the one who will get the hot drinks!" she replies, a greedy grin on her face.

Amused, I watch her leave the store smiling. During my friend's absence, I uncover the huge, luminous snowman that used to stand outside the store every Christmas behind a bunch of antiques. Each time we walked in front of it, we would hear the sound of Santa's chime, followed by a "Merry Christmas" in a Santa Claus voice. I hope it still works! My grandfather was very proud of it. This discovery reminds me of how cruel the absence of Grandpa Joe is. With teary eyes, I drag the snowman to the entrance when Capucine returns accompanied by Sonny, their hands loaded down with steaming cups. They seem to get along well, as I see them joking around. In his black jeans adorned with a steel chain, Sonny has a look that doesn't go unnoticed. Very heavy metal rock, but without resorting to the basic clichés, it's a style he has perfected. This big guy looks like a modern Viking with his long hair shaved on the sides and his blond beard. Also adept at tattoos, his hands feature very colorful patterns to which are added skull-shaped metal rings.

His ice blue eyes land on me kindly.

"Need a hand, Line?"

"Oh, I won't say no Sonny, but I need a drill to affix it in front of the door."

"Don't move, I'll be right back."

He puts the cups down near the cash register and returns ten minutes later, equipped and ready to help. Capucine ogles him openly while he performs the installation of Snowy. I watch Sonny and see a smirk floating on his lips. Clearly, my friend once again lacks discretion, which makes me smile in turn.

"And there you go! You can turn it on."

I hold my breath in hopes that it's not broken and… fabulous. It works wonderfully! My big guy immediately lights up, letting off a white light that contrasts with the red scarf he wears with pride. Measuring almost five feet, this imposing decoration suddenly comes to life by tilting its head back, while letting fly with a "HO, HO, HO! Merry Christmas!"

All three of us standing in front of the window, we witness the snowman spectacle like little kids. My pleasure, however, was short-lived. Jordan walks past us, takes a look at Snowy, and exclaims furiously, "Is this some kind of a joke? Are we going to have to endure this monstrosity?"

Paralyzed by Jordan's new outburst, I even forget to breathe and take a step back.

"Jordan!" Sonny immediately intervenes. "You—"

"Don't get involved, Sonny!"

He turns around without even looking at me, rushing out of our building. I stare at the door that closes behind him and feel the anger rising in me. "What an asshole!"

Sonny comes over and puts a reassuring hand on my shoulder. "Line, don't take it personally. He… Shit! It's just that the Christmas decorations… It's not his thing, you know."

"What's his thing then? Antipathy? Crudeness? Spite? Maybe bullshit?"

"He's not a bad guy, Line." he insists gently but with conviction.

"Not a bad guy?!" Capucine interjects. "He still ki—"

"Capucine, please stop it!"

My friend stops right there, understanding that I am hurt.

I turn to Sonny, who seems taken aback, and say loudly, "Fuck Jordan Miller!"

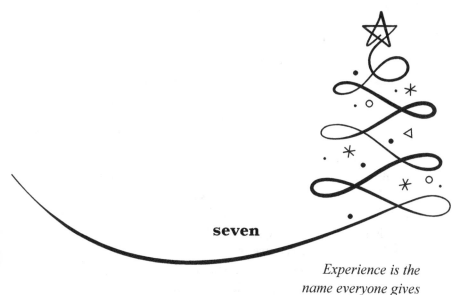

seven

*Experience is the
name everyone gives
to their mistakes.*

Oscar Wilde,
Lady Windermere's Fan

Jordan

I violently slam the door to my apartment. To say that I am angry is an understatement as I'm dealing with a torrent of emotions pouring into me. Ever since last night, I have been struggling to get her out of my head and what do I see on this fucking sidewalk but that damn Christmas anathema!

Seriously!? Will I have to endure this abomination?

As if installing these ridiculous decorations everywhere were enough to bring joy to our hearts. Bullshit! Mine has been two sizes too small for a while now and if there is a time of year that I can't stand, it's Christmas. The only thing I have in common with all of this is the coldness. The one that has covered my heart.

And she… she… she settles in here and plans to make her shop one of those extravagantly luminous displays that I despise!

Damn! I hate her as much as I want her!

That kiss last night brought me back to the cruel reality. I have no place in her life. In a moment of weakness, I abandoned myself to my desire for her, and she responded to it with all the sensuality that I had anticipated. But I can't bring her into my life. Everything opposes us. She would suffer too much. And if, to keep her away from me, I have to behave like a big asshole well so be it. I'd rather have her hate me than get attached to me.

I let myself fall on the couch, nervously playing with the steel rings that adorn my fingers. I shouldn't have given in and tasted her soft lips, and here I am in torment facing the memory of her body pressed against mine. Fists clenched against my forehead, I try to chase away the image of her big eyes. A small noise catches my attention and I see Stringer, standing on the living room table, observing me with curiosity. He didn't show up when Line came even though he's always free to roam around here. I extend my hand, and he gently climbs on it, making his way along my arm to come and nestle on my shoulder. I close my eyes for a moment, trying to find a semblance of calm, when a few knocks on the door disturb me. I grumble and don't answer. But the knocking gets louder and louder and Sonny's voice reaches me. "Jordan, open up! I know you're here!"

Stringer comes down from my shoulder and takes refuge in my room. Exasperated, I get up and unlock the deadbolt, then go back to the sofa.

Sonny comes in, closes the door behind him and comes to sit next to me, looking worried. "What is happening to you?"

"You know very well! This is not new."

"Yes, but Line, damn it! Do you realize how you behaved with her? You can be stupid sometimes, but that's not you, Jordan. What happened between the two of you? And don't tell me it's about your car, it's obvious that's not what the issue is."

"Just leave me alone, Sonny!"

"No way, man. Give it up! You don't have to be a psychic to see that you hurt her."

I sigh loudly and end up confessing. "Damn it, Sonny, I fucked up! I… I kissed her."

My friend stares at me, sketching a smile and calmly resumes, "If you call that fucking up, I wouldn't mind fucking up every day."

"No, Sonny! You don't understand! I kissed her and immediately pushed her away. She… she's not for me."

He listens carefully to my words, raises his eyebrows

while stroking his blond beard, then sighs as if distraught by my confession. "Jordan, you have to get back on your feet. You are not going to be happy if you just keep screwing Elise indefinitely. *She* is not for you. But Line, she's a good girl. It may be time for you to get out of this nightmare."

"I can't do it. Then to top it all off, she flaunts her fucking decorations right under my nose!"

"Hey, you can't ask the whole world to stop celebrating Christmas because you're in pain. And where are your beautiful sentences?! 'I don't want drama here, it would quickly go to hell. Go find chicks to bang somewhere other than in the neighborhood.'?!"

"It won't happen again, Sonny. I'm going to stay away from her," I say without much conviction.

By saying these words, I know that I lack credibility.

Which is not lost on Sonny. "Yes, well, if you can swing it. Only two yards separate you. At least try to make peace with Line. For everyone's sake. Who knows? Maybe you'll manage to become friends?"

I look at my friend without saying a word and by the way he moves his head, I understand that he knows: becoming friends with Line is not going to alleviate the desire that I have for her.

When Sonny leaves, I inform him that I am taking the rest of the day off and hole up in my place to mull over our conversation. When the afternoon ends, I keep an ear out for footstep noises in the hallway. Sonny is right, at least I have to apologize to her, otherwise the tensions will make our neighborhood a battlefield. At the very least, I try to convince myself that this is the only reason. In truth, I blame myself. For wanting her, for having kissed her, for having rejected her. At 7 PM, Line's light step resonates, and I wait for her to face her door to open mine. "Line…"

"I think we said it all, Jordan. Leave me alone," she replies without even turning around.

"No! I want to apologize, Line. I shouldn't have kissed you only to push you away. I'm sorry."

She turns and looks at me with self-assurance. "Great! And is that supposed to be enough for me to forgive your boorish behavior?"

"Shit! Won't you even try and listen a little? I'm telling you I'm sorry! It will not happen again. Can we make peace or do you want to declare war?"

"What the hell do you expect from me, Jordan? You have been playing with me from the start! You pull me in only to push me away again. You have to make up your mind!

"I want to make peace, Line. We are adults. I screwed up. Damn, I admit it. But don't you think we can find a solution rather than hating each other?"

"A solution?" she says, turning around. "And what does 'Mister Two-Face' have to offer?"

Ouch! Right where it hurts! Her reddened eyes sparkle with anger but also with sadness. I hurt her, and it twists my guts. She cried because of me.

"Line, please. I... I didn't mean to hurt you. It's—"

"Too late!" she interrupts by finishing my sentence for me.

Hands pressed into the pockets of my jeans, I clench my fists. But I refuse to leave on a bad note. "Look, I'm really sorry. Maybe we could..."

She raises a skeptical eyebrow, waiting for the offer I am about to make. With a heavy heart, I start talking as my ambivalent feelings are tearing me apart. "... behave like civilized people. Maintaining good neighborly relations would be more pleasant than constant tension, wouldn't it?"

She stares at me without letting the slightest emotion show through. "Do you really want us to behave as if none of this happened?"

"Yes, Line," I say as my brain screams the opposite.

"Do you know that good neighbors are cordial to each other? That they help each other? That they are kind to each other?"

"Damn it, I know all that, Line. Please, is it possible to forget what happened and start again on good terms?"

"Good terms?" she answers skeptically, crossing her arms.

I nod my head without looking away to encourage her to give in to my request.

"Only seven days before December. Do you agree to come with me to find a Christmas tree?"

"A Christmas tree? Are you kidding me?!"

"That's what I thought, nothing is sincere about you, not even your words," she says, turning to her door.

"Hold on! Okay, okay, that's fine, I'll take you to get your fucking tree."

She turns around, displays a sly smile and extends her hand to me in a very courteous manner. "Very well, Jordan Miller, good neighborly rapport."

We shake hands then she goes into her apartment without looking back.

Ah, shit!

She managed to bamboozle me so that I would go get a damn Christmas tree with her. I am planted in front of her closed door like an idiot and I realize that she has just pulled off a fantastic poker move!

***

As promised, the following week, I find myself with her in the car, taking in her boundless enthusiasm. This spontaneity in her attracts me.

"This is my favorite time of year, and buying a tree is a tradition to be respected," she says out loud.

I can't help but grumble into my beard. "Oh, Joy! Great!"

She glares at me then tells me where she wants to go. "There is a Christmas market on Lord Street. I'm sure to find the most beautiful tree there."

"A tree is a tree."

"Hey, I'm warning you, you are not going to spoil this moment for me! Stop bellyaching," she says, sticking the tip of her finger under my nose.

That tiny little finger just makes me want to suck it. "Take your finger out of my face, Line!"

"Oh okay, party pooper! You can be such a Grinch sometimes!"

"I never said I was Prince Charming."

"What the hell is your problem? What are you? Frustrated? Relax a little."

"There is no problem. But please stop confusing frustration and self-control."

My answer has the effect of making her shut her trap for a moment. Surprised by my words, she stares at me with her big green eyes, trying to analyze the meaning of my last remark. I park the car and look around the huge market and its snowy surroundings. *But what the hell am I doing there?!* Line hops all over the place, exclaiming, "Love it! Love it, love it, love it! Do you know that this market has over fifty crafts and food stalls from around the world?! Five continents united in the same place! Isn't it fabulous?"

I roll my eyes, slamming the car door. "Yeah, beautiful. But you know what? I didn't come to travel around the world, Line. Get your damn Christmas tree and we're out of here."

She shrugs, clings to my arm and draws me toward the entrance to this nightmare. We are in the heart of an ostentatiously opulent village whose chalets, woven with fairy lights, play Christmas carols. It's sickening. All this bullshit gets on my nerves. Line goes from stand to stand, talks to the craftsmen with unconcealed merriness. It almost seems like she is purposely prolonging my ordeal! The stall in front of which she now stopped offers various interior decorations and she goes in search of ornaments for her future tree.

"Well, Jordan, wanna hold my balls while I'm looking for the garlands?"

"And you. Wanna hold mine?"

I walk away, muttering, thrusting my hands deep into my pockets. I see her come back five minutes later and looking annoyed, I suspect my comment was not well received.

"For fuck's sake, Jordan. Can't you make an effort? Do you have to be so rude?"

"Hey, relax Cupcake, you dragged me here."

"Precisely, we can enjoy it a little, right?"

"I just want to get out of here! Can't you just pick a tree already?"

With a scowl, she walks with a determined step towards the salesman behind her and chooses a tree of rather imposing size. She pays and I go ahead to take her spiny thing when some sort of elf shakes her little bells under my nose. "Happy Holidays! Taste our gingerbread!"

Exasperated, I run my hand over my face, ready to lose it. "You, you fucking little imp, get the fuck out of here or I'll sink your bells so deep that you'll have to shake your ass to hear them chime!"

"Jordan!"

Shit, she heard me.

Once the tree is loaded in the back, I start the car and the trip back home is completely silent. After my confrontation with the leprechaun, I suffered Line's anger but against all odds, I also apologized. And I was the first one surprised. Not for what I said to the other puppet, no, I meant that. But for showing bad faith.

When I walk through the door of her apartment to drop off the purchase, I realize that this is the first time that I have set foot there since she moved in. My eyes scan its interior, looking over the large room in the living room. I like what she did with this place. It's relaxing and cozy. She chose neutral tones that harmonize perfectly with the place. Even if closed boxes are still lying around here and there, its layout is almost complete. "I see that you have made good progress, it's already great here."

"Thank you, Jordan. Can I get you a cup of coffee?"

"With pleasure," I reply, watching her take off her long coat and scarf.

I almost choke on seeing her outfit. *Holy shit! What is that?*

In a single heartbeat, my blood rushes to concentrate at the most pleasurable and sensitive point of my anatomy. My dick throbs in my jeans and my wheezing almost gives it away. Dressed in a small gray skater skirt that reaches her mid-thigh and a small matching lace top, she is to die for. My eyes go up along her tapered legs and rivet at the edge of the fabric that sways against her thighs. I have to get out of here as quickly as possible. "Never mind the coffee, Line. I gotta go."

And without waiting for her answer, I hasten to leave and take refuge in my home. I lean against my door like the devil is after me. Well, of course, the devil wouldn't give me such a hard on, but it's a witch that has reduced me to this state! I have to pull myself together quickly, and the only solution is to grab my phone and quickly dial a number. "Elise?"

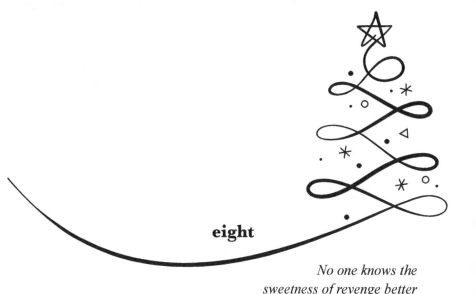

eight

*No one knows the
sweetness of revenge better
than he who has been wronged.*

Étienne Pasquier

Line

Jordan and I have been avoiding each other for the past few days. Ever since our trip to the Christmas market, he seems to be grumpy again. We politely greet each other but it doesn't go any further than that. He left so suddenly last time that I don't even know how to act around him. I keep asking myself questions about this strange and attractive man, without managing to get a handle on him. I would like to succeed in unraveling this mystery, it intrigues me, and I find myself looking for him when I pass in front of the window of the Hipster Maniac. As for me, I am getting my bearings at the store and I'm making great progress. Capucine and Victor came to see me at the store and were surprised by all of the changes.

We also went to dinner one evening near the Albert Dock, from where we can see Liverpool's ferris wheel adorned with all of its festive lights. The Albert Dock is a complex of floating docks and warehouses and our little pre-dinner visit bestowed a lot of amazing information. After the port was built, Liverpool served as a gateway to the rest of the British Empire and a place of arrival for exotic products such as brandy, cotton, tea, silk, tobacco, ivory, and sugar. It's now one of the most important tourist attractions in Liverpool and UNESCO has declared it a World Heritage Site.

This evening with my friends gave me a chance to clear my head, but it was also an opportunity for me to be able to confide in them. We talked about our respective plans for Christmas. I then realized that this Christmas would be the first that I would spend on my own. I also realized that I had decided to start decorating my tree which still sits, bare, in the middle of my living room. Of course, I couldn't avoid questions about my bizarre neighbor. Finally, I got to tell them about my progress at the store. Today, even though I still have papers to put in order and the inventory to close, the doors of the Magic Cave can reopen before Christmas.

The only downside is Elise's screaming and yelling every night. And when it's not her not disturbing my sleep, Jordan is the one sneaking into my dreams! Each appearance more scandalous than the next. Since we exchanged that kiss, my mind doesn't seem to want to get rid of his memory. And every time I meet him, my heart begins to pound. And to think that this caveman has the power to ruin my life indirectly. And tonight's hullabaloo is seriously starting to get on my nerves!

But this time, it must stop. My patience has its limits.

When the nympho moans for the first time, I take out my secret weapon. *It's you and me Jordan Miller. He who laughs last, laughs best!*

Midnight has just struck when I start to hear the screams of the nympho. I get into position, adjust my chin rest like a pro, raise my arm, and start a long screeching bow on the strings of the violin that I found in a corner of the shop. The irritating sound which escapes from it sounds like a mix between a cat who has caught its tail in a door and the strident noise of a fork scraping across the bottom of a plate.

Terrible. But oh, so enjoyable!

I throw myself into torturing this poor instrument with indescribable satisfaction. Elise's vocalizing immediately ceases. There followed a raging scream from Jordan. The latter wasted no time in banging on my door with fury. I let him sweat a little, then finally open the door to admire the results.

Jordan, his hair in disarray, dressed in simple unbuttoned jeans, probably thrown on in a rush, seems to only moderately appreciate my musical prowess!

"But you're completely crazy! What is this hellish noise?" I shove my instrument under his nose with a victorious smile. "I present to you 'Alfredo Silencio Illico!', my new friend. Whenever your girlfriend decides to disturb my peace, Alfredo and I will respond by disturbing your coitus. The 'Coitus Interruptus in D Major!' Is that clear enough?"

"For crying out loud, where are you getting ideas like this? Are you telling me I can't fuck in my own home anymore?!"

"No, go ahead and dip your noodle if you want, but put a damper on it! I don't have to endure your nightly exploits. If you need an audience, find a club!"

Jordan seems to be fuming, and his gaze hardens. An unspeakable satisfaction spreads within me. With pursed lips, he comes a little closer until he grazes my ear. "You don't know what you're exposing yourself to, Line. Don't fuck with me."

The door of his apartment opens, and Elise suddenly appears in the doorway with only a T-shirt on. Thin, with long thin legs and a busty chest, she seeks to recover the attention of my neighbor which I have cleverly diverted. "What are you doing, Jordan? Come on, come back," she whines imploringly.

Without even turning around, he coldly gives her a "Put on your clothes and get out, Elise!"

In light of Jordan's brittle tone, she doesn't even try to protest and goes back inside. I watch all this go down without the slightest hint of remorse. It even makes me smile. Our eyes lock. He eyes me scornfully, furious. "Satisfied?"

"Since peace and quiet have been restored, yes, I'm satisfied!"

I slam the door in his face and go back to bed. Obviously, that night, I don't fall asleep right away. The image of Jordan, half naked, coming out of a bed, haunts me until the wee hours of the morning.

* * *

The next day, I finally decide to take care of my tree which stands in the middle of the living room still wrapped up. I bend each branch to restore it to its original volume. I take the time to hang each of the decorations, with calculated precision. Little metal angels, resin stalactites that look like icicles, golden stars. Accompanied by the melancholic notes of Jacob Lee, I quickly let myself be immersed into the song "Secrets." The tree begins to look quite festive as I cover it with ornaments while drinking a honey-cinnamon tea. From time to time, I step back to get an overview and continue my task tirelessly. I carefully unfold the most fragile balls which I hang delicately. When I hold the one I bought on Lord Street in my hand, my heart sinks and a tear rolls down my cheek. A glass ball similar to an iridescent soap bubble whose ephemeral beauty can break at any moment. Like the fleeting moments of sweetness that Jordan knows how to show when he is not hiding behind a mask of arrogance. Why is he doing this? What hurt him so badly? My thoughts are interrupted by a few knocks on my door. I quickly wipe my eyes with the back of my sleeve and open the door to a smiling Timothy.

"Hello, Line! We were worried, we haven't seen you at the store."

As tall and broad-shouldered as Jordan, under his navy blue duffle coat, I can see that he is only wearing a T-shirt with his faded jeans. Touched by his concern, I smile at him and move over to let him in. "Come in quickly, it's freezing cold in the corridor."

"Ho ho ho, I understand now," he says, advancing towards the tree.

He turns to me and seems to suddenly notice my reddened eyes. "Hey, is everything all right?" he asks, frowning.

"It's okay, Timothy. It's just that decorating a tree by myself immerses me in sometimes painful memories. It's a thing that we usually do with family, but since Grandpa Joe's departure, I find myself all alone. It's hard. I miss him."

Timothy walks towards me, looking worried, and puts a comforting hand on my shoulder. "If you need anything, Line, we are here for you, you know. And I can help you decorate it, this tree!"

"You want to help me?" I say, moved by so much kindness towards me.

I can imagine a loving nature in this man with tender eyes.

And I am sure that we could become very good friends, like with Victor.

"Certainly! When I go to see my family for the holidays, the tree is already done."

I make us coffee and spend the rest of the morning finishing the decorations.

"You've known each other for a long time you and—"

"I have known Jordan since we were children. Our parents were neighbors. We both followed the same path. Same university, same passion for our profession, he is like a brother to me."

"I see. But you talk about your passion for your job when what you do with wood is just... extraordinary. I saw the counter you made at his place, it's incredible how you managed to preserve the beauty and the very essence of wood, I'm really impressed."

He interrupts my sentence with a gesture. "Did you... go to Jordan's?" he asks me, tilting his head to the side, looking surprised.

Damn! So much for discretion! I lower my head while blushing but nevertheless try to give him an honest answer.

"We... ate together the other night, I was coming back from the hospital where I volunteer. It was late and he came home from jogging with food in his arms. We met in the hallway, and he offered to share his meal."

"Well, a little innovation can't hurt. I'm impressed!"

I squint, unsure of where Timothy is coming from.

"It's been a while since Jordan invited a girl to share a meal with him."

"Well not exactly. There's Elise!"

Timothy runs his hand behind the back of the neck and resumes, hesitating. "Elise is not... invited to eat at Jordan's, Line. They..."

"Yeah, yeah you're fine, I get it. Besides, it's actually quite difficult not to get what's going on."

"What I mean, Line, is that the fact that Jordan asked you to share a meal is a first for a very long time."

"What aren't you telling me, Timothy? Why is Jordan so... rebellious?"

"Line, it's not up to me to tell you about it. It's up to him to explain it to you."

"Forget it, anyway, I don't care. He made it clear to me that he has no place for me in his life. Are you going to spend Christmas with your family?"

OK, my strategy of changing the subject is not the most subtle. Besides, Timothy doesn't seem to be fooled, but with gallantry he lets me do it and smiles while continuing to hang figurines in the shape of barley sugar. New knocks on the door sound as we finish placing the star at the top of the tree. There is definitely a crowd today! I open the door and come face to face with Jordan. In his cream-colored Irish turtleneck, he is breathtaking. This sweater accentuates the broad build of his shoulders, and the sight of him so desirable right here on my doorstep makes my heart skip a beat. His outfit is complemented by trendy jeans and a pair of Stan Smith shoes. He glances over my shoulder, and that is enough to convince me that he is looking for his friend. "What the hell is going on here? Tim, I just sent you to check up on her, not to stay!"

I stare at Jordan in amazement. He… worried about me? I am flustered, and the confusion must be visible on my face.

He looks into my eyes and without breaking eye contact, speaks to Timothy again. "Sonny needs you downstairs."

Timothy grabs his jacket and complies. Passing in front of me, he kisses me on the forehead, and winks at me.

"Thank you for this delicious moment, Line. I loved it."

He walks past Jordan and taunts him while the latter squints, growling.

Jordan pushes me inside and closes the door behind him. Suddenly, the air is charged with a very palpable tension. We are both alone in my home. My thoughts become jumbled and jostle under the intense gaze pointed at me.

"What moment was he talking about, Line?"

"Were you worried about me?"

"Line, answer me!"

"No," I answer stubbornly.

"Fuck, Line! Yes, I was worried. Are you happy now? I didn't see you open the shop. We thought you could be sick, since you spend your days locked up in the cold of the Magic Cave."

"Are you spying on me? And if so, why didn't you come yourself?"

"I'm not spying on you! I'm looking after you. *We* are looking after you. And I didn't think you would answer me."

I am touched by this mark of attention and try to appear as detached as possible in order to hide my inner turmoil.

"You have a point. You want some coffee?"

"LINE!"

"OK fine, fine! We decorated the tree together. And how is that any of your business?"

"Are you poaching my partner to decorate a damn Christmas tree?"

"I didn't poach anyone! You sent him to me because you're too stupid to come yourself. What is it, Jordan, are you mad because I screwed up your evening yesterday? So let me remind you that in good neighborly relations, there are the words 'good' and 'neighborly'!" I say, getting angry.

He smiles and replies, amused. "Oh it's okay, you made me pay for it, yeah, with your *Coitus Interruptus*."

We stare at each other for a long time, as if each of us refused to give up on this improbable exchange.

Then, becoming much more serious, he asks quite abruptly. "And that's all?"

"That's all what, Jordan?"

"With Tim. Is that all that happened?"

Is he out of his mind?

Who does he think he is? I don't owe him any explanations! What's with the third degree? He was the one who made Elise yell last night. He's starting to get on my nerves, this bearded buffoon! "Oh well no, that's not all, you see, he also savagely took me against the buffet. Damn, if your buddy isn't in really good shape! A real bulldozer!"

In two steps, Jordan closes the distance, hugging my waist in order to push me back against the wall. His body pressed against mine, fists clenched over my head, forehead against forehead, he tries to control his jagged breathing. My halted breath mingles with his as the beating of my heart pulsates in my chest.

"Damn it, Line. Stop," he whispers softly. "Please… stop provoking me. I'm just trying to protect you."

"From what? Protect me from what, Jordan?"

"From... me, Line."

Framing my face with his hands, he plunges his eyes deep into mine, and I see his torment unleashed. His face is only a reflection of the pain he is trying to fight off. The sight of it freezes me and grips my heart. I put my arms around his waist and press my face against his chest, hugging him harder. His hand reaches out to caress my hair, and we remain glued to each other for a long time. His heartbeat seems to calm down and gently, he releases me to place a tender kiss on my forehead. My heart explodes, and a tear trickles down my cheek.

"I have to go now."

In silence, he steps back and leaves my apartment.

Finally! For the first time, Jordan dropped his mask. I saw the broken man. I'm overwhelmed.

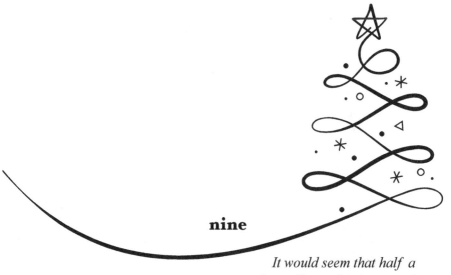

nine

Jordan

I join the guys at the shop and I barely get in the door when Sonny gives me this look of mutual understanding. Timothy, far from being intimidated by my furious look, stands in front of me, arms crossed, looking more than satisfied. The feelings that flurry within me are contradictory. Angry at not being able to control my emotions. Relieved to have had that moment with Line. Thrown off guard by the desire I have for her. We face each other for a long time and in the shop empty of customers, you could almost hear a pin drop. "Are you proud of yourself, Tim?"

"As proud as I can be. Whether you like it or not, Line is a classy girl, and I won't let you destroy her. If she needs me, I will be there, as I am for you, Jordan. And if what she needs is someone to decorate the Christmas tree with her because her grandfather is no longer there to do it, then I will do it. Because we all agree you're not going to be the one helping her with that, right?"

At first, I am surprised by his harsh words then I admire him, proud to have him as a friend. "I expect nothing less from you, Tim. Thank you."

"And for the record, I didn't say anything to her, Jordan. However, she suspects that something is amiss. You won't be able to dodge her questions for very long."

"I know…"

Customers start coming in again and continue to walk in until closing time, after which we go for a drink at the Graffiti Lounge & Bar. I get back home around eleven taking care not to make noise on the stairs so as not to wake her, but as soon as I enter the building, I hear music blaring in her apartment. And not just any music: Jenn Johnson with "You're Gonna Be OK." These few words are like words of hope and encouragement to me. As if Line were sending me a message through her door. Should I read something into it?

Once safely in my apartment, I continue to think about Line's strength of character. A fiery and combative temperament. This girl is a tornado that blew into my life only a few days ago and yet she already holds an important place in it. She doesn't back away from me, she confronts me, forces me to react. Impressive! An amazing little piece of woman who has incrusted herself into my lonely universe with finesse, pushing me to question my personal choices. I am tired of struggling. Should I try? Should I give Line a chance?

As incredible as it may seem, I find myself smiling as I open my fridge and grab a beer. I take my phone out of the back pocket of my jeans and send a message to Line.

[Nice music]

[Do you want me to lick it for you?]

I smile when I read the strange message Line sends back to me. Definitely, autocorrect doesn't fail to spice up our conversations!

[It's harassment dear neighbor]

[Grrrr! Do you want me to LOWER it?]

[No, I want to listen to it with you]

She increases the sound slightly and, leaning against my door, a beer in hand, I close my eyes. When the music ends, I decide to continue this exchange and stay with Line a little longer. I don't feel ready to leave her.

[My turn now]

The song I choose is a Colton Haynes/Travis Atreo cover of "Craving You" by Thomas Rett. This version has a more languid tempo but becomes increasingly louder, crossing our respective walls. I imagine Line leaning against her door, adopting the same position as me. I can almost feel the warmth of her body on my skin, the subtle scent in her hair. I want to knock down the wall to hold her against me again. I breathe in, I breathe out. She can't imagine what she's making me endure. And yet, even if it may seem crazy, I like that. I like what she makes me feel.

My phone vibrates on my thigh almost immediately.

[Excellent choice]

[Excellent choice of dress today]

[Mr. Miller, would that be a compliment from you?]

[Good night, Cupcake]

[Good night, Jordan.]

Lying on my bed, I'm trying to analyze how I came to send these texts to Line and I come to the only plausible conclusion: I needed to be connected to her before going to bed. To ground me before facing another tumultuous night.

I wonder... Would she be able to silence my demons? I close my eyes and fall asleep imagining the snow falling outside the window.

Around four in the morning, I wake up again in a sweat, with the memory of big glassy eyes staring at me accusingly. I seem to feel an icy breath brushing against my neck, like that of a last sigh. I tremble violently and uncontrollable heartbeats tear my chest apart. Like a dead man walking, I make my way in the dark to the bathroom where I slip under the hot jets of the shower, the only thing capable of temporarily pushing back the weight of my guilt as one would rinse out foul stains by throwing buckets of water at them.

I let my thoughts go numb, my tears flow, and weariness overwhelms me. I only come out once my breathing stabilizes. Like every morning, the mirror cries out to me to pull myself together. I grab my razor and try to tame my beard. I put on a tracksuit and leave my apartment to go running. The first frosts of winter give way to a more biting embrace than the previous days. The night ends and in its freezing cloak, I make small strides beneath the flakes that begin to fall. My hoodie protects me from these frozen caresses which flit gracefully before my eyes. I accelerate, letting the cold penetrate my lungs. Two hours. Two hours of running to get rid of these images that clutter my head.

I stop at Starbucks and sit down in the corner. The first customers, the most early-morning customers, begin to parade before my eyes. I bring the steaming cup of coffee to my lips and savor this moment in which I gradually regain a certain control over my mind.

When I push open the doors of the Hipster Maniac Liverpool, Sonny is already there and is setting up. Like all of us, we can say that he really looks the part for this job. His shaggy mop of shining gold hair falls on his piercing blue eyes. His beard, much denser than mine, is perfectly groomed and the many tattoos that cover his body complete the picture. Timothy has a more discreet but no less effective style with the fairer sex. His thick brown hair goes perfectly with his tender eyes tinged with green, and his square jaw proudly sports a precisely trimmed beard. He joins us a few minutes later, holding pastries from Sayers the Bakers, the bakery he loves so much on Williamson Square.

"Guys, there's a party Saturday night at the L1 KTV Club! Jordan, I'm counting on you to bring Line and Capucine. Find a way!"

"I'll let her know, but I'm not promising anything!"

I don't know what Line will think about it or if she will agree to come, but I must admit that the idea of spending a little time with her… excites me.

"Tell it to the Marines!" Sonny intervenes, his eyes bright. "If you apply yourself and you don't behave like an ignoramus, there is no reason that they would refuse to accompany large and beautiful fellows such as ourselves."

"What's your take on Capucine?"

He responds with a smile that leaves no room for doubt. "She's already crazy about me."

Timothy bursts out laughing at the sight of Sonny's deeply convinced expression, while hanging up the white protective blouses adorned with our embroidered logo.

"What about you, Jordan? Is the hatchet buried?"

"When do we get to hear the bell?" adds Sonny.

In the afternoon, I receive a phone call which gives me a good excuse to go see Line at her shop. Taking advantage of a lull, I run directly to the Magic Cave. I find her crouching in the back room, dressed in a large sweater and a scarf that goes around her neck several times. She seems absorbed in reading a book and even the uproar produced by the snowman at the entrance has failed to break her concentration. I refrain from mentioning it and move towards her. "Hey, am I bothering you right now, Cupcake?"

She jumps and looks up, revealing her little red nose.

I crouch down next to her and grab her hands. "Damn Line, you're freezing! Are you trying to get sick?"

The only answer is a loud sneeze, and that's all it takes to worry me. I put a hand on her forehead and see that the fever is already there.

"It's just a little cold, Jordan, nothing serious."

"And letting yourself freeze here is the smartest solution you could come up with? Get up, you're going to humor me and go home and go to bed! You need to be in shape this weekend."

She questions me with her eyes. "Timothy and Sonny want us to spend the evening together at the L1 KTV Club. They asked me to invite you, and Capucine too. It's a music club, there's a great atmosphere there."

She squints and looks at me insistently.

"What?"

"Do you really want me to come?"

I sigh at her worried look and try to reassure her as best I can. "Yes, Line, I would be happy for you and your friend to join us."

"Okay... aaaachooooo!"

"Okay, you look terrible. I'm taking you home, you can barely stand up."

Without further ado, I lift her in my arms and get ready to go out before she objects. She shivers and her teeth chatter, snuggling against my chest. Shit. She seems so fragile. Troubled, I hug her closer to me, trying to warm her up a bit. Seeing her in this state shakes me up.

"My boooook... Take my book plea... AAAAAchoooo! Please."

I yield to her request but grumble under my breath. Is she completely reckless or what? Acting as if this book is more important than her health. Fucking nutjob!

By the time I arrive on our floor, Line is deeply asleep in my arms. I don't have the keys to her apartment and, refusing to wake her up, I have no choice but to keep her at my house so she can rest quietly and in warmth. I stoked the fireplace this morning and the apartment is bathed in gentle heat. I lay her down gently on my bed and cover her with the blanket. I put the book on the bedside table, while lingering on the blue illustrated cover. *The Little Prince*, by Antoine de Saint-Exupéry. My eyes find their way to Line's face, whose regular breathing at least has the merit of reassuring me a little. She must recover and rest. I see her as vulnerable and fragile right now. She moves me. A strange feeling invades me. A protective feeling towards Line. I leave the apartment quietly and return to the barbershop.

"Hey there, you took a while, didn't you?" Timothy says, smiling.

"I'm leaving you guys. Line is sick. I wanted to take her home, but she fell asleep in my arms. So, I put her in my apartment in the meanwhile. Sonny, call a heating repairman, make sure he comes as quickly as possible. Threaten him if necessary."

"No worries, happy to. Jordan? She is okay?"

"Yes, I think, but she has a high fever. She's exhausted."

Timothy walks over to me and gives me a compassionate look. "Take care of her, Jordan. We'll take care of the salon and the repairman."

I thank them then tiptoe back home and start to prepare an "ailing nutjob special." As I start getting busy, my thoughts drift towards the young woman lying in my bed. Seeing her like this in my world, in my bedroom, so fragile, it troubles me. Oh, of course, I could just as easily have put her on the sofa, but my steps led me to my room without me trying to hold them back. I could also have called her friends, Capucine or Victor to take over, but I was unable to bring myself to do that. Something prevented me from doing it. I take care of her, no one else. And however much I try to see the logic in all of this, I can't. I just wanted her to be there, I wanted her to be okay. I'm still surprised by this decision.

Of this inescapable need to protect her, when I know that it would be so much better if I kept my distance. When was the last time I prepared a meal for someone?

Six years...

I've been living on autopilot for six years already, exhausted from those nights that are way too short, where the ghosts of my past come to haunt me every time I close my eyes.

I buried myself in a place where guilt sets the tone and condemns me to exile.

To those who begrudge me my silences, I simply reply: "I don't half talk because I'm half dead."

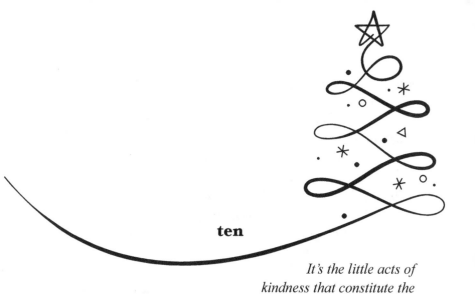

ten

*It's the little acts of
kindness that constitute the
most magnificent relationships.*

Unknown Author

Line

When I open my eyes, Jordan is sitting near me and gently wipes
my forehead with a wet cloth. I feel groggy and the fever is still
there running through my veins like a burning river. He's right,
I'm in bad shape. I feel confused and I find it hard to stay awake.
The room I am in is unfamiliar. I am dizzy. The drawn curtains
barely allow the light to filter in, but I can see a large chest of
drawers in brown wood and a walk-in closet. The huge bed in
which I find myself is covered with a chocolate-colored quilt that
comes up to my chin. But what I find appealing above all is the
fragrance that emanates from it. This scent, I recognize it well
now. His. The sheets impregnated with his smell envelop me and I
give in to the pleasure. Then I snap out of it and I sit up suddenly.
"I... I'm... in your room?"

Very uncomfortable with this situation, I chew my lips
nervously.

"Hey hey, relax, Cupcake," he says soothingly. "Yes. You
fell asleep in my arms, and I didn't have the keys to your house.
So I brought you here."

"Hmm... I..."

Surprised but also moved by Jordan's initiative, I'm at a loss for words and run my hand over my hot forehead.

"How are you feeling?"

"Terrible, I feel muddy. My head is spinning. My body aches all over."

"The opposite would have surprised me, Line. You have a very high fever. Here, drink this! It will relieve your aches and help your fever go down. Do you want me to call a doctor?"

"No, I don't think it'll help. It's just a bad cold."

Feverishly, I grab the glass he hands me and swallow. It is so bitter my face distorts in disgust.

"Yuck… Gross!"

He smiles at my reaction and shakes his head, amused. "It's good for you, Cupcake. I fixed you a tray, I'll go get it," he says, getting up.

"Uh, Jordan. Please tell me you changed the sheets! Because the memory of your girlfriend screaming…"

My comment probably took him off guard. He cocks an eyebrow while stroking his beard then runs his hand through his hair. This gesture raises the bottom of his T-shirt, revealing his firm abs drawing a plunging V under the belt of his jeans. I shudder at this sight and look away before he catches me. Then he breathes in, out, plants his warm gaze in mine and responds hoarsely. "Line, first: Elise is not my girlfriend. And second: no one but me lies in my bed. Now enough with the third degree, I'll go get you your meal."

I watch him leave the room with a strange feeling. Is it the fever or does Jordan seem really worried about my condition? He is bewildering. I try to sit up in bed, but each of my movements is painful. I growl at this sad observation.

When Jordan returns, he holds a tray containing a bowl of soup, a large glass of water, and some applesauce. He helps me sit up a bit and places a cushion behind my back before placing the tray on my lap. Baffled, I look at the tray and blush, moved to see him being so considerate. This is in such contrast with the personality he usually displays. The first spoon is a marvel of flavor. "You really have to tell me where you buy your soup, it's delicious!"

I see him blush in turn as he runs his hand through his beard, embarrassed by my remark.

"I made it while you were sleeping. I had some fresh vegetables in the fridge so…"

"You… you cooked this soup for me?"

"And the applesauce too. Eat!"

"Thank you, Jordan, I—"

"It's okay, no big deal, it's just a meal. That's what neighbors do, right?" he blurts out in a gruff tone reflecting his embarrassment.

I'm amazed. The more I learn about Jordan, the more his personality intrigues me. It looks like two people cohabitate in him. One hateful, wild, and cold. The other, attentive, delicate, and protective. Why is he making such an effort to keep the second at bay?

Once I finish eating, I am once again dizzy and shivering. Jordan immediately suggests that I lie down while as he sits on the edge of the bed. I reach out for my book but he pushes it away so he can grab it.

"Why is this book so important to you, Line?"

"Grandpa Joe read it to me every evening after the death of my parents. I loved listening to him tell me this story. It's not just any book, Jordan. It's the most translated book in France after the Bible. It's a tale full of melancholy, one that fosters dreams, but it's also filled with powerful and inspiring messages. You read it?

"No."

Jordan then opens the novel at my bookmark and begins to read aloud a passage from the book. His deep, deep voice envelops me like a cocoon, and I listen as his words calmly lull me.

"The first evening, I fell asleep on the sand a thousand miles from any inhabited land. I was much more isolated than a shipwrecked man on a raft in the middle of the ocean.

So you can imagine my surprise, at daybreak, when a funny little voice woke me up. She said,

'Please, draw me a sheep!'"[3]

---

[3] excerpt from chapter 1 of *The Little Prince* by Antoine de Saint-Exupéry

Half asleep, I look up at Jordan and watch every line of his raw-looking face. "Jordan, would you have drawn a sheep for me?"

"Draw a... sheep? Uh, no, I don't think so. I would probably have proposed a game of leapfrog instead!"

He gives me a rakish smile and kisses me tenderly on the forehead.

"Sleep, beautiful rose, if you want to bloom again tomorrow."

At this point in my life when I feel so exceedingly vulnerable, for him to be caring for me like this is deeply disturbing but it also gives me a sense of security. I close my eyes and drift off immediately, unable to resist the sleep that's been looming over me any longer.

I have a restless night. The fever is toying with me, I wake up several times drenched in sweat. And each time Jordan is there, taking care of me, giving me a drink to keep me hydrated, making sure I get back to sleep.

When dawn arrives, I am surrounded by powerful arms whose tattoos seem to dance before my eyes. Snuggled against Jordan, I realize that he joined me in bed after the last time I woke up. I savor this moment where pleasure and emotions merge. His beard touches my neck in a delicious caress, and his warm breath flirts with my ear. His muscular body glued to mine completely envelops me and it is with regret that I refrain from kissing him. I feel him wake up behind me without making a move. With his pelvis pressed against my butt, I feel his imperious erection come to life. I stifle a small hiccup of surprise when his deep voice breaks the silence. "I know you're awake, Cupcake."

"I didn't want to disturb you, Jordan."

"Go back to sleep, Line. It's early."

He hugs me tighter and I let myself go against him. I go back to sleep almost immediately so that I don't wake up until much later when he gets up to go and fix lunch. I can clearly see by his somber expression that the caveman has resurfaced again. This saddens me, I join him in the kitchen and without a word sit on one of the stools. Although I am still a little groggy, I feel much better and the fever is gone. He puts a cup of coffee on the counter and pushes it in front of me.

"How are you feeling, Line?"

Destabilized by his somewhat abrupt tone, I try not to let it show. "Better. Thanks, Jordan."

I bring the cup to my lips with a trembling hand and he doesn't fail to notice.

"Line, I'm sorry for earlier. I—"

"Don't apologize, I know it's a perfectly normal reaction for men when they wake up. I'm not completely clueless."

He says nothing but continues to stare at me while I finished my lunch.

When I get up, he slaps his forehead and says, "Oh, I almost forgot! Yesterday, I came to the store to tell you that our cars are ready. We can go get them tomorrow evening if you are free."

"Perfect, but what about the estimate?"

"All taken care of, Line! Come on, get moving. We have shops to open."

I get down from the stool, and he accompanies me to the door.

"You didn't have to do what you did. Thank you for everything, Jordan."

He puts a hand on my cheek and places an innocent kiss on my nose. "It was unusual, but I don't regret it."

"Unusual? What do you mean?"

"I repeat, nobody sleeps here, Line."

"Excuse me, but Elise definitely came here several nights."

He sketches a contrite smile but doesn't back down. "No one sleeps here. Especially not Elise. You are the first to spend the night at my place, in my bed, for years."

This revelation is like a bolt of lightning. "Come on, why do you refuse to be happy? You have beautiful things in you that you force yourself to hide! But I saw them Jordan! I saw that you are not who you pretend to be."

"Line, you don't know what you're talking about. What you see is just a ghost. I'm no longer that man. I'm far from perfect and—"

"So what? No one is perfect; I don't care if you're perfect!"

He closes his eyes and exhales loudly, running his hand through his hair. "Don't push it, Line. You had better leave now."

He kisses me tenderly on the top of my head and opens the door to let me out.

***

Later, curled up on my couch, I think back to what Jordan told me before I left. I can't resist asking him one last question. I take out my phone and quickly write my message.
[Why Jordan?
Why are you shutting yourself up?
What if you gave yourself the opportunity to try?
Isn't it important for you to be happy?]
The answer I receive is not what I expected, but the depth of its content feels like a confession.

[Supposing I know of a flower that is absolutely unique,
that is nowhere to be found except on my planet,
and any minute that flower could accidentally
be eaten up by a little lamb,
isn't that important?[4]]
By quoting this passage from *The Little Prince*, he demonstrates two things. He read the book overnight and he wants to protect me again and again. Protect me from himself, at the expense of his own happiness.

And with this message he proves to me that he is a Prince.

---

[4] excerpt from chapter 7 of *The Little Prince* by Antoine de Saint-Exupéry

eleven

The heart. We often use this word that so eloquently says what it does not mean.

Maurice Donnay

Jordan

She attracts me like no other lover and pointedly refuses to disengage from my thoughts. That night was a true test of self-control! I took refuge in reading this tale to avoid spinning my wheels as I contemplated her sweet face on my pillow. I discovered a crystalline fragility in her. Grandpa Joe's departure was an ordeal that she is still struggling to overcome. Feeling her frail body huddled in my arms, I was bombarded with strange mixed feelings of fear and possessiveness. Because yes, not being able to take it anymore, I lay down next to her, so eager was I to breathe in each fragrance that perfumes her soul. I got drunk on the sweetness that characterizes her, burying my nose in her golden hair. No ghost came to cut my night short. My only distress was the temptation to give in to my desire for her. This appetite which has been devouring me ever since she is came into my life.

The loneliness that I inflict on myself may seem deadly in itself, but how could I blow out her flame and draw her in among the shadows that inhabit me? It's in a daze that I push open the doors of the Hipster Maniac Liverpool.

The snow is falling hard outside, and a thick layer begins to cover Mathew Street. Cars are idling and pedestrians are struggling with each step, to avoid slipping on the road. Peering through the window, my eyes are lost in the contemplation of life when Timothy puts a friendly hand on my shoulder. "Jordan, are you okay?"

I hesitate before answering. I shrug my shoulders and go back to the counter to get some coffee before perching myself on a stool. "It was a long night, Tim. I've been up since four in the morning. I maybe closed my eyes for an hour at most."

"How is she?"

"Better."

"So, let me ask you again, Jordan. How are you?"

I see from his insistent gaze that I'm not going to get out of this.

"What do you think?" I reply wearily. "Look outside! Every single snowflake hurts so much. Fuck! I hate this shitty season. It's hard enough the rest of the year, but this is the worst time of all."

Timothy grips the back of my neck with his hand and exerts pressure as if to transmit a little of his strength to me. His support is whole, fraternal and precious.

Sonny arrives and shakes his hair to get rid of the snowflakes strewn on his head. He puts down his leather jacket and joins us, understanding in the blink of an eye the subject of our conversation. His face darkens and he comes to sit near me. "You know we're here man. Always!"

"I know!"

Wishing to change the subject, I get up and clap my hands.

"Go, go, go, go! We have customers coming. Let's get back on track guys!"

***

Each scissor stroke, each stroke of the comb, allows me to keep a semblance of calm, at least in appearance. Hours pass and my friends are not fooled by my fragile state that I hide from the eyes of others. At three, taking advantage of some downtime, Line pushes the door of the Hipster Maniac Liverpool and comes to get a hot drink. Immediately, Sonny and Timothy greet her and ask her how she's doing. I stand back and pretend to clean the clippers.

"Glad to know that the fever has gone down. Not too tired?" asks Timothy.

"I feel drained right now. Since we woke up at six, it's starting to take its toll! I'm sure I'm not the only one feeling this way…"

I lower my head to place a bottle of cream near one of the rinsing tanks when Timothy absentmindedly lets fly: "Jordan, when we spoke earlier, didn't you tell me that you had been awake since four?"

Damn it! Tim just stuck his foot in his mouth. I can already feel Line's gaze on me.

I look up and my gaze clings to hers.

Then she understands.

This morning was not just a case of morning wood.

No, it was pure, unadulterated desire! Deep and unsustainable.

By her expression, I know she knows. Her cheeks are covered with a pink tinge that unsettles me.

I grumble between my teeth, unable to hide my irritation. "Oh! We are not in a tea room here! When you're done gossiping, maybe we can get back to work."

Line doesn't reply but turns on her heel and leaves hastily. Great! What could I have said to her? "Sorry but you got me hard all night?" I can easily imagine the face she would've made. In some cases, silence is preferable, even if mine is a habit. Sonny squints as he stares at me long and hard, trying to understand what had just happened. I ignore him and resume my activities but don't fail to notice the sidelong glances that my two friends exchange.

Timothy ends up asking, "Waking up at four, huh? Why does Line think you woke up with her?"

"Shit!"

Sonny stands in front of me, arms crossed, waiting for a response. "Because I was comfortable, and I don't want her to know!"

"Why?"

I hate when they do this. "I don't want her to get her hopes up unnecessarily. I'm just trying to protect her."

"And you, who protects you, Jordan? Maybe you should give her a chance to see who you are."

"You mean who I was! No. Bad idea. Forget about it and mind your own business."

At the end of the day, I still don't know what to do. Do I need to clarify certain points with Line and talk to her face to face or keep going as usual? Totally undecided on what to do, my mind is a jumble of questions. Why does her presence plague me so? How has she managed to get under my skin at this point in my life? And above all, how am I going to get out of this attraction that I have for her? I'm obsessed with her. I know that if I give in, it will be even harder. For her and for me. So, I just watch her and content myself with her vicinal presence.

I drop the grate of Hipster Maniac Liverpool and greet Tim and Sonny who are leaving together towards Rubber Soul, the bar located a few yards away from here. Going up the stairs that lead to my apartment, I see Line who is apparently preparing to leave. She pauses, obviously embarrassed to run into me. Damn, how beautiful she is in her little gray skirt! I stroke my beard, scrutinizing her graceful body. Our eyes meet and time seems to stand still in this dark stairwell. "You're leaving?" I ask in a voice that I hope sounds detached.

"Obviously."

"Line…"

"It's fine, Jordan. You don't need to make any excuses. Apparently, you like me but not as much as you like what you have with Elise. Right?"

My blood just boils. How can she, even for a single instant, compare herself to Elise? She is so much more than that! I join her on the stairs and my arm grips her waist, drawing her to me while I lean my back against the wall. "I forbid you to compare yourself to her, Line!" I say, brushing the corner of her lips. "What do you want from me?"

She then presses against me and crosses the last few centimeters that separate our lips. I can't resist any longer and devour that perfect mouth. My tongue is wrapped around hers, and we taste each other without restraint. I lose my mind as our kiss becomes more intense and passionate, revealing this hunger for her that growls within me. My hand slides under her skirt to reveal red lace boxer shorts covering her firm and plump butt that I caress with delight. She shudders, letting out an exquisite little sigh. Her hand slides through my hair as our kiss intensifies. This girl will be the death of me. She has this insolence that attracts me and this candor that melts my heart. In the middle of this stairwell, our bodies are searching for each other, to the tune of our short breaths. My erect dick threatens to bust through the seams of my jeans in torment. With great difficulty, I manage to pull myself together and gently grab Line by the shoulders to push her back. The glimmer of a dare shines in her eyes. "Line, damn it!"

"Are you going to continue to deny it?"

"I'm not denying anything, but it's not a good idea! The fact that I want you doesn't change my position. I have nothing to bring to the table. I can't offer you any kind of commitment, just a sexual relationship based on desire. And you deserve better than that."

She wraps her little arms around my waist and places her ear on my heart which is beating frantically in my chest. Her eyes then come to meet mine which are staring at her with difficulty.

"One day this heart will awaken, and I will be there!"

I take her in my arms and rock her gently before reluctantly letting her go.

* * *

Another night full of nightmares deprives me of sleep, confirming that Line has no place in my life. I get lost in a maze of memories, strangled by guilt. Like the sinner who suffers his penance, I tirelessly endure this sentence without rejecting it because no action can atone for my sin.

The next day is painful and it's with bags under my eyes that I go pick up Line to go to the garage. No comment on her part about my exhausted features, but rather a look filled with concern. This benevolent aspect of her personality moves me. Soft and attentive, she can see suffering even when it is hidden. After a while, she starts the conversation innocuously. "The heating tech called, he will be there Monday, first thing in the morning."

"That's a good thing, Line. It couldn't go on like that."

"Yes, I'm happy. I will be able to finish putting everything away under better conditions. Jordan. Do you hear that noise at night too?"

"What noise, Line?"

"Like something banging. It's pretty nondescript to tell the truth."

My face tightens and I grip the steering wheel even harder. "Probably a draft."

She dons a skeptical pout but does not insist any further. After informing me that she would be at the club with Capucine and Victor on Saturday evening, I park and we each collect our reconditioned vehicles.

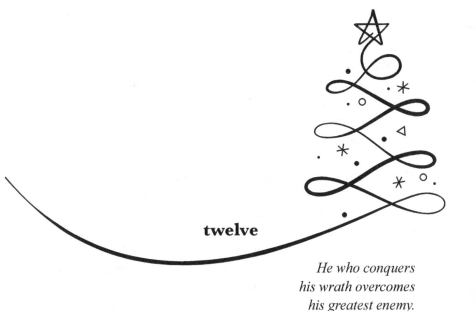

twelve

*He who conquers
his wrath overcomes
his greatest enemy.*

Publilius Syrus

Line

The weekend approaches; Victor and Capucine can hardly wait. I admit that it has been a long time since we went out, and this evening will be an opportunity to introduce Victor to the boys. While we finish dolling up with Capucine, the latter can't help but ask, "So, have you made any progress with your hipster hunk?"

"Not really, but he isn't as wild as he seems after all. But secretive, yes. For sure!"

Capucine doubles down and adds, mischievously, "He made her homemade soup! He's a very gallant caveman"

I burst out laughing at Victor's impressed reaction. "Right, but… it was only because I was sick!"

"Well, in any event, he took care of you. That's a good start."

Except that if Jordan continues to persist, it won't go anywhere!

We meet the boys in front of the L1 KTV Club around 9:30. At the entrance, the boss gives them a big bear hug, confirming that they are regulars there. Already, people are crowding the dancefloor, while the stage is occupied by a couple singing a catchy tune. The lights of the club's pink and blue neon lights give it a super cool trendy pop style. Victor offers to pay for the first round. Jordan sits on one of the benches and shifts to leave me a seat. As for Capucine, she sits down between Timothy and Sonny.

When Victor returns with the drinks, I notice a guitar case lying on the ground.

Timothy leans over to answer my unspoken question. "It's mine, I used to come and play here," he says simply.

He informs me that he started playing at a very young age, and that for him, it's just a hobby although he still indulges in it regularly. So now I discover another talent of Timothy's, in addition to that of working with wood.

We cheerfully toast in a relaxed atmosphere and get to know each other better. This is how Timothy admits to having family in the south of France and that he stays there regularly. He is therefore perfectly bilingual, which pleases Capucine who informs him of her dual citizenship. Sonny can't help but add his two cents. "And that's why we love him so much! Every time he comes back, he teaches us expressions from there. Like stuffing the envelope or getting your head wet."

I look around this unfamiliar place and I must admit that it looks good! The padded black leather benches lend a rock vibe to the decor. The tables, illuminated from the inside by blue neon lights, add a very trendy touch. Good idea of the owner to have mixed karaoke club and disco.

Sonny approaches us suspiciously, as if he didn't want other eavesdroppers to hear what he had to say to us. "Have you heard the rumor running around the neighborhood? It seems that the other evening, in the middle of the night, people heard a terrifying sound. One of those strident sounds that freezes your blood, scary, don't you think? Didn't you hear anything?"

Jordan's lips quiver, as he smirks at the memory of dear Alfredo Silencio. He gives me a fleeting look, then gets up and heads for the bar. My heart races suddenly, filled with a strong emotion, my eyes following his sexy and self-assured swagger. This complicity in his eyes. This silent exchange that just happened belongs only to us.

He could have teased me in front of the others. But he preferred to keep quiet and not reveal anything about this episode, to make it a secret. Our secret. I suddenly realize that Jordan, when he doesn't play the provocation card, knows how to show great modesty. He only reveals what he wants. If, in the beginning, I considered him a brute, I now come to realize that his personality is actually quite complex and he's about much more than just provocative crudeness. This truth smacks me across the face. He camouflages his profound nature by hiding it under the skin of an ill-bred ruffian.

Capucine suddenly gets up all agitated, like she's got ants in her pants. "Oh, this song is great, come dance with me, Line!"

I let her drag me onto the dance floor where a hoard of people is writhing and wriggling to the pop. We dance for a long time, having an absolute blast. What a joy to rediscover simple pleasures! Tonight, I feel like a teenager discovering the delights of disco, dancing with her girlfriend, letting herself go, savoring the singular atmosphere of a night out with friends.

Classic rock notes then resonate, and I am about to go sit back down, when a hand grabs me with authority.

Jordan, standing in front of me with a mysterious look on his face, begins to lead the dance with astonishing mastery. I would never have suspected that he was such a good dancer and, even if I am not really gifted, he guides me with grace. Some even stop to watch us as we twirl around with ease. Truth be told, I couldn't dream of a better partner! When the music ends, he doesn't let go of me and pulls me towards him possessively. The next song is a fabulous Chester See slow dance, "Who Am I to Stand in Your Way," and I find myself enveloped in his powerful arms. I don't try to break away, preferring to savor the warmth emanating from his body pressed against mine.

As we blend into the crowd, I suddenly feel cut off from the rest of the club. As if we were alone in the world. Isolated in our bubble. He tightens his grip and takes me on a languorous journey to which I surrender. His hand comes to caress my hair, urging me with delicate pressure to let my head rest against his chest. From that moment on, I only follow a single rhythm. That of the beating of his heart.

Fast, faint, but steady.

I feel his chest swell, and a long sigh escapes his lips. His thumb tirelessly caresses the hollow in the small of my back, in a soft and comforting movement. When was the last time I felt this safe? For the first time, I feel at home, curled up in his arms. In this precise instant, I know that this will lead to unspeakable suffering but tearing myself away from this embrace is beyond my control. Everything pushes me towards him like a centrifugal force that throws us together. As if our paths were destined to cross. For better or for worse. Because the duality that lives in Jordan is omnipresent and looms over us ready to burst.

My thinking is interrupted by the soft timbre of his voice, which makes every bone in my body shudder. "What are you thinking about, Line?"

I lower my chin and stare at the ground.

With the tip of his index finger, he lifts face back up until my gaze meets his.

"Line…"

"You're… different, Jordan. You… I see another side of you."

He exhales deeply and seems tormented by my words.

"I wish this moment would never end, Line. But what you are seeing now no longer exists. I'm not the person I used to be, and I have nothing to offer you. You would suffer, and I don't want that. You deserve so much more. So many things separate us."

"Jordan… you refuse to live fully."

He plants a kiss on my forehead, as if trying to comfort me. "In your book, the little prince says, 'If someone loves a flower of which just one example exists among all the millions and millions of stars, that's enough to make him happy when he looks at the stars.' So, come on Line, let's go join the others."

Suddenly, I feel Jordan tense up. His eyes fill with black anger. I turn around and try to figure out what is making him react like this when I see a man arguing with the boss who seems to be refusing him access to the club.

In the blink of an eye, Jordan forges his way through the crowd and pounces on the waxy-faced guy who has just forced his way in. I then witness a scene of extreme violence, where blows rain down like a tsunami. Nothing seems to be able to stop this burst of brutality. Timothy and Sonny immediately jump out of their armchairs and try, with a great degree of difficulty, to contain Jordan who is beating the guy to a pulp. Each seizes him by a shoulder, and they manage to disengage Jordan, who struggles frantically. Victor joins them to lend a helping hand, but Sonny beckons him to stay with us. Timothy yells at us to go home and calls out to the boss to walk us out. "No way!" I protest, trembling. "We stay here with you. We are waiting for you.

Just then, Jordan breaks free from the hands of his friends and once again begins to pummel the guy who collapses on the ground. I'm petrified; such violence is beyond me. My brain tells me to get the hell out of there, but my body won't let me go.

Timothy glares at me and reiterates his order. "Damn it! Get out of here. Don't make me say it again! Line, do what I tell you!"

Suddenly, I realize that the man that Jordan is beating up on stares at me deviously, and I realize that Tim wants to protect us by keeping us out of harm's way.

The owner stands in front of us then takes us out through a service door under the watchful eye of Sonny who makes certain that we are leaving the premises.

Once outside in the freezing cold, I'm in a daze. What just happened? I am dumbfounded. And just like Capucine, embarrassed and worried.

Only Victor seems more concerned than frightened. While driving me home, he irritably blurts out, "What the hell was that?"

"Huh? I have no idea."

"This guy… something's fishy."

"You… you know him, do you?"

"Not personally, no. I don't associate with those kinds of people, but I know them by sight and reputation. That guy is a junkie, Line, a fucking addict. Hanging out with him is a terrible idea."

This new information pales me. When did Jordan's path cross that of an addict? Why did Jordan attack him? Apparently, they've crossed paths before. But how?

I take leave of my friends and once alone at home, I put on a white cotton nightie and curl up on the couch with my slanket. A thousand questions hit me all at once. I find myself trembling with all my limbs. I never thought Jordan would be capable of such aggressiveness. Nothing seemed to be able to stop him and his two friends had a hard time making him let go. The blustering brutality came on so suddenly! It left us terrified. I try to think of a logical explanation for Jordan's untenable violence. Where did it come from? What could drive this mysterious man to that point? His driving conflict brings out such ferocity that he seems totally out of control. I am worried about him but also about the secrets that shape his life.

I listen for noises in the hallway, waiting for Jordan to return, but the fatigue hits me unexpectedly and I fall asleep. I am awakened much later by a familiar strange noise. The one I hear regularly at night. I get up and carefully go out into the hallway. Relentlessly repetitive, the noise doesn't stop. I suddenly look at Jordan's closed door and hear music coming from within, I realize that the noise is coming from his apartment. "Jordan?"

But no one answers. However, it's clear that the noise is coming from his place. Driven by worry, I put my hand on the doorknob and after a moment of hesitation, I turn it. The door opens as if it were beckoning me to enter. The notes of Ruelle's song "Rival" resound eerily, plunging the living room into an atmosphere charged with apprehension. I slowly enter the apartment, short of breath. I call out once more. "Jordan?"

Still no answer. Only the sound of incessant blows. I make my way through the dark apartment, following the hammering sound, to the bathroom where a weak light filters through the half-open door. My heart pounding, I arm myself with courage and approach the opening. I freeze on the spot.

The scene is positively petrifying. Thick steam fills the room and I discover Jordan, from behind, completely naked in the shower, pounding the wall in despair. The jets of hot water trickle down his body, and his sobs mingle with the sound of the blows on the wall. My heart breaks in the face of his suffering. My eyes burn as the tears fall from them. I walk slowly towards him and whisper in a single breath, "Jordan…"

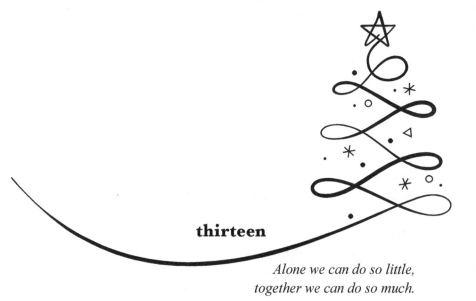

thirteen

Alone we can do so little,
together we can do so much.

Joseph P. Lash, *Helen and her*
teacher: the story of Helen
Keller and Anne Sullivan

Jordan

I shudder upon hearing her voice behind me. My whole body feels her presence and stiffens. I turn my head slightly to the right without turning around, a visible sign that I am aware of her presence. After a moment of hesitation, she steps forward to position herself against me. Her hand rests flat on my shoulder while her mouth lays a tender kiss between my shoulder blades. I flinch beneath her delicate touch. Motionless, I allow her to continue, tormented by the strange sensation it brings on in me, then after a few minutes I decide to turn around slowly to face this waif of a woman who stands in front of me, who walked in on me in a moment of absolute distress. My red eyes latch on to her gaze, and in her shimmering eyes I see her utter determination. She looks like a warrior that will never back down. Fascinated, I observe her at length, scrutinizing her silhouette, the shape of her, lingering on her firm chest which rises and falls at regular intervals.

Slowly, I let a finger slip from her neck to the plunging neckline of her nightgown, now soaked by the water falling on us. In victory, I grab her right breast, erect under the transparent fabric. At my touch, her mouth opens and emits a sigh. With my other hand, I grab her by the waist and draw her to me possessively as my mouth descends to that provocative little nipple. I press her against the shower wall, to continue teasing her hardened nipple. I suck ardently, nibble, delight in its sweetness. I slide a hand on her butt and grip firmly. Each of my gestures is slow but abrupt under the heat of desire that spreads within me. I plunge my eyes into hers. I want the assurance that I have her total, unconditional consent. She is simmering beneath my touch, in the agonizing expectation that I continue. I do, however, feel the need to clarify things before taking ownership of her body. "It won't change anything we've talked about, Line. No commitments, no questions. It won't mean anything. If that's not okay, there is still time for you to back out."

She nods and, not being able to hold back any longer, I lift her as her legs come to curl around my hips. I feed on her luscious now-open mouth, letting my tongue penetrate it to entwine with hers. She overflows with femininity, offering herself to me with such elegance that my desire is increased tenfold. Still glued to one another, I leave the shower stall and go over to place her on my bed. Looming over her, I stare at her unremittingly, languid between my sheets. My eyes roam over every curve of her body, laid bare under my insistent gaze. I perceive her embarrassment as I take my time to look at her so patiently. But when she rubs her thighs together, I realize that this discomfort is born of desire. And those pink spots on her cheeks ignite my desire. I crawl above her, remove her nightgown and my already-hard dick flutters at the sight of her willing body. I lick my lips, reveling in this vision. I want to make every inch of her milky skin sizzle. To take her down pleasure-filled paths, to hear her cry out with pleasure. Tonight, I want her to be mine, and even if it drives me mad, I will take my sweet time satisfying my hunger for her. Every second Line spends in my bed will be spent pleasing her. My face is lost in the back of her neck where I breathe the soft scent that permeates her flesh. My beard caresses her skin; it makes her shudder. I savor the taste on my tongue, revealing a delicate and intoxicating flavor. I move slowly, feeling her squirm under me.

Her small but exquisite chest captivates me, and I play with her nipples with immeasurable calm. I continue my descent, leaving wet furrows with the tip of my tongue, blowing on it to watch her skin bristle. Each shiver passing through her makes my cock throb even harder.

Once I make it past the curve of her belly button, I straighten up and slide off her thong without taking my eyes off her. I rest one of her legs on my shoulder and kiss the inside of her thigh while my hand moves towards her intimate parts. In a slow and tempting gesture, my index finger follows the fold of her slit in slow motion and she arches her back in response. For God's Sake! She drives me crazy. I rest her leg on the bed and grip her waist to draw her closer to me. I then begin to savor this delicate flesh with ardor, my tongue delving into every corner of her wet pussy. Her moans fill the room, she braces herself and I really need to get a grip if I am going to continue my feast. I start in on her pink pearl and insert two fingers inside of her, feeling her monumentally strong contractions on them. "Yes, beautiful. Let yourself go."

My fingers start moving around inside of her, caressing every corner of her private cave while my tongue tirelessly continues to tantalize the nerve point that overlooks it. I could feast on her forever. The tremors that shake her body now beget a smile of satisfaction as the orgasm passes through her with force. She is the perfect representation of raw eroticism. Feminine from head to toe, overflowing with pleasure. Her cries resound within me like a delectable delicacy as the aroma of her joy graces my palate with its presence. She barely has a chance to catch her breath when I flip her over onto her stomach in one, quick gesture. My hand lingers, caressing her back, to finally touch the arch of her buxom butt. My lips explore this body undulating underneath me, responsive and vibrant, punctuated with her sighs. With one hand, I enclose her delicate throat where I feel her pulse beating and with simple pressure rotate her face towards me. Her full lips part, letting out a breath of pleasure. Our eyes meet, revealing a crude and sensual mutual desire. My teeth sink into the most tender part of her neck, nibbling, sucking, leaving small pink marks here and there. She lets me mark her skin, arches under me and whispers in a smoldering groan while pressing against my cock.

"Again!"

I cover myself with protection while savoring the view of what awaits me. I draw her to me so that she raises her pelvis and sink into her with a liberating cry. Every movement of the hip is intoxicating, revives me, and pushes away the images that clouded my mind when she arrived. I chase my demons back and forth ever more strongly. So narrow, so hot… I dive into her, again and again, and with each movement, our bodies clap against each other. My fingers sink into the tender flesh of her hips which I cling onto with force. Every moan she emits makes me harder and I speed up my movements as if I wanted to lose myself in her indefinitely. Is it possible to die of pleasure? If so, I ask for eternal damnation. Sweat pearls on her body shaken by my pounding. She comes in a liberating blast, and my name spews from her lips with force. The vision of her that I have in this precise moment, ass on high, short of breath, makes it hard to hold back any longer. I liberate myself by growling with an intensity that overwhelms me. Only our jagged breaths can be heard now. I lie down next to her and take her in my arms, where she snuggles immediately.

I caress her hair, unable to prevent myself from ceaselessly cuddling up to her after this moment of incredible intensity in which she gave herself to me unabashedly. Silence fills the room, and her calm breathing confirms that she has fallen asleep. I am more shaken up than I care to admit. Like a flashback that keeps looping back around, I remember every moment of our embrace. Her long sighs at my caresses, her voice strangled in orgasm, the way her body undulated between my hands. One word comes to mind: phantasmagoric. And yet she is there before my eyes, in my arms and in my bed. Without a word, she knew how to pull me from the darkness in which I was flailing a few hours earlier. Just how to disconnect me from the hatred that was bubbling up in me after my fight with Styx. I'm in trouble! Because a salient question now arises.

What now?

How am I going to handle this? My mind is struggling to focus with Line up against me. Her perfume envelops me and soon my eyelids close, my face buried in her neck.

When I open my eyes, the bed is empty, cold. I spring from

the bed to go look for Line. The bathroom is empty and there is silence in the living room. Then on the kitchen counter, I find a note placed in such a way it couldn't be missed.

No commitments, no questions.

Shit! This is not what I was expecting.

Why did she leave like that? I'm totally taken aback by her reaction. I would have preferred that we not part ways like this. Did I hurt her? Was I too abrupt? All of a sudden, I feel terrible for giving in to my lust.

Damn!

I used my unhappiness as an excuse to let myself go.

I throw on my jeans and go across the hall to knock on her door. "Line, open up!"

Silence.

"Line!"

Nothing, I can't hear anything. She's not there but it is only eight o'clock. Where could she be so early on a Sunday morning? I go home and slam the door. I send her a text, but it remains unanswered. The day goes by and Line still remains silent. I find myself pacing around in circles like a caged lion all day. Leaning on the kitchen counter—her note in plain view—I crack my neck, relieving the tension that builds up there. I feel guilty. I should never have let this happen.

During the evening, I receive calls from Sonny and Tim wanting news. After the altercation at the club, they had a really hard time calming me down. With the help of the boss of L1 KTV, they isolated me in a back room so they could get Styx out, that bastard. I ignore my late-night misconduct and try to reassure them.

When night falls, I sit on my bed and grab the wooden box that Timothy carved with such finesse, which I keep hidden under the box springs. I lift the cover and take out the photo with trembling hands. My eyes land on this face which seems estranged to me.

What did you do to me?

Many say that pain subsides over time. *My ass!*

Tears run down my cheeks, and my heart bleeds endlessly. The pain consumes me. I put away the picture with the medallion resting at the bottom of the box and put it back in place under the bed. I am in for another tormented night.

As usual.

No respite.

Except for those two nights spent with Line. But on those two nights, I barely slept a couple of hours. In other words, not much. It's with great difficulty that I emerge the next morning. I swallow my coffee and put on my sneakers to go running before opening the shop. My strides are long, sustained and rapid. I run out of breath, push my limits, failing to get rid of my deeply annoying problem. To say that I am upset by Line running away is a candy-coated euphemism. I did specify that I did not want any involvement, but that was no reason to up and vanish! Her silence worries me, and I blame her for putting me through this. Why? I was honest with her when I accepted her advances, so what happened? Why did she cut and run? Why is she not responding to my messages? For nearly two hours, I exhausted myself, pacing through the neighborhood streets as they were quietly waking up, not knowing what to make of all this.

I notice that shops have started stringing on lights in their storefronts, illuminating the windows with a multitude of colors characteristic of this approaching holiday season. It annoys me even more, and my bad mood kicks up a notch. I'm a bundle of nerves and even my intensive jogging doesn't help appease my state of mind. I absolutely need to speak to her, to understand why she is hiding behind this wall of silence. This is driving me crazy!

I sit on a bench and try to calm my breathing down. I'm trying to figure out what I can say to make her understand, but nothing comes to mind. If I tell her of my guilt, she will look at me in disgust. I don't care to see contempt and disappointment in her eyes. I couldn't bear it. Not after the night we spent together. I would rather have her hate me than tell her the truth. But I also want answers, to know why she left without warning. I need to clarify our relationship. We made a mistake, of course, but I don't want it to screw up the mutually beneficial bond we have established. I get up and continue my run, making a brisk beeline for the Magic Cave. When I push open the door, I find her deep in conversation with some guy, all smiling, who is unscrupulously checking her out. My blood boils suddenly.

Who the hell does he think he is?

"Line, I need to talk to you!"

She jumps at my petulant outburst.

"We'll talk later, Jordan, I'm busy as you can see," she replies through clenched teeth.

I lose patience and raise my voice. "LINE!"

The guy in question decides to play the hero and step in. "The lady told you she would talk to you later."

"You there, a word of advice. Shut the fuck up or your tonsils will be saying hello to your asshole. Got it?"

Line intervenes and stands in front of me, furious, hand on her hips. "What's the matter with you? GET OUT OF HERE!"

I turn my back to her, trembling with rage, and kick that strepitous snowman rolling around on the sidewalk.

"I hate you!" she yells to my back.

Well, that's it. It's over!

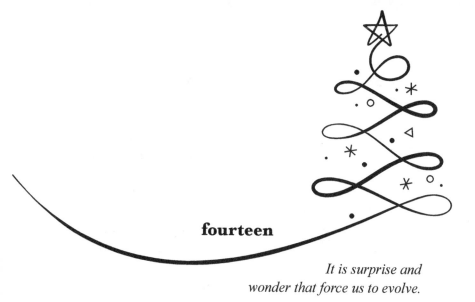

fourteen

*It is surprise and
wonder that force us to evolve.*

Edgar Morin

Line

I woke up with every muscle in my body aching, remembering the intensity with which Jordan had taken me. He took me on paths of pleasure the likes of which I had never known. He is driven by such a ferocious appetite, that sharing his bed is a dizzying experience. His desire is raw, sensual, animalistic. Last night in his bathroom I found a damaged man. Beyond the anger, there was great fragility. The kind that eats away at you, that surrounds you and compels you to waste away slowly.

Who is this man that hides behind a mask of arrogance by day only to reveal himself as being on the brink of a breakdown when no one is around? I awoke to a feeling of unchartered sensuality in the arms of a man whom I still desire. However, I also realized that what it ignites in me is dangerous, addictive. It would be too easy to fall in love with this man who is averse to any serious relationship. And the pain I felt when he said *her* first name stung me deeply, like a slap in the face. The bottom falling out of my peaceful little world. He made love to me with incredible intensity yet in his sleep, he dreams of another.

I am racked with pain.

I am not strong enough for this.

I deliberately offered myself to him, and I have no regrets whatsoever. He was hurting; I was there. But like he said: no commitments, no questions. So, this morning, I preferred to take off before he got up, to avoid an embarrassing scene. However, spending the day at home, a stone's throw away from him, was too much. I needed to be elsewhere, to think things over, and above all to shake off the storm of emotions stirring within me.

I left. Straight to Capucine's. And in my rush to leave this place and get as far away as possible, I dropped my cell phone in the street. It got smashed on the sidewalk. RIP my phone.

Now I'm angry! Livid! How dare he come to the Magic Cave and behave with such crudeness and animosity? I hate him! He broke my snowman in a deliberately vicious gesture. Oh, I'm mad at him alright. He came barging in there like a maniac, interrupting my conversation, spewing threats. What was he thinking? That because we spent a night together, it gives him the right to come into my store and insult people? That I am at his disposal? Seriously?

Just goes to show he doesn't know me very well. I don't need him in my life. Not that way, anyway. After his cataclysmic visit, I couldn't even look the heating guy in the face. The only good thing that came out of this chaotic morning is that my hot water heater works again.

The day seems endless. Each moment is a struggle to dispel the images of his body that keep coming back to haunt me. Sculpted to perfection, firm, invigorating, and powerful. Covered with tattoos in various and colorful patterns intended to mesmerize. Salient muscles, a body to die for.

I hate him!

Even more!

I won't be the one playing the hysterical groupie. I refuse to let my life be dictated by the shenanigans of some egocentric bearded brute!

At the end of the day, I hoist Snowy into the dumpster. He's completely trashed. My anger soars. I dash furiously out to my car and head to the mall to buy a new cell phone. Surrounded by holiday tunes, late-night boutiques are swarming with shoppers. I wander the aisles at length, taking advantage of this reprieve that will prevent me from running into Jordan. Having purchased my phone, I can't resist the urge to indulge myself. And between clothes, lingerie, and various flavors of ice cream, my monthly budget just took a serious hit!

A few hours later, I'm on my couch, a jar of ice cream on my lap. I revel in its caramel flavor while calling Capucine.

"So tell me, Gremlin, how is it going with the bearded man?"

After a deep sigh, I tell her all about this catastrophic encounter today.

She listens to me patiently, trying to quell my anger and manages to comfort me as always. However, her obsession with bearded men in general is insufferable.

"Your neighbor may have a nasty temper, but he is drop dead gorgeous."

"Great, good for him, Capu. Just as long as he drops dead somewhere else."

"Him maybe, but you, it would do you good to come across a man who knows how to take care of business. And now that you have tasted it, you may not be able to go back. Every girl should have a bearded man up her sleeve."

"Uuh, Capucine. You know you're talking about human beings, right? Not decorative objects?"

"Who said anything about decorations? I'm talking about sex toys!"

"Capucine!!!"

"Come on, bearded men, they're a dime a dozen. I'm sure I can find you another one! Well, I gotta go, Gremlin. Don't eat after midnight and be sure to stay dry!"

I smile as I think back to my friend's last words. This god-awful habit of waking up in the middle of the night to snack dates back to my college years, when the stress of exams kept me from sleeping. Since then, at the slightest annoyance, my sleep has been punctuated by trips to the kitchen.

Inadvertently, I can't help but try to listen in on what's going on across the hall. But silence reigns. The silence is almost palpable. Nary a noise that would betray Jordan's presence. I sigh spitefully and sink deeper into my sofa. It pisses me off to be sitting here waiting for him.

My dirty mind isn't making my job any easier. I have to be careful not to think about him anymore. I dig around in a box and finally find what I'm looking for. An album that I have not yet completed. I grab the shoebox containing the mess of photos that are patiently waiting to find their place.

All these memories leave a smile floating on my face.

A photo of Grandpa Joe and me when I was 8 years old: I straddle my grandpa on all fours, and the expression on my face is priceless. I dreamed of having my very own pony, but since we had neither the means nor the space for one, Grandpa Joe had renamed himself "Pony Joe." And he played that role to perfection. He would have done anything to make me happy. Despite the absence of my parents who were taken away much too early in an accident, he knew how to give me the foundations of a solid and loving family. I take another photo and come across a picture of Victor, Capucine and me at graduation. We were so proud! It seems so far away. Life doesn't always give us what we look forward to. As a child, we develop theories about what our future will be and life happily interferes with our projects. So we improvise.

It's just after five o'clock when I hear the sound of Jordan's door keys. I am tempted to rush to the door to call him out on his bullshit, but I hold back. Why? I don't know. Well, yes, I do. Seeing him again would only rekindle the memories of that incredible night. Besides, he may not be alone. I couldn't bear it. Fleeing him is the best option.

* * *

The following days are like a parody of Benny Hill, the scenes where everyone flees from everyone else. I wait until Jordan leaves before I go out and come back before he does. I scrupulously try to avoid him. It's childish, I know. But there are two of us playing this little game. He, too, has shown extreme caution. I don't even hear music coming from his apartment anymore and I haven't been to Hipster Maniac in four days. However, Timothy came to see me. He tried to get information from me about the state of war between Jordan and me. Tim even tried to apologize for the destruction of Snowy: "He's hot-tempered, Line, and the seasonal festivities only make things worse. Don't be mad at him. He's not as bad as he seems."

Sonny also stopped by, but he came to the shop bearing hot chocolate. At least, that's the excuse he found to tell me how unfortunate it was that the tensions between Jordan and I were still running high. Of course, he regretted that his friend took it out on my animated figure, but like Timothy, he made excuses for Jordan.

That evening, I returned late from the hospital, held back by a discussion with Jeff who heads our association. He entrusted me with the responsibility of organizing Christmas at the hospital. And this project delights me. Being able to bring a smile to the faces of these little munchkins all hooked up to wires and tubes brings me immeasurable joy. I climb the stairs mechanically, lost in my thoughts of setting up this project, when I arrive at the landing and freeze.

Snowman is there, enthroned beside the door to my apartment. Impeccably repaired. You can hardly notice the large crack that has been carefully sealed. I stay there for an eternity, inspecting it from every angle. I did not anticipate this. I open my door and as I enter the apartment, my cell phone beeps with a text from an unknown number.

[I'm sorry. Jordan]

How did he get my new number? He's apologizing? But why? For the snowman or for... Suddenly, his door opens and he appears in the doorway, his face serious, his eyes ringed. His stature is so imposing that I feel very small. With shaky legs, I remain frozen in front of him. My heart is beating like crazy but I'm trying to keep face.

"Were you planning to run away from me like that forever?"

"It's you who—" I start, outraged.

"I shouldn't have, OK! But running away from me is not a solution. I still live here, and you are still my neighbor. Maybe we can talk about it?"

Arms crossed over his chest, he looms over me, full of confidence as I tremble like a leaf. How the hell am I supposed to handle this when my whole body goes haywire at the mere sight of him? "We will discuss it, but not tonight. I'm tired and I want to go to bed."

Far from letting himself be discouraged, he comes even closer up to the point where I feel his body brushing against mine. His scent envelops me and images of us in bed begin to rumble around in my head. He tilts his head forward, brushing the back of my neck with his beard and whispers confidently, "What bothers you most? That I sent your thingamajig flying? Or that we fucked?"

Faced with this unexpected question, I retreat in silence, looking away from his eyes as anger invades me. My cheeks catch fire, and my breath gets caught in my throat.

"Answer me," he insists.

"You had no right to take out your anger out on my snowman!"

"Fuck, Line, you left without warning. I sent you a message and you didn't reply! I was pissed off. It was Sonny who told me that you no longer had a cell phone."

I stare at him, taken aback. "Sonny?"

"Yes. Apparently, he had Capucine on the phone. Why did you leave like that?"

Choosing to dodge the question, I continue standing up to him. "You didn't need to make such a big stink at the store!"

"Your friend didn't have to interfere in our conversation."

What? Is this a joke? Friend?

"A conversation? That's your idea of a conversation? And, for the record, he's not my fucking friend, that was the heating guy! But, damn it, what's wrong with you?"

Jordan squint as he lifts my face to him with his fingertip. "Do you regret it? Line, look at me!"

"I… I didn't know what to think after… after… Well, basically, I thought it would be better for me to leave rather than to suffer embarrassing looks when you got up. You made it clear that you didn't want anything serious, right? I didn't want to impose."

"Fuck, Line. You… OK, look. I didn't mean to hurt you. Go on and get some sleep, Cupcake."

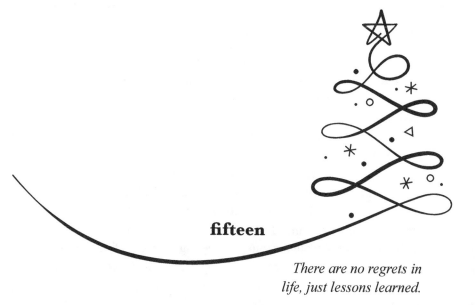

fifteen

There are no regrets in life, just lessons learned.

Jennifer Aniston

Jordan

I am trapped in my remorse, having locked myself in this empty cage alone. So far, I have been pretty successful at pushing people away. It didn't bother me. Worse, I didn't care, preferring to hide behind a frosty facade. But this little nutjob reaches in beyond my barriers. I try to keep her at bay, but having her next door is not as easy as I originally thought. I remember the many discussions with Grandpa Joe who read me like an open book. He had been there for me, offering advice and support. "I'm sure my little Line can melt the ice around your heart," he used to tell me jokingly. But, was he really kidding? The more I know about this little scrap of a woman, the more something in me crumbles. She managed to make a breach that evening she surprised me in the shower. Goddamnit! He must be having a good laugh from up there watching me torture myself over his little cupcake.

I can't help but wonder how Line is feeling. Is she as upset as I am? Does she think about that night as often as I do?

Sitting idiotically on my couch, the images of an action movie scroll by without me paying the slightest attention. My mind is elsewhere. It's stuck in my neighbor's home.

When I went out that night and saw her snowman in the

trash can, I felt really guilty. Me and my temper! I retrieved it and managed to thoroughly repair the damage. I wanted to restore her memory of Grandpa Joe and prove to her I'm not that bad basically. I'm just… broken.

But then again, couldn't she have simply said that that asshole was the heating repairman?

I sigh and slide a Blu-ray into the player, hoping to divert my mind from the thousands of questions that pervade my thoughts. Why do I feel like Line isn't telling me everything? I've had this strange feeling ever since I saw her eyes avoiding mine earlier. As if she was intentionally keeping something from me. What is she not telling me? I do everything to keep her at a distance and now that she is actually backing off, it aggravates the hell out of me. What on earth is wrong with me?

Maybe it's time I go back to Abigail. I have held out so far, but I'm losing my resolve. I need to let go so I can release this terrible pressure that is suffocating me. Words once buried deep inside are yearning to break free. I absolutely have to go see her or I will lose my mind. She alone has what it takes to calm me down. Without judgment, without rebuke.

***

The next day, I let Sonny and Timothy know that I'll be out all day. The advantage of working together is that we can easily adapt our schedules to everyone's benefit. I slept very little last night, largely preoccupied wondering if I was really going to go back to Abby. But by morning, I had made up my mind. It's what I need. After going for my morning run, I take a quick shower, put on jeans, a black shirt, a sweater, and a pair of boots. I prepare a small plate for Stringer who is nowhere to be found, then go to Thomas Steers Way which borders Chavasse Park, a must-see park where many families come to relax. When I arrive at my destination, I remain for a moment in front of the intercom of the gray building towering over me. Full of doubts, I hesitate, and my thoughts are all over the place. But I quickly chase these doubts away and press the button whose inscription is all too familiar to me: "Abigail Loxford."

I hear a crackling noise, then the hall door unlocks. I rush into the corridor, walk up two flights of stairs, until I find myself in front of a wooden door. I knock four times, hoping that the code hasn't changed. When I hear the latch open, I hold my breath and then my eyes land on her.

"Jordan, I thought I'd never see you again."

Hands in the pockets of my jeans, on edge, I can't help but make an affable remark. "Only fools never change their minds, Abby."

Abigail faces me, a victorious smile on her face. In her tailor-made suit and with her long-manicured nails, she looks like one of those hoity-toity women on *Desperate Housewives*.

"What brings you here? I thought you said we were over."

At her honeyed tone, my jaws tense, but I suck it up. Our last meeting had clearly offended her. She had not at all appreciated my decision to cease all contact before opening the salon. "I had to come, Abigail. I can't manage my life anymore."

"Come in. You know that my door is always open for you. What do you need, Jordan? I'm listening."

I walk through the door, carefully avoiding physical contact. I am not there for her, but for what she can do for me. As I enter the large room, I look around. Nothing has changed. The same rug with tribal patterns. The same mirrored coffee table that reflects my tired face. It takes me back. Abigail watches me without saying a word. She lets me revisit the place, inspect each decorative element without interrupting.

I sit on the sofa, take off my sweater and roll up the sleeves of my shirt, getting ready to silence my demons.

Abigail comes back, with a swagger in her step on her varnished high heels, holding in her hand a wooden box which she places on the table.

"Relax, Jordan honey. It's going to be fine. Let me do this."

A few hours later, I come out again, with uncertainty in my step. I float in a thick cloud of pseudo-comfort. With Abigail, I can let myself go, I have full confidence in her know-how. She knows how to take me from one world to another. She provides me with what I need when the void becomes too vast. It has been three years since I've been here. Since the opening of Hipster Maniac to tell the truth. I had stopped so I could devote myself to this professional project with Tim and Sonny. We worked like hell to start our business, not counting the hours. And today, we have something to show for it. It's working well for us, professionally speaking.

Each of us has baggage, each of us tries in his own way to stay on course. But most importantly, we have found each other, and our friendship is unwavering. Too many collective tribulations, too much pain drowned in drunken evenings. Some see us as party animals when we are really just survivors of a vitriolic life whose thorns left us with permanent scars. My steps take me to the park where I lie down on the thick, frosty grass. It's freezing cold and I am the only one sprawled out. But I'm not ready to go back, I need more time. I observe the comings and goings of passers-by, listen to the song of a bird perched on a branch, smile at the sight of a child throwing a tantrum for a donut...

My phone rings when my eyes are drawn to a silhouette that I know all too well. Styx. Damn! What is he doing here? I reject the call without even looking at who called and put my phone back in my pocket. I will make this asshole pay if it's the last thing I do. Discreetly, I get up, careful not to be spotted and decide to follow him from a distance. I become nauseous as anger overcomes me. I have to contain myself, breathe, exhale, make sure he doesn't notice me. From afar, I follow his steps, observe him walking like a madman straight towards Hartley Quay. Holy shit! I know where he's going before we even get there. That bastard is going straight to the Albert Dock warehouse complex. I will not follow him there. Going back there is just impossible. I stop myself in my tracks, watching him go. My shoulders sag under the weight of guilt and I turn away before I can even catch him in the act. One day, I will find the strength to corner him. But that day is still far away. I try to regulate the beating of my heart by calling for calm.

On the way back, my mind wanders again towards that little green-eyed nutjob across the hall. At the mere memory of our embrace, the discomfort that I suddenly feel in my jeans brings me brutally back to my senses. Hmm... My mind wants her, but my body wants her even more. I long to lose myself in her until I can't take it anymore, to revel in her body and the music of her moans.

I'm dying to see her eyes veil again as her orgasm overwhelms her. Damn, this chick is making me lose my self-control. A cold shower would be very helpful to calm the throbbing between my thighs. I hurry back home to hide. Only fate decides to play tricks on me. No sooner do I cross the threshold of the building than I come face to face with Line. Fuck!

Hands in my jean pockets, I try to adjust my jeans discreetly so as to hide my embarrassment while feigning nonchalance. "Hey there, Line. Aren't you working today?"

"Yes, but I came to get a tea bag from my apartment. Is everything okay, Jordan?"

"Yes, of course. Why do you ask?"

"You weren't at the shop today."

"Ah... Uh... Yes, I took a day off. One of the perks of being your own boss."

"Oh, OK. I think I'll take a day off this week too. I want..."

There, she completely lost me! I'm not paying attention to her anymore. Just her pronouncing the word "want" makes me lose my mind. My dick is on the verge of exploding in my pants and she chooses this moment to shoot the breeze. *Sweetheart, if you only knew what I wanted at this precise moment, you would run away before I could catch you.* OK, this is a sad state of affairs. My cock is doing the thinking for me. I need to get the fuck out of here and fast. "Okay, bye. Gotta go! See you later, Line."

She seems taken aback by the abruptness of my words and disappears to let me pass by before leaving to go back to her shop. Damn! In terms of tact, I'll have to do better next time. Oh, well. It was either that or me pressing her against the wall of this godforsaken hallway. I run up the steps and finally lock myself in my apartment.

In no time, I'm in the shower, my dick in my hands, stroking it at regular intervals. Each thought of Line only increases my violently pulsating desire. I can see myself sinking into it roughly, reveling in her sighs, languid in the middle of the crumpled sheets of my bed. My hand tightens more firmly on my penis, increasing the pace to the rhythm of my desire. It doesn't take long for me to shoot the wad with all my strength, in a groan of satisfaction that has been stifled for too long.

Damn it! When was the last time I jerked off? I must not have been more than 15 years old. However, I must admit that this girl makes me hard like no other! Her tight ass and bright eyes will be the death of me. A *big* problem, to say the least!

Once showered and dressed, I sit in front of a cup of coffee and look at my phone. Sonny tried to reach me. Damn, I missed that call. I dial the number to the salon but Timothy answers, "Hipster Maniac, hello."

"It's Jordan, Tim! Sonny called me earlier?"

"Oh yeah, nothing serious, just a problem with the delivery of grooming oils. Can you try to contact the supplier?"

"OK, I'll take care of it!"

"Hey, Jordan! Everything is alright?"

"I'm fine, Timothy It's all under control…"

Yep, my last sentence wasn't very convincing. Especially in light of my recent activity. No matter how hard I try to keep a straight face, right now, it's all completely out of hand. Even my determination to keep away from Line. To be honest, I want her under me, on me, in front of me and everywhere in between.

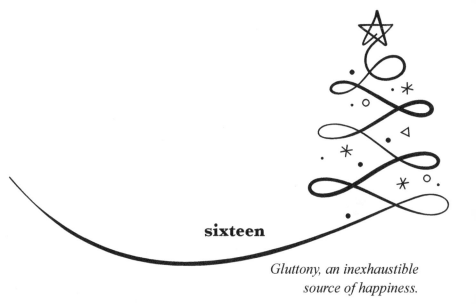

sixteen

*Gluttony, an inexhaustible
source of happiness.*

Pierre Hermé

Line

The fleeting encounter with Jordan in the lobby of the building left me bemused. I return to my shop with the feeling that he couldn't wait to get away from me. These constant mood swings are starting to get on my nerves. Not only does he continuously haunt my thoughts, but every encounter is an ordeal. Destabilizing and intoxicating. Oh, damn it, what's happening to me? Since when do I fall head over heels for a man I have only known for a few days? Especially one who clearly doesn't want to be in a relationship!

In spite of it all, I can't help but hope that he changes his mind.

Relentlessly, I immerse myself in Grandpa Joe's accounts, sort his papers, and realize that filing was not his thing. But after long hours of hard work, I have confirmation that the Magic Cave is doing just fine. That's enough to make me smile again.

I am interrupted by the phone ringing in the shop. "Magic Cave, hello!"

"Hi, Gremlin, I'm pleased to inform you that the phone line in your shop is working perfectly!"

"Capucine! You're unbelievable. Is that why you are calling?"

"Nooo, but since I wanted to talk to you, I said to myself, I might as well see if her phone works."

"I admit that I hadn't thought about that yet."

"Well now it's done! Okay, but I'm actually calling about something else entirely. How would you like to curl up in front of *The Great Spy Chase* this evening? That famous French film I was telling you about with the bearded spies. We can make hot chocolate with marshmallows. Okay, it's not really a Christmas movie but you gotta see it!"

"Capu, you are miraculous! I just spent the entire day up to my ears in the books and a relaxing evening would do me a world of good! Victor is coming too?"

"No, not tonight, he had something else to do apparently."

"Oh! Well, it will be a girls' night then."

"Great! It's going to be awesome! I'll meet you at the store."

"OK, see you soon."

After hanging up, I feel relieved. Capucine has this strange power to bring back my smile with a simple phone call.

I have a good hour ahead of me before she arrives, and I take this opportunity to ponder the hospital's Christmas mission. I will need a Santa Claus, if possible an elf as well, and maybe organize some activities for the children. As for the decorations, I will find everything I need at the association office. I'll discuss it with Victor, he knows our stock like the back of his hand.

When I look up from my spreadsheet, I jump in fear when I find Timothy standing in the middle of the store, arms crossed. I was so absorbed in my work, I didn't even hear the door chime. "Tim! Damn, you're worse than a ninja! I didn't hear you come in."

"I can tell, yes, but I didn't want to interrupt you, you looked so concentrated," he replies calmly.

"I'm preparing Christmas for the children at the hospital."

"You impress me, Line. You are perfection personified! And Jordan, is he still as stubborn?"

I look at Tim with a smile and retort jokingly, "Well, maybe not but he's damn well close."

Capucine arrives at this exact moment and her smile widens when she sees that I have company.

"Hello, both of you! Look, Line, I had a raided the marshmallow aisle! We are going to have a blast tonight!"

She hands me a bag overflowing with pink and white treats, which I take with sparkling eyes.

Timothy looks at us confused, darting his eyes back and forth between me and her, before he spots the sweets.

"Capucine is planning a French film, chocolate, and marshmallow evening," I explain.

Visibly interested, Timothy's eyes widen like saucers. "Oh, no way! Which movie are you going to watch?"

"*The Great Spy Chase*!" she replies proudly.

"With Lino Ventura?"

"You've heard of it? Ah yes, silly me. Of course, you have! Your French origins!"

"It's been ages since I've seen it. It's a wonderful movie!"

Capucine and I look at each other in silence. It seems that we are both thinking the exact same thing. "Timothy, do you want to join us tonight?"

Tim's face is plastered with a dazzling smile and the childlike joy it exudes is a pleasure to behold. "Heck yeah, I'm down! But are you sure you don't mind? Maybe you wanted to have a girls' night in?"

"Not at all, it will be fun," says Capucine. "Let's say 9 o'clock at Line's?"

"Sold!"

On that note, he leaves the shop smiling and returns to the barbershop.

Less than two minutes later, Sonny hurls the door open and rushes in. "Are you having a party and didn't invite me? I'm mortally offended!" he exclaims, theatrically donning an air of outrage.

Capucine bursts out laughing and can't resist messing with him. "Uh, Sonny, do you speak French?"

"Well, no... but... you can translate for me, right?"

Impossible to resist this adorably childlike expression of Sonny's. I can't leave him hanging any longer and invite him to join us this evening.

OK, I'll take a rain check on girls' night. At least this will help take my mind off of things!

It's funny to see them both, as close as two brothers and yet diametrically opposed. Tim is a quiet force, a shoulder to lean on, always there with good advice and a kind word. Sonny is more dynamic, loves sketchy jokes, and partying. As for Jordan…

Shit! I really have to get him out of my head.

After closing the shop, Capucine and I go up to the apartment where I take a long shower while she busies herself depositing the evening's delicacies in bowls. When I leave the bathroom, she has placed trays on the coffee table in the living room. Small toothpicks decorated with pink ribbons abound. I burst out laughing as I picture the face of those two guys with a pink ribboned toothpick in their hands. I look at my friend while trying to catch my breath, but the laughter is contagious, and we find ourselves guffawing like a couple of teenagers.

"It couldn't possibly be more girly. They may turn around and leave."

We are still riding the wave of our hilarity, giggling nonstop when someone knocks on the door. "Capu, can you get that? I'm in the kitchen taking out the cups."

My head is still in the cabinet when a firm hand pulls me away. Jordan, in all his splendor, stands right there before me.

"The guys dragged me with them. But if it bothers you…"

I try to regain my composure under Jordan's inquisitive look. "I'll take out an extra mug."

"Line, are you sure?"

"And you? Are *you* sure? Do you really want to spend the evening here?"

His gaze pierces through me because he knows perfectly well that I am referring to his constant mood swings. His eyes become veiled but with a movement of the head, he confirms his consent. A strange feeling then flows through me. Yes, he hurt me, however he is taking a step forward by coming here this evening. That he wants to spend this evening by my side is reassuring. My heart is racing.

Very well, the *bearded spies* are all here! Let the party begin!

Clearly, the plan for this evening has deviated from the original. They all good-naturedly settle into the living room while Capucine and I take care of serving the steaming cups of hot chocolate. Before I sit down, I realize that I have forgotten the cinnamon and so I make a quick trip to the kitchen. When I return, the only spot available is next to Jordan. The glances exchanged between my friends confirm that this was well calculated on their part. I wrap myself in a blanket to place a barrier between our two bodies. Yes, I know, it's ridiculous and totally unnecessary. Timothy took his place on the carpet and Capucine and Sonny are on the bean bag chairs. We dim the lights, and the movie begins. From the start, we all burst out laughing in response to Sonny's incessant interruptions: "What is he saying? What did he say? I don't get it?! And there, him, what's *he* saying?"

I must say, it is quite the challenge to stay focused on the movie with Jordan's presence at my side. I can hardly sit still but half an hour into the movie, he delicately draws me towards him. With no intention of resisting, I allow myself to curl up to him and all the tension accumulated throughout the day magically evaporates. Insidiously, my caveman slips his hand under the blanket and comes to meet my shoulder which he gently caresses with his thumb while watching the movie. Does he have the slightest idea that this simple gesture sparks transcendental turmoil within me? This moment of tenderness moves me to no end. A quick glance at his face confirms that he knows exactly what he's doing; that slight smile floating on his lips doesn't lie!

As I get up to prepare a second round of hot chocolate, Jordan follows me into the kitchen. I shrewdly try to avoid his gaze but didn't take into account his persistence. Trapped between the sink and his massive body, I have no choice but to look at him when he raises my head towards him with his fingertip.

"Are you enjoying your evening?" he says to me in that rocky voice of his.

"I am. And you?"

"It's… innovative!"

He places a kiss on my forehead, and we return to our friends. Capucine is starting a second movie to which I don't pay attention. Again, curled up against Jordan my eyes slowly close, and I fall asleep.

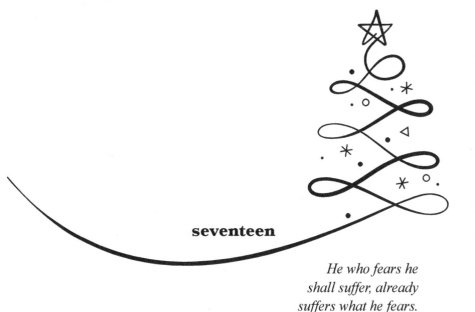

seventeen

*He who fears he
shall suffer, already
suffers what he fears.*

Michel de Montaigne,
Essays

Jordan

A few days have passed since the evening at Line's with the others. Again, I pull back while my body is practically begging for it. But it's even worse than before. When I am near her, my heart races uncontrollably. She's like this catchy repetitive tune, an earworm that becomes an obsession without you knowing why. My fingers tremble when I touch her, but I refuse to let myself go. I am well aware that I am not being fair. Taking advantage of her one day: brushing against her, caressing her, cuddling her. Then running away the next: distant, innocuous. Yes, I'm running away, I'm fleeing my desire for her. But what has become of me? I don't want to make her suffer and yet that is exactly what I am doing. I see it every time our paths cross. That sad, faded look in the back of her eyes. Those same eyes that were all cheerfulness and light in the beginning. I have become an expert in emotional coercion.

I sigh, exhausted by my own thoughts, when a clearing of the throat invites me to raise my head. Timothy and Sonny stand before me, arms crossed, looking at me with a weird look. The rush hour having come and gone, we take advantage of the down time to do some cleaning in the shop. "What? What's up with you two?"

To tell the truth, it's more like a bark than a question.

"Jordan. What are you doing, damn it?" Sonny, on the offensive.

"Unless proven otherwise, I'm working right now, aren't I?" I respond while counting bottles of oil.

Timothy jumps in before Sonny can answer. "Come on, don't play dumb. You know good and well we are not talking about work. We mean Line! Damn it, she's not a yo-yo! And you had better respect her! Otherwise, I swear I'll knock the living daylights out of you. You can either get out of her life or give her a place in yours. But you better make up your mind, and quickly!"

In gestural punctuation, he shakes his fist right under my nose.

"A piece of advice Tim: mind your own business. How do you expect me to make room for her when that space is occupied by another?"

Suddenly, I look up and see Line on the doorstep, certainly here to get something hot to drink.

From her look, I get that she overheard everything. "I... I... But... What is going on with you guys? Sonny? Tim?"

Eyes wide and white as snow, she steps shyly forward and puts a hand on Timothy's shoulder. "Timothy, please, don't..."

Lowering his fist to his side, Tim takes a step back.

"Line!"

Her eyes clouded with tears, she turns on her heels and bolts, followed by Timothy. I remain motionless, staring at the wide-open door through which the cold air rushes in. Acerbic applause snaps me out of my stupor. "Well done, man! It was already sad, now it's downright pitiful. That was your best shot at reconnecting with life and you just ruined everything!" adds Sonny.

"What are you trying to say? You think I'm enjoying this?"

"OK, so make a choice but make it fast!"

I challenge him with my eyes, but I know he is right. Now, I'm not only dispirited, I'm enraged. I suddenly feel like I'm suffocating. In anger, I tear off my barber jacket and throw it on one of the shampoo stations before walking out. Sonny doesn't even try to stop me. He tells me just as I walk past the door, "Don't worry about it, I'll close up and leave my phone on!"

I walk aimlessly for several hours. Just to get away from it all, to escape. I end up landing in a bar where I sit at the counter. I take advantage of this deserted place as a temporary refuge. Leaning on the counter, hands around my head, I feel the overwhelming weight of my inability to extricate myself from this impossible situation. After half an hour, the waiter approaches, sympathetic. "Shit day?" he says to me.

"Shit life would be more accurate," I answer laconically.

"A girl?"

"A woman. Or rather women, plural."

Serving me another glass of bourbon and another one for himself, he raises the glass and makes a toast. "To women: those who make us laugh and suffer, love and curse. To women that make us hard to the point of hysteria!"

I look up at him, smiling at these articulate words of wisdom. "Amen!"

Sitting there on that stool, my mind gradually seems to calm down. It's only much later that I return to my apartment. After giving it a great deal of thought, I come up with an idea. Crazy maybe, but worth exploring. It would require some planning, and I would most likely have to leave for a few days. But it might just be a necessary, important step that would enable me to move forward and try to save myself. As neon lights replace the light of day, I sit on my sofa waiting for the sounds of footsteps on the stairs. I forgot that it was Thursday. Line is probably at the hospital and won't be back until late. It's her volunteer day, and this simple fact fills me with affection. What an extraordinary woman. She is overflowing with admirable qualities: kindness, generosity, humor, knowledge, innocence, sensuality, honesty, dedication... Compared to her, I don't have much going on. But I have this desire to cherish her, to protect her and above all to bring a smile back to her lips. I get up and call Stringer, but he refuses to come out. It happens sometimes. You know, he and I really do have a lot in common.

In the morning, my eyes swollen from my nightmares, I'm slowly emerging in front of a cup of coffee when I hear a few knocks on the door. Still wearing a tracksuit, I open the door to a

Timothy in no better shape than I am. I hate it when we argue. I sigh and tilt my head to the side.

"Are you going to let me in?"

I step aside and invite my friend to sit in the living room.

"Jordan, I'm sorry—"

"Stop! I don't hold that against you, on the contrary. Only a true friend has the courage to stand up to me like you did. I know that my behavior towards Line is appalling, and I..."

"She is hurting, Jordan. She doesn't know what to think."

"Have you talked to her?"

"Yes. At length. I found her in tears at the back of her shop. You need to do something, Jordan. Talk to her, try to explain yourself. If you don't tell her everything, at least try to settle things down and make her understand that you really are a good guy."

"And how do you expect her to have anything to do with me once I've told her everything, huh? She'll cut and run for sure!"

"You don't know that! She might understand, listen, sympathize. You can't let her think you are playing around with her. Because that's not the case, is it? Am I right?"

Rubbing my beard with my hand, the pain grips me with full force. "No, Tim, it isn't. Quite the opposite. But I'm scared. I'm afraid I'll back out again. And what if I can't... I already feel guilty about the little snippets of happiness I feel when she's around. We know when the pain starts but do we know if it ever really stops or if it sticks to us indefinitely?"

"Dude, you'll get there eventually. What scares you the most?"

"She's too omnipresent."

"You're too much! You don't even spend that much time together."

"Exactly! It's when she's *not* there that I can't breathe. She is on my mind every minute of every day."

"Jordan, you're smitten!"

"I know. And what's worse, she chewed me up and spit me out, bro!"

We hang around for a while talking then he leaves to open the shop while I jump in the shower. This serendipitous morning meeting allowed me to put words to my fears. One step up.

At the store, we have several appointments, and the morning passes in the blink of an eye. Around two o'clock in the afternoon, taking advantage of a moment of calm, I gather my courage and decide to go find Line at the Cave. Spurred on by Sonny and Timothy, I go out and cross the few yards that separate our shops. The most bewildering thing is that despite my apprehension, I can hardly wait to unburden myself.

I push open the door. A strange silence fills the room. Normally, I hear Line rummaging around on the shelves even if she is in the back of the store. I call out but no one answers me. I walk forward with this bizarre feeling, a bad feeling, that something is wrong. Panic suddenly grips me when I see her, lying on the ground, a spilled cup by her side. Her waxy complexion revives my deepest demons, and I start to scream at the tops of my lungs. Sonny and Timothy come running and stop dead in front of Line's inert body. Kneeling beside her, I take her in my arms, my whole body shaking. "She... she's breathing. Call a doctor! Quickly!"

Timothy is the most reactive and immediately dials the emergency number. The paramedics arrive a few moments later although it seems like an eternity to me. Suddenly, she opens her eyes, seems totally disoriented, and starts panicking.

Fuck!

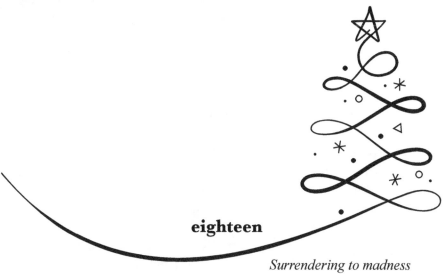

eighteen

*Surrendering to madness
takes as much effort as spending
your life trying to remain sane.*

Jean-Pierre Richard

Line

What the... I... Holy cow, everything in here is moving!

As soon as I open one eye, I close it again. The world is
spinning around me...

Weeeee! It's like a merry-go-round, only nauseating!

My thoughts are running amuck, and I don't even feel like
chasing after them. I try to sit up, but a mysterious force pushes
me back down on... on what, by the way?!

Oooh! It's spinni—

"Miss? Miss, can you hear me? Do you understand what
I'm saying?"

*Aargh! Who is that? I wish he'd shut up. I'm trying to sing!
What was that I was singing? You put your left foot in, you take
your left... shake it all about... do the hooooooooookey pokey...
that's what it's all about...*

"Miss Thomas, please stay still!"

I try to sit up again but everything is soft.

My knees are soft!

And... I burst out laughing.

"LINE!"

The powerful voice suddenly resonates throughout the room. I gather my thoughts but it's really hard. I just want to laugh, to laugh and laugh and laugh…

I suddenly feel two straps pressing on my arms. Strong. Powerful. No, those aren't straps, they are hands. Tattooed, massive, and familiar. In front of me, a man with a white beard places this contraption on me.

"Come on, let me examine you!"

Oh? Santa Claus is here with his long white beard and he even has… headphones!

"Sooo cooooooool! Santa Claus is really groovy this year. Hey, Santa, what are you listening to? Go ahead, turn it uuuuuuuup!"

Other voices reach me from my left.

"Oh, my! She's completely out of it!"

"Yeah, totally tripping!"

I turn my heavy head to the side and discern two more heads leaning over me. "Oooooh, the *bearded spies* are here toooooo!"

The old bearded guy gets angry and orders me to shut up, looking deeply annoyed.

"Ho, ho, ho! Cheer up Santa, or you'll end up like the Grinch. Where is he, by the way? Oh right, he's behind me!"

I hear him grumble and he tightens his grip on me.

I lean over towards Santa Claus and whisper with confidence (well at least I *think* I am whispering), "Watch out Santa, the Grinch, he's surly. Plus, he haaaaates Christmas. I think he has a problem with balls, Christmas balls…"

And I start laughing again inexplicably.

Jordan shakes me slightly and urges me to calm down. "For God's sake, stop it, Line!"

"You, I'm not talking to you. You're stupid!"

Seemingly at the end of his rope, he starts yelling at me. "And you got high!" he shouts.

"Maybe. Buuuuut for me at least, it's temporary!"

"Jordan," Sonny intervenes, "maybe you and Tim should go for a walk and—"

"No way, I'm staying right here! I'm not leaving her side!"

He barely gets a chance to finish his sentence when a nurse

walks in and wordlessly gives me a shot which immediately puts me into a deep sleep.

* * *

I awake in a hospital room that is silent and plunged into darkness. Disoriented at first, I try to understand what I'm doing there. Everything is blurred, as if awaking from a nightmare. However, my train of thought is disrupted by the silhouette that I make out on the armchair near the bed. Jordan stares at me with his black eyes. The exhaustion portrayed on his face is a horror to behold and I can say with absolute certainty that he isn't in the best of moods. I fidget, uncomfortable, then finally ask him, "What are you doing here, Jordan?"

"What do you think? What the fuck am I doing in this hospital room? Are you even aware of what happened?"

His dry, hard tone goes hand in hand with his stringent attitude.

"I'm having trouble remembering. I…"

"We found you face down on the floor of your store, Line! What the fuck were you thinking? Do you have any idea how worried we were?"

"What on earth are you talking about? And stop barking at me, I have one hell of a headache!"

My head between my hands, I try to relieve the pounding that is raging inside by pressing on it. My mouth is as dry as if I had just crossed a desert. I feel drained and getting into it with Jordan now is beyond my strength.

The door opens on a doctor who enters, chart in hand. "Hello, Miss Thomas, do you remember me?"

I stare at him, looking for an answer, but nothing.

What, am I supposed to know him?

"I'm the doctor who checked you in upon your arrival. What do you remember?"

"Uh, I was in the shop, and I wanted to make myself a cup of tea. I found some in a box that belonged to my grandfather. After that, it's all a blur!"

"Miss Thomas, after analyzing that tea that you drank, it

appears that it was anything but tea! It was actually an infusion of psilocybin, in other words: magic mushrooms. In a nutshell, you were tripping on shrooms. And given the state you were in when you got here, I can only advise you to avoid going down that road again."

I can't believe what I'm hearing. I try to remember but draw a blank. I am horrified. What was Grandpa Joe doing with that stuff? "I assure you doctor, I had no idea. And what's going to happen now? Can I go home?"

"It's best that you stay under surveillance tonight. But if someone can stay with you, I have no problem with you being discharged."

Jordan gets up and speaks to the doctor authoritatively. "I'll watch over her tonight!"

"In that case, you can go but you do need to sign the discharge papers at the front desk."

The situation suddenly took an unexpected turn. Of course, the idea of spending the night here is far from appealing. But spending the night with Jordan?!

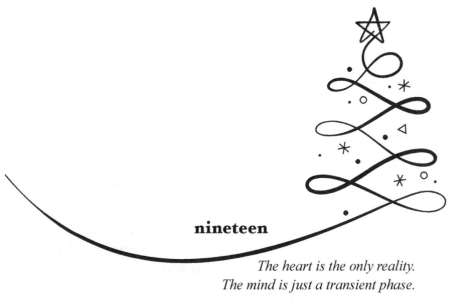

nineteen

The heart is the only reality.
The mind is just a transient phase.

Ramana Maharshi

Jordan

Nothing could stop me from taking care of her tonight. Not even her. When I should be doing everything in my power to get away from her, it's impossible for me to rid myself of her. No matter how much she glares at me with her furious eyes, whether she likes it or not, tonight I will be by her side. I will not take any risks. Once was enough for me. Once and my life took a sharp turn for the worse.

"Don't feel obligated to watch over me, I'm much better," she groans.

"I don't feel obligated to do anything, Line! I told the doctor that I would look after you and I intend to keep my word. Don't try to get out of this. I won't change my mind, you're stuck with me tonight."

Grumpy, she sinks into the car seat and pouts as she pointedly ignores me. She ends up falling asleep and I let her rest so recover her strength. She wakes up slowly as I park. Still a little confused, she stumbles slightly as she gets out of the car and leans on the hood. I make sure she regains her balance by standing next to her and we then climb the stairs in silence. As we arrive on the landing, I feel her hesitate. "Open the door, Line."

"You can still back out, Jordan."

My decision was made the minute I found her livid, lying on the floor of the Magic Cave. No matter how many ploys she enacts to get rid of me, she's wasting her time. I put my hand in her jacket pocket, grab the keys before she has time to protest, and open her door. I close it carefully behind us, locking it as a precaution. I don't want to rush her, I remain silent, I want her to feel reassured by my presence here, not trapped.

She ends up turning to face me. She is still really pale, and dark circles adorn her big eyes. The sight of her like this makes me shiver. Other images suddenly overlap in my head, rekindling my anger at her carelessness. I close my eyes to chase away those troubling images. When I open them again, Line is standing by the sofa, arms crossed, looking at me with concern. "Jordan? Are you okay?"

I pull myself together immediately and nod. "I'm fine. It's just that... No, forget it." I sigh. "So what do you want to do?"

"Uh, I think a shower will help. Do you mind if I..."

"You're at home, Line. Take all the time you need. If you'll allow me to use your kitchen, I'll fix us a snack."

"Oh... Um... Yes, yes, of course. Whatever."

She turns around then heads for the hall. Suddenly, anxiety overcomes me, and I can't help saying a little too curtly, "Line, don't lock that door!"

She turns around and stares at me, looking confused and embarrassed.

"You might get woozy. Don't worry, I won't come unless you call me!"

She blushes brightly and rushes into the bathroom. When I hear the water running, I try to cook a balanced meal so that she can bounce back as quickly as possible. I find fresh vegetables and chicken breasts in the fridge. When she appears, her hair damp and wearing an oversized T-shirt, I lose my breath. God, she is beautiful! She looks so fragile right now. Gently, she approaches and lifts the lid on the simmering pot. As well as Tim and Sonny know me, they would be amazed to see me cooking in this apartment awash with Christmas decorations. However, in this precise moment, the decor doesn't bother me because it reflects

Line's personality perfectly. Fragile and bright.

"It smells divine!"

"Glad to hear you have an appetite, Cupcake. It's ready, we can sit down at the table."

"Why do you call me that?"

I extend my hand to serve her a plate. "Questions later. Right now, eat while it's hot."

I inwardly thank her for not insisting because that would mean the beginning of a long-drawn-out discussion.

Twenty minutes later, we clear the table like an old married couple. To be here with her is strange. Strange but far from unpleasant. I thoroughly enjoy it, even if I still refuse to admit it out loud. "I have to go get some sweatpants. I'll be back."

When I leave, I leave both of our doors wide open. Less than two minutes later, I am back at her place. I find her comfortable in the living room, her head resting on the armrest in front of the TV. "Line, may I use your bathroom?"

"Yes of course, the towels are in the cabinet, under the sink. Help yourself."

As I observe Line's bathroom for the first time, I linger over every detail that constitutes her personal space. The perfume bottles, the creams, the scent of her that permeates the room. The shower stall reminds me of the time when she surprised me at home in a moment of weakness. I can see myself caressing her, exploring her body for the first time. An intense desire begins to grow within me as I think about it, but I cast it aside, well aware that now is not the right time. Line is vulnerable and I refuse to take advantage of her. I want to, though. In fact, I'm dying to.

I shower quickly so I don't leave her unattended for too long. I can't help it, she has really gotten to me. When I get back to the living room, I find her all curled up and asleep on the sofa. I gently lift her in my arms and take her to her room which can be seen through the half-open door. Carefully, I put her on the bed and cover her with her comforter. I want to caress her sweet face, but I change my mind for fear of waking her up. Quietly, I slip away and go back to the kitchen. I brew myself a cup of coffee and remain swathed in darkness for hours on end, bombarded by memories. In the stillness of the night, I look out the window at the flakes that are starting to fall. The apartment is quiet, lit only by the soft light of the Christmas tree in the living room. My hands grip the edge of the sink so tightly that my knuckles turn white. Suddenly, I feel a presence; I feel observed. I turn around, and there she is. Line. A few inches away from me, arms dangling by her side, her long hair falling silently around her face and over her shoulders.

Her eyes lock onto mine as she takes a step forward. I don't move. We face each other quietly, eye to eye, wordlessly. She looks like she's floating in her billowing terracotta T-shirt that comes down to mid-thigh. I feel like my blood is starting to boil and it's got me completely discombobulated.

Like a fearful doe, she cautiously and slowly advances until our feet touch. Then, without further ado, she puts her ear to my chest and listens to the messy beating of my heart. This simple gesture of hers has always had incredible power over me. It calms me down. Engulfing me in her itty-bitty arms, she comforts me with dazzling sweetness. This little angel is irresistible. I put a hand on her head, stroking her honey-tinted hair and sigh as I give in to the joy. The delicate touch of her embrace moves me to no end, filled as it is with absolute charm. I tenderly kiss the top of her head and when she lifts her head to look at me, I become lost in her gaze. This silent face-to-face is worth a thousand words.

My hands take hold of her hips, and while my primary goal is to get her out of my way, my fingers caress her graceful curves as if they had a mind of their own. My grip tightens as I draw her closer to me. My hands slide down to grab her firm, plump butt, all the while moaning with pleasure. I can't fight it. She is so cute, so obstinate, so real, so… I'm so shaken up that words to describe her escape me. What she awakens in me is beyond desire. It's like a breath of fresh air, the very breath of life. "Don't ever do that to me again, Line. I thought I was going to lose it."

"You've been through this before?"

"Questions for later."

Silencing her with a kiss, I lean over and lift her up. Instinctively, she wraps her legs around my hips as if our two bodies were meant to fit together.

As I head for the hallway leading to her room, I continue

kissing her eagerly. Her sweet mouth, tantalizing me like forbidden fruit, is mine for the taking. By the time I arrive at the foot of her bed, I feel like I'm on fire.

I try to somehow curb enthusiasm so as not to get swept away but it's a lost cause. I don't even notice the decorations anymore, focusing only on Line. My whole body clamors for her. And when I put her down on her bed, I immediately feel cold. This fleeting separation creates an immediate void. I need to regain the warmth of her skin again. Much more than simple desire, it's a visceral need. Her touch. I don't know what kind of magic it beholds, but it is fundamentally soothing.

Without looking away, I take off my clothing, piece by piece, so I can finally fill that void. Kissing her thin ankles, I gradually move up her legs as my fingers linger on her silky skin. My mouth delights in tasting her, inch by inch, discovering her bare thighs under her large T-shirt. The lace of a turquoise thong winks at me and my ascent continues, sliding my hands to the firm curves of her busty chest. Like a forbidden fruit, I savor her proudly hardened nipples while listening to the melodious song of her long sighs. She shivers, comes to meet my caresses, undulating her body with supreme sensuality.

It's an invitation to a dream in which I can escape reality. My desire is fierce, and it requires a monumental effort to hold it in. I can't any longer, my fingers find their way under the elastic of the lace that taunts me.

I give her no respite, plunging into the warmth of her intimacy, caressing every nook and cranny, lingering in the most erogenous zones. I torture her with delight until she abandons herself with an exhilarating cry. I want her to be mine, giving her all to me and delirious with delight. Quickly, I slip on a condom and with one clean snap, the thong is history. Kneeling between her thighs, I devour her with my eyes and what I see in them makes me lose control. Reciprocal, carnal desire. This insatiable hunger for surrender. I grab her ankles and place them on my shoulders before sinking into her in a firm, deep movement. The groan that escapes my throat expresses all of the primal pleasures I feel within my body. She lets out a cry of surprise under the firmness of my assault but encourages me to continue by undulating her pelvis lasciviously. So, no longer holding back, I let my desire for her speak, gratifying her with ever more powerful thrusts.

Eagerly, I inundate her with my presence as I watch her squirm and cling to the sheets. Eyes half closed, she gasps when with my thumb I caress her clitoris as I come and go. I want to see her break and surrender completely. I want her wholeheartedly, and to see her faint with joy. My desire is bestial and hungry. The heat that spreads through me is spirited, spreading. I bite the inside of her thigh and smile at her with insolence. She arches and her moans grow louder, excited and sensual, filling the room with a shamelessly erotic and shameless atmosphere. Abruptly, I flip her over and pull on her hips to bring her pelvis to me. Sliding my hand along her back, I reach her neck and make her lay her head on the mattress then work my way back down to her hips, letting my fingers linger over her sweaty skin. A groan of satisfaction escapes me as I look at her tantalizing ass pointed towards straight at me. I cannot help nibbling the soft roundness and hear her giggle at the sensation. Clinging firmly to her hips, I return to her, leaving the mark of my fingers on her flesh. I fill her again, deeper, and resume my vigorous momentum. Her fingers clench the sheets, trying to keep up with me. The small hoarse cries that she casts forth multiply my pleasure tenfold and I begin to caress the dark little halo that is eyeing me. Her reaction is immediate, her excitement doubled and accompanied by blissful sighs. I am at the breaking point. I slowly enter as I intensify my movements. The orgasm sweeps through me with such intensity that it surprises me with its strength. I feel her come at the same time, contracting her muscles around my cock, trapping it in an embrace that finishes me off. Our pleasure resonates in unison and we fall flat on top of each other, out of breath.

Time passes by and we remain pressed against each other without feeling the slightest inclination to move. The moon is full tonight, and its light floods the room. Her hands caress my back lavishly before tracing the dark lines of the tattoos that cover my chest. Suddenly, quizzically, she stops, and I wonder why. "Line? What is it?"

"What is this mark?" She asks in a trembling voice.

I look down and, on my left pec, I notice a long scratch. I run my finger on it quizzically. "I don't know Line, I hadn't noticed. It was probably Stringer who inadvertently scratched me."

She seems to be weighing my words, deciding if they are good enough for her. I earnestly insist, seeing her riddled with doubt. "Line, don't go imagining things. I haven't seen anyone. I assure you."

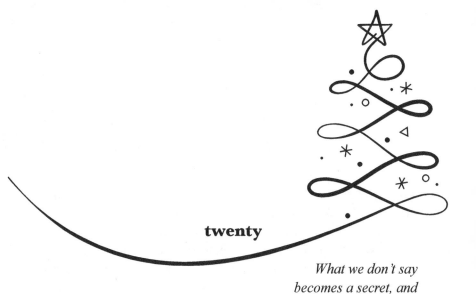

twenty

What we don't say
becomes a secret, and
secrets often create shame.

Eve Ensler,
The Vagina Monologues

Line

After a quick shower, we fall asleep, cuddled up against each one another.

My sleep is interrupted less than an hour later. By my side, Jordan sleeps peacefully, and I sit up in bed, trying to figure out where that noise is coming from.

Crrrrr…

I roll up the sheet over me, as the noise is starting to seriously stress me out.

Crrrrr…

Suddenly, two shiny little eyes stare at me from the foot of the bed. I let out a shrill cry and wiggle my legs like a madwoman. Jordan snaps out of his sleep and turns to me on high alert, all haggard looking. "What the hell are you doing? Are you demented or what?"

"There's a thiiiiiing on the beeeeed."

He turns on the light as though I were in the middle of an episode of paranoia and bursts out laughing when he discovers his ferret trying to nest in his T-shirt. "Stringer, buddy! Hey, what are you doing here little man? You missed me?"

Turning towards me, he gives me a half-amused, half-contrite smile and holds out his arm onto which his pet climbs without being asked. In passing, a small scratch appears on his forearm.

"You see? Nothing serious, it's just Stringer. He must have sneaked in when I went to get my tracksuit. Hey! Look!" he says, pointing to the mark left by his four-legged friend. Hidden beneath the sheets, I stick out my head a bit and actually see the red scratch then stare at Stringer as if he were about to jump on me.

"Well, it's time for you to get to know each other. Stringer, this is Line. Line, this is Stringer. Come on, say hello, a little pat…"

"You're kidding, right?"

"No, Line. Come on. Give it a whirl."

"What if he bites me?"

"He doesn't bite. Well, not people he likes anyway."

"Who says he likes me?"

"He would have bitten you already. Come on, give him a little pat then stick your arm out."

I take my hand out of its hiding place, swallow hard, and look at Jordan apprehensively. I am not at all at ease. He, on the other hand, seems to enjoy the scene that is playing out before him. He chuckles but still encourages me to reward his ferret with a caress. When the tip of my fingers touch his silky coat, I'm amazed. I expected it to feel rough, but it doesn't. Its softness is fascinating. He rubs his snout against my hand, sniffs me, rubs again. When I extend my arm, he jumps on, climbs all the way up, and settles in on my neck. I don't move, amazed by this little fur ball snuggling on my neck.

Jordan laughs then, touched, looks at me and proudly announces. "You see, he likes you."

Stringer tickles the tip of my nose then approaches my lips which he inspects affectionately, which makes me smile like a child. Jordan rolls his eyes and starts fidgeting by my side. "OK, now that's enough!" he hisses.

He walks towards me, takes his four-legged friend back and addresses him, looking him straight in the eye. "Don't get carried away, my friend. She… she sleeps with me! She is MY female. And you… you sleep on the T-shirt. That's non-negotiable."

He grabs the T-shirt and places it at the foot of the bed on his side before placing Stringer on it.

I stare at him, feigning indignation at the term he used. But I'm also taken aback by what it implies. "Your… *female*?"

"Yep," he answers mirthfully.

Then, in a more serious tone, he whispers softly, "I want to try. But I can't make you any promises."

What a bombshell! He reaches his hand out to turn off the light, turns around and takes me in his arms, placing one leg over me to wrap me up completely.

"Now sleep."

* * *

BAM! BAM! BAM!

I painfully open one eye. What the fuck is it now?

BAM! BAM! BAM!

I wake up with a sudden jolt, intrigued by the incessant racket. The bed is empty, and I can hear the water running in the shower. Jordan woke up earlier than I did. I get up and realize that the constant banging is coming from the hallway. I open up and find Timothy knocking on Jordan's door.

"Fuck, open up! Jordan!"

"Uh, Timothy? What's going on?"

He turns around and seems surprised to find me there.

"Shit, Line! Sorry, I didn't mean to wake you up, but damn, Jordan *has* to get up! We have a huge problem and His Royal Highness is stuck to the sheets!"

Sonny barges in recklessly. "So he's up?"

Suddenly, the door opens behind me, revealing Jordan wrapped in a small towel. Tim and Sonny drop their jaws.

OK, this is extremely embarrassing.

"Uh, maybe we could take this little meeting inside? It's chilly out here."

So, we all enter my apartment. It's barely six thirty. My mind is racing. Too much information to process all at once. Yesterday,

Jordan and I took a step forward. But where are we this morning? What does he want now? And me? What am I ready to accept? And now there's a family reunion on my doorstep. "Tim, Sonny, you want some coffee?"

They simultaneously respond in the affirmative and take a seat in the kitchen.

"Jordan. Coffee?"

"I would prefer shorts," he quips under his breath, looking deeply troubled.

"What? Shorts?"

"Go put on some shorts, damn it! I'll take care of the coffee."

Suddenly, I lower my eyes and realize that, in my rush to get out of bed, I'm only wearing a T-shirt that barely covers my thighs. Mortified, I start to blush and, raising my head, I notice Tim and Sonny smiling blissfully from ear to ear as Jordan gratifies them with simultaneous slaps on the back of the head.

"Hey! Lower your eyes or I'll poke them out!"

The two of them do so snickering, and I run into the bedroom to put on something more decent. I hear raised voices in the kitchen and, as I head back, I have the sinking feeling that I'm intruding on their conversation. I arrive just in time to see Sonny handing Jordan a bag. When he sees me, he hastily grabs it and stuffs it deep into his pocket, jaws clenched. They look at each other in silence. These three have a mutual non-verbal understanding, it seems I'm the only one in the dark. Timothy then explains what's going on. The store was vandalized last night. The window is broken, and the chairs lacerated. I glance at Jordan who seems on the verge of a violent breakdown. As his fists open and close, the tension emanating from him seems to invade the room.

Do what you have to do. We'll take it from here," says Sonny.

He nods and then draws me into the hallway leading to my bedroom. "I have to go. Can you take care of Stringer for me?"

"Yes, but... uh... Are you okay, Jordan?"

His cold, absent gaze worries me. He mumbles something that resembles a "yes," looking away.

"Where are you going, Jordan?"

"To my supplier's."

"What did Sonny give you?"

His jaw contracts again and he responds tersely. "Nothing that concerns you, Line."

He kisses me on the forehead then leaves me standing in the corridor. He puts on his coat and leaves the apartment with his two friends by his side.

Once alone, I collapse on the sofa without knowing what to think. Jordan's attitude. The looks exchanged between those three, the unspoken words. That murky, secretive atmosphere in the kitchen. I let out a sigh of weariness. The lack of sleep isn't helping, but I decide to pull myself together and go to the store.

On the sidewalk, Sonny and Timothy assess the damage to the facade and look up when they see me leaving my building.

I'm uncomfortable, embarrassed. I know I saw something I shouldn't have seen. I don't know what to say. I step forward and contemplate the damage. The window is broken, and things are even worse inside. Whoever did this was merciless. Broken bottles, armchairs ripped open, debris strewn all over the floor. It looks like a tornado blew through the shop. Timothy sees that I'm completely discombobulated and tries to reassure me. "It's going to be okay, Line, we just need a good cleaning crew. And the window can be changed within a couple of hours."

"Shit! Was any money stolen from the shop?"

"No, we don't keep cash here. It was just a gratuitous act."

I look at him, perplexed, without knowing what to say. "Jordan is already gone? I can give you a hand if you want, I—"

Sonny and Timothy exchange a look and I understand that I'm not going to get any information out of them. Sonny gives me a smile which is nonetheless comforting. "We'll be fine, Line. You can go on to work. We're going to start cleaning."

I nod and rush into my shop. Mechanically, I start filing the last of my grandfather's papers. Now that I have a broader view of the situation, I am optimistic about the stability of the business he left behind for me. And there is something else that concerns me: Christmas for the children at the hospital. It is imperative that I start looking for freelance entertainers. I decide to call Victor to bring him up to date on our stock of decorations. A Christmas without garlands is not Christmas at all. And these children deserve our very best to help them get through all the suffering they have to endure. "Victor? It's Line, tell me, can we go over what we have so far for Christmas at the hospital?"

"No worries, I'm not working! You want me to come to the shop? That way, we'll get to see each other."

"That would be great, Victor. I didn't get much sleep and a helping hand would be much appreciated."

"I'll be there in half an hour. See you later."

He hangs up, and I stare at my phone, torn by an urge to call Jordan. But something is telling me not to. I feel a strange uneasiness when I think of Sonny, the bag, them looking like kids caught in the act, and Timothy's eagerness to change the subject. When did everything start to go wrong? Last night I offered myself to Jordan. Again. And we have actually made progress. Jordan was relaxed, more spontaneous. Then there was his confession as he was falling asleep. He wants to try. Our relationship increasingly resembles that of a budding couple, and yet there are still things hidden from me. Things Tim and Sonny know about but refuse to talk about. Even though they try to console me, I am still worried. Memories come back to me from that evening at L1 KTV and from Jordan's rage when he saw that guy. That Styx. A dealer. The mere thought of that term and all that it suggests freezes my blood.

What am I getting into? Am I totally crazy? However, I'm not dreaming. This bond between Jordan and me is very real. I feel it. I see it in his eyes, like last night, but also in his way of standing close to me. But nothing is simple with him. So what? Should I prepare for the worst at his side? Am I tough enough for that? I don't know.

But one thing is certain: I will not tolerate lies. I rub my eyes, exhausted by all these questions running through my head. Jordan entered my life, broke through the gates to my heart, and settled there. Yes, it's obvious. A simple and strange truth is now clear to me. I love him. Never before have I been so attracted to anyone. And I'm not talking about mere physical attraction. It's his profound personality that attracts me. The one I see beyond his mask. The one he hides but struggles to keep hidden when we are alone together. He is intense and passionate. Sweet and wild at the same time. Complex and compassionate. A cornucopia of character traits that makes my heart sing every time my eyes land on him.

The doorbell chimes and Victor walks through the door. His usually jovial face seems troubled. I walk towards him and take him in my arms, like always. "Hi, Victor. Is everything all right?"

"Hi, Line, I just walked past the shop. What's with the mess?"

"They were vandalized last night."

He mumbles something and puts his jacket on the counter. He seems angry but I don't know why. "Are you sure you're okay, Victor? You seem... upset."

"I just talked to Sonny. I find it odd that Jordan didn't hear anything. His apartment is right above the shop, right?"

"Uh, yes. Yes, but he was at my house last night."

"All night long?" he replies, almost choking.

"Yes, all night. And for your information, I'm of age and have had all my shots!" I say, blushing. "But if it makes you feel any better, he was watching over me, on doctor's orders."

I then begin to tell him about my experience down the rabbit hole, my dizzy spell, and my short stay in the hospital. Worried about me, he has loads of questions. I answer them all, reassuring him that everything is okay. We then get down to the tasks at hand: taking inventory of the decorations at our disposal and calling around to find entertainment. However, my thoughts keep turning back to Jordan. So many questions remain unanswered.

twenty one

*Make big decisions
with your HEART, small
ones with your HEAD.*

Omid Kordestani

Jordan

I've been driving for over an hour. I still have a little under 400 miles to travel before I reach Inverness, a town on the northeast coast of Scotland, where the River Ness joins the Moray Firth.

It's the largest city and the cultural capital of the Highlands. More than seven hours on the road and my thoughts are jostling every which way. It's chaos in my head.

Memories come to the surface uninvited. *She* loved this place. She was ecstatic when we went for a walk on the moors of Culloden, site of the famous battle of the same name which, in 1746, put an end to the Jacobite uprising. The Scottish monarchs, the Highlanders, the Jacobites, and the English competed for the city, so that today there are hardly any important buildings left that date before the 19th century. We loved coming here and laying down on these vast, green plains. She evoked with passion this part of history that fascinated to her so. A dark and tragic story in itself. Just like ours.

A warm tear rolls down my cheek. I wipe it with the back of my hand. With foggy eyes, I chase my demons. Now is not the time, I must stay focused on the road, on the reason for my trip and on what I will be able to do when I return. I think of Line. I have to end this. It's too much for me. I am tired. So tired of all this. All this darkness that engulfs me. Line doesn't deserve that. She deserves to be happy on the dawn of her new life. The miles pass, linear, and the landscape changes little by little, giving way to more soothing scenery. I stop for a bite to eat at noon. I'm sitting in a brasserie about to order today's special when my phone rings. "Timothy, any problems?"

"No, everything is going well. I'm calling to find out how you're doing. How's the traffic?"

I smile at my friend's attempt to get information out of me. "It's all good, no problem. Do you have an actual question or are you just going to beat around the bush?"

I hear him muttering into his beard on the other end of the phone. "Oh, alright already, calm down. I was trying to be tactful, but if you insist. When do you plan on telling Line what's really going on? No, 'cause I swear to you man, when she opened her shop, she looked pretty pitiful. Victor is with her right now."

"Victor?"

"Yep, we exchanged a few words before he joined her. He's a good guy."

"Well, your 'good guy' doesn't seem to like me very much."

"It must be said that his first impression of you was to see you beat up on some guy. So, judging strictly from the optics, it's totally understandable. He just wants to protect Line. He offered to help, and I think he can be useful."

I stroke my beard while listening to his take on things. Quite convincing, I must admit. "Yeah, and he's right."

"And speaking of Styx, how's that going?"

I cringe at the mere mention of that asshole. "Everything is right on track. I went to Devon, and I gave your cousin what he needed before I left. I think we're good."

"Let's hope so!" he replies with determination. "Hey, Jordan. Go easy on Line. I know you want to spare her the shitshow, but she has feelings for you."

"Precisely Timothy, that's why I'm going to put an end to it. Well, I gotta go. My steak is getting cold. Let's keep in touch. Talk to you later."

"Bye."

I scarf down my meal and hit the road with a hovering concern: what say once I get there. How am I going to handle this? It's been six years. Six long, godforsaken years. The pain is still as sharp, branded on my soul. To take my mind off of my misery, I turn up the volume to "So Cold" by Ben Cocks playing on the radio. As if fate is forcing me to face my problem. This song about home, abandonment, the pain of loneliness, and tears couldn't be better suited to what I am about to encounter. With bitterness and the crushing weight of grueling guilt, I continue my journey into my past.

It's dark when I arrive in Inverness and I park in the lot of the motel where I reserved a room. I walk into the dimly lit hall when fatigue hits me like a ton of bricks. After a visit to the reception desk, I retrieve the key to my room and go lie down on the spacious bed waiting for me.

I am overburdened. I feel like I'm suffocating in this room, as if these walls were slowly closing in on me. I get up and go into the shower. My neck is completely stiff after driving for so long, and the stress, plus the lack of sleep doesn't help. Lack of sleep. That night with Line. Her body pressed against me, disconcertingly genuine. She's like a blinding light that is oh, so far away. I exhale several times, desperately trying to get a hold of myself. When I think about her, my thoughts become jumbled. I grab a towel and immediately leave the bathroom. I sit on the bed and dial Line's number. She picks up on the third ring. "Good evening, Cupcake. Is everything going well with Stringer?"

"Good evening, Jordan."

Oops! I sense something is wrong by the tone of her voice. "Line, what is it?"

"Stringer... He..."

"Stringer what? Did something happen to him?"

"To Stringer, no. But to my G-strings, yes!!! Hell, you could have warned me that your ferret was a fetishist! He ate most of my panties."

"Ah... um... uh... Surprise!" I say, trying to downplay the situation with humor.

Indeed, he carries his name very well, that little perv has

the annoying tendency to nibble on female underwear. That said, I admit that he has very good taste in that regard. Line's voice pulls me out of my thoughts.

"It's not funny! Jordan, tell me you'll be back soon to get your rat from hell. And by the way, where are you and what are you doing? What's with you leaving in a rush like that?"

Ouch! The question I dreaded. I can't see myself having this conversation with her over the phone. No, the day I put my cards on the table, it will have to be face to face.

"I think I'll be back in two or three days tops. At least I hope so. I'll explain everything when I get back."

"What? Are you serious? Are you really going to leave me hanging?"

"Look, Line, I'm exhausted. I need to sleep and—"

Beep, beep, beep…

She hung up on me. Shit! I grab the pillow and hurl it across the room in anger. I'm in no condition to fight over the phone right now, damn it! Right now, all of my fears are directed towards one person. How will I manage to overcome this? What am I going to be able to say? And when I look into her eyes, what will I see?

Anger?

Sadness?

Shame?

My apprehension stems from more than just fear. I am terrified and my heart races at the very thought of it. In the end, it would be so much easier to turn around and keep hiding out like I have been doing for six years now. But I can't, I can't anymore. I have to face my reality. For me, for them, for Line.

I go down to the hotel bar and down a few drinks in order to lose myself in an alcoholic haze so that I might find a semblance of sleep.

***

As the sun diffuses its first rays, I emerge with difficulty from a night full of nightmares. Today will be a long day: painful, and intense. But it will also mark a turning point in my life as I know it.

Leaning on the hotel bar, I have a large black coffee and

try to clear my head before setting off. Here too the Christmas decorations are out. The hotel has a festive atmosphere, and a plethora of golden garlands hang in every corner. In the background, a jazzy version of "Jingle Bells" can be heard. My phone rings, pulling me out of my morning torpor.

"Hey Jo, what's up?" Sonny asks into the receiver. "Got there safe? How are you feeling?"

"Being here stirs up a lot of things."

"Yes, but that's the goal, right? So, what time do you plan on going to see Langley?"

"I'll be on my way right after I finish my coffee. Langley is an early bird, I'll be there as soon as they open. How about you on your end?"

"We're making progress. The window has been changed and we got the place cleaned up. The painters should be here around eleven. Everything will be good to go by the time you get back. And Timothy went to get us some oils since everything was ransacked. Don't worry about us here, we can manage. Just focus on the reason why you're there in Scotland. Come on, dude! You can do this!"

I run a hand over my tired face while listening to him speak. His support warms my heart. We hang up and I leave. I still have a little bit of time ahead of me. First things first, head to Hank's old store, "Langley—Father & Son," our supplier for the store. That's the only place we can find the barber chairs we want. Working with wood and iron, this specialty artisan creates unique, one-of-a-kind pieces. Usually, Timothy takes care of this, since they are both passionate about woodworking. And their conversations often go off a tangent. When I arrive in front of the large metal gate, Hank walks towards me as if he had seen a ghost. "Well, I'll be damned! Jordan Miller! In the flesh!"

His limp seems to have gotten worse since the last time we saw each other. He gives me a big hug before staring at me with curiosity.

"So, Jordan? What brings you here to Inverness?"

"I'm just passing through, Hank. We had an incident at the store, and we need new chairs."

"Shit, that sucks. Follow me, let's see what we can come up with!"

We enter the workshop where the scent of freshly cut wood shavings blends with the smell of solder. We review each detail of my order and after two hours quibbling over details, we finalize the work order for the new chairs.

As I am about to leave, he can't help but ask, "Jordan? Are you going to go see her?"

The carefree atmosphere that prevailed up to now suddenly vanished and gave way to obvious discomfort. Hands deep in my pockets, I turn to him and look at him in the eye. "That's actually why I'm here, Hank. It's about time, I think."

He nods without taking his eyes off me. His handshake is firm and encouraging. I get back into my car and psych myself up as best I can to take the plunge.

I drive through the city anxiously until I reach the long dirt road crossing the moorland. I am bombarded with memories. The images snap, crackle and pop in my head like fireworks. The driveway seems endless, but when I see the flowery gray stone facade surmounted by a slate roof, my heart skips a beat. Then suddenly it starts racing and I feel dizzy. My eyes start tingling, on the brink of tears. I inhale deeply then park next to the bed of heather that stands out, purplish pink, from the tall green leaves.

Determined to see this through to the end despite the fear squeezing my heart, I slowly walk to the front door. The die has been cast.

I knock three times and hold my breath when I hear steps approaching from inside. The heavy wooden door opens slowly and when her eyes meet mine, my whole past is laid bare.

"Jordan," she says in a trembling breath of emotion.

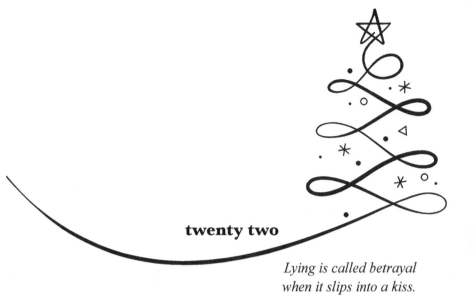

twenty two

Lying is called betrayal
when it slips into a kiss.

Anne Barratin, *Along the Way*

Line

When I wake up, I'm still furious. Ever since my phone call with Jordan yesterday, I have been fuming and not even the music resonating in my living room can calm me down. I'm like a pressure cooker ready to explode. I wander around my apartment, a mug of coffee in my hand, and try to pull myself together. But what is he thinking, damn it? That he will be able to lie to me and play it off as if nothing happened? Because yes, I am sure he is lying to me. His two friends' story is super sketchy, and they are clearly protecting each other. I am pissed off. He didn't even bother trying to reach me this morning. OK, so I hung up on him last night, but he deserved it. If he thinks he can push me to the sidelines when he sees fit and only come to me when it's convenient for him, he doesn't know me very well. I'm not another Elise! I'm not going to play this toxic game, no matter how much I love him and how many demons he is battling.

My thoughts are all over the place and yet, despite my anger, I'm still worried about him. He refuses to tell me where he is or why he left. What the hell is he doing? I'm angry, but I don't want anything to happen to him either. The mere memory of his fight with Styx sends a shiver down my spine.

These last two days sure have been an avalanche of sensations. And to top it all off, I can't seem to find performers for the children's Christmas Eve show. Everyone Victor and I contacted yesterday is already booked. So here I am at an impasse and that only adds to my bad mood. In order to clear my head, I decide not to go to the store this morning but rather to go shopping to find gifts for Victor and Capucine.

Before leaving, I cut an apple and put it in a small plate for Stringer. That rascal may have nibbled my underwear, but he's so adorable with his beady little eyes that I can't stay mad at him. He never left my side last night. Curled up on the sofa in tears after Jordan's phone call, he snuggled up against me and nuzzled me with his little snout as if he wanted to ease my pain. Once the door of my room is closed, I grab my bag and go look for presents for my friends.

My first stop will be Beauty Bazaar for Capucine. This cosmetics store is my friend's favorite; she spends hours there. I decide to buy her that perfume I know she has been wanting for a while as well as a gift card for body care products in the relaxation and massage section. I know that with these gifts, I can't go wrong. Capucine is Liverpool's proverbial girly girl. Now it's Victor's turn! I think I have an idea for the perfect gift for him. I head over to Gower Street in hopes of lucking out at the Beatles museum. Victor, like Timothy, is passionate about music and also plays the guitar. Well, he used to practice regularly anyway. I can't even count the times that he would sit out on the lawn near the cafeteria between classes and play. And we can all agree that the guitar is a weapon of mass destruction when it comes to luring the ladies. Victor had quite a fan club and they were all insanely jealous of Capucine and me. Just like actual groupies, some wouldn't think twice about harassing us. Of course, it all went right over Victor's head. Only music mattered to him. Until the day he suddenly stopped playing.

I enter the shop next to the museum and begin to look through everything in search of the perfect gift. Finally, after several minutes, I find exactly what I was looking for. Beautiful Beatles guitar covers. Since Victor stopped playing it, his guitar has been gathering dust and that saddens me, especially knowing how talented he is. I look all of them over and then, on a whim, also decide to get one for Timothy. Even if it does irk me that they keep making excuses for Jordan, Tim and Sonny welcomed me with great kindness. As I am paying for my purchases, I realize that I will have to find a gift for Sonny too. I leave the museum, immersed in my thoughts, when a squeaky voice calls out to me. "Well, well. Who have we here?"

I look up and come face to face with the guy Jordan fought at the club. My blood freezes and my heart start racing. This guy really gives me the creeps with his skinny body and his crooked smile, which actually looks more like a grimace. Instinctively, I step back to increase the distance between us, but he advances towards me like a vulture circling in on its prey.

"Hey cutie, what are you doing so close to the Albert Dock? Is your friend not with you? Huh? Tell me, where is this dear Jordan?"

I gather all my courage and try to force my way past him, but he blocks my path with his body and won't let up. His foul breath makes me nauseous.

"What? Do I scare you? But I can bring you happiness. You must like it, right? If you hang out with Jordan, you must be pretty familiar with narcotics, right? Don't you want a hit? Come on, the first one is on the house."

I free myself from him and, this time, manage to get away. "Leave me alone! Jordan too!"

"I'm not done with him. You can tell him I said so!" he shouts as I run away, breathless with fear.

I run smack into someone and scream, thinking that Styx had caught up to me.

"OOOOH LINE! Calm down! What's wrong?"

I look up and realize that it's Victor.

I throw myself into his arms, shaken by shivers, but I can't string two words together. He hugs me tightly and begins to rock me gently while whispering words of reassurance in my ear. When I regain control of my breathing, I start to explain. "It's... it's Styx... He..."

"What the fuck did he do to you? I swear I'll kill him if he touched you," he says getting angrier by the minute.

"He didn't touch me, Victor, he just threatened me. I was just leaving the Beatles museum when he accosted me. He... he recognized me. He knows I'm with Jordan. He said he was not done with him... and..."

I burst into tears. Too many emotions are jostling, and I stop the tears from overflowing. Victor takes my hand and makes me look up at him. "First, as long as I am here, nothing will happen to you and second, he has no chance against Jordan. Finally, Line, did you see how that piece of garbage is built? He's got one foot in the grave. He's nothing but skin and bones. There's more meat on a sparrow's kneecap than on that lowlife."

"He looked so hateful, Victor. He scared me."

"He and Jordan have a score to settle, that's for sure. I guess he still hasn't given you an explanation for all this?"

"Indeed, he has not. Jordan is so secretive when it comes to talking about his past. And about his present situation too."

Victor looks at me confused. "What do you mean by 'his present situation too'?"

"Last night, I had him on the phone. He refused to tell me where he was and what he was doing there. He made it clear to me that it was his problem, not mine. But for fuck's sake, his shop is vandalized and he just up and leaves, without a word, and he expects me to be okay with it? I don't know what to think, Victor."

He tightens his grip on my hands to bring me some comfort and continues calmly. "You have to protect yourself, Line. I will always be by your side whatever you decide to do, but you have to make a decision because as things stand now, this relationship is unhealthy. And I don't want to see you suffer."

"I know. Thank you. I think I'll head home. But, incidentally, what are you doing here?"

Victor's embarrassment is obvious, and he is slow to answer, which annoys me even more. "Fuck! You are keeping secrets too?!"

"Come on, Line, knock it off. I was just in the neighborhood, walking around. Why are you getting on my case?"

"Because I'm sick of being lied to and tired of people hiding things from me. I've had it up to here; I'm going home. Bye, Victor!"

I take my leave with a determined step and head towards my apartment. This day seems endless. I climb the stairs to my apartment on autopilot and come face to face with a woman on Jordan's doorstep. Her slender and classy look momentarily takes my breath away. Tall, thin, her blond hair is impeccably styled in an elegant bun. She is a very beautiful woman. She turns around and stares at me steadily, scrutinizing me from every angle. It's embarrassing.

"Hello," she says in a velvety but confident voice.

"Hello, can I help you?"

"I came to see Jordan. You probably know him…"

I can't tell if she's deliberately messing with me or if she is just being snooty. "Well, since we live across the hall from each other, that would be the obvious assumption, Miss?"

"Loxford. Abigail Loxford. And you are?"

"Line Thomas."

"Ah, yes. The antique dealer, right?"

She lets out a derisive little laugh that infuriates me. "What am I supposed to think? What's so funny, Mrs. Lox-whatever?"

She suddenly drops the facade and stops playing around. She assumes an air of victory and glares at me with sheer contempt. "Jordan always comes back to me. I have what he needs, and I give him what he wants. You will never get with him. You have no chance, my dear. He always relapses. He will have his fun with you, but will come back to me. Like he always does. Oh, and he forgot this at my house the other day."

She throws it at me with disdain and I recognize his turtleneck sweater immediately. The bitch then turns on her heels and heads down the stairs with consummate class, which annoys me even more. I dream of seeing her trip and fall miserably. But instead, I hear the front door open and the click-clack of her dizzying heels on the pavement.

What the hell was that? I'll be damned if it isn't just one thing after another. Is this some kind of contest?

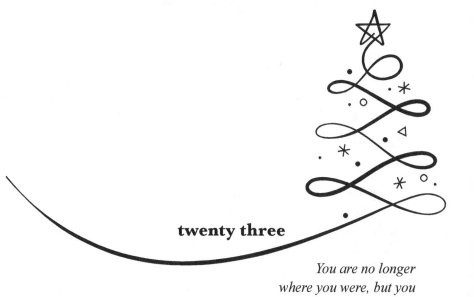

twenty three

*You are no longer
where you were, but you
are everywhere that I am.*

Victor Hugo

Jordan

On the way back, I have a bad feeling. Relieved and comforted that I reconnected with my past, but also terribly anxious and worried thinking about what lies in store for me now. The familiar scenery that abounds brings back so many memories. Today, covered in a thin layer of snow, its beauty is increased tenfold.

When I arrived and the door opened, I was paralyzed by emotions, unable to utter a single word. As if time were standing still. We spent a long moment looking at each other, in great detail, attentively, trying to convince ourselves this moment was real. Only when she hugged me did everything resurface: tears, love, guilt, and forgiveness. We spent several hours trying to make up for lost time, voicing all the unspoken words, realizing that we now have a future, comforting each other.

Nothing had changed: same decor, same jasmine scent wafting around the rooms, same photos displayed on the living room mantelpiece. As if I had jumped back in time. Only our eyes, filled with sorrow, disclose the passage of time and the pain endured.

Now I feel drained but liberated. All is not over yet, though. I have a long way to go before I can successfully reconcile with the person I used to be. Now, I can't wait to see Line, to discuss and clarify everything for her. It will not be easy, I know that, but it is high time that I came clean. I am aware she suspects something is up and that unintentionally, my silence hurts her. Does she have any idea of what I am about to reveal to her?

I try to think of a way to present the facts to her. But where to start? How will she react? In my mind, over and over, I try to find the right words to say so that she will understand. No mean feat… I just spent six years caught in a downward spiral. I know I can move forward now. I just have to take control of my life so I can build the future I crave.

Will I have the strength to do it? I like to think I will. I hope so. I will do everything in my power to get there. Where there's a will, there's a way.

Slowly, the light of the day dims in front of me and I feel exhaustion taking over. I decide to stop at a motel and hit the road again after a few hours of sleep.

* * *

Once I spot Matthew Street, I sigh in relief. It feels so good to be home! After hours on the road, I am drained. I drive up the street and park not far from the building. I get out of the car, and the neighborhood, usually so lively, seems eerily quiet despite the fact that it's already 8 AM. That being said, with the cold front that has been sweeping through England since last night, I am only half-surprised. People probably prefer to stay home rather than face the snow that has started to fall heavily.

Walking past the shop, I immediately notice that it is closed. Then, checking on the Magic Cave, I spot a faint light towards the back. Good, Line is already in, I will have that conversation with her right now. Waiting any longer would constitute an unnecessary step back. I inhale deeply and walk towards her shop decisively. For one brief moment I stand motionless on the doorstep, then I turn the door handle and enter. A heavy silence welcomes me, and I move forward slowly. "Line?"

Not a single sound. I call out again but there are no signs that anyone is here. The floor creaks as I step forward. Outside, the flurries intensify, and the snow starts falling in large flakes. She seems to be missing. My mind panics.

Yet, the light and the open door…

Something is off, and a nasty feeling takes a hold of me viciously. Shaken by my growing anxiety, I run to the stockroom. With each step, my fear increases, and no sooner do I get through the door than I stop, frozen, barely able to breathe. My head starts spinning, and my heart starts to race in an attempt to tear through my chest. My legs seem to cave under me, and I struggle to stay standing. I am petrified; I think I am going to be sick.

Among the boxes, Line's body is sprawled, her complexion pale, her hair partially covering her face. My whole body shakes violently as I rush to her side. I fall to my knees. I hold her cold hand in mine, and check in vain for a pulse that is not to be found. I keep checking for it, again and again, in several different spots but to no avail. The needle in her arm seems to taunt me like an old movie stuck in a loop. I feel sucked into a black hole, and I howl in pain. I can't seem to stop screaming. Sobbing uncontrollably, I throw up, I call for help, take her in my arms, rocking her desperately, hold on to her, refusing to face the facts. She is so… cold.

Not again. No! Not Line!

I simply can't go through this again. It seems my head is about to explode. My blood has frozen in my veins, and I feel its biting cold throughout my entire body. Why? The answer comes to me with disturbing ease.

Life is like a whore that has taken you hostage: She toys with you, crushes you with her power even though she is barely hanging on by a thread herself. I feel my heart tightening terribly, a blood-curdling cry of pain rips through me and paralyzes me. The fire brought on by all this pain courses through me, and my vision blurs. Unable to fight it any longer, I fall, unconscious, wishing for only one thing. To join them. Both of them.

At times, it seems I can hear noises in the fog where I lock myself up.

Please, let me be with them. I want to stay with them. Let me go with them!

Then, nothing. Once again, I was not up to the task.

I am empty.

Completely empty.

Empty without them.

Suddenly, without warning, I feel sucked back up, as if being wrenched away from a place to which I was pointlessly clinging. Sounds suddenly become louder, and I start to discern movements around me. I open my eyes and a voice pulls me out of my drowsiness. Through the veil blurring my vision, I make out a shape leaning over me. I thrash about instinctively, trying to push away this person who is preventing me from joining them.

I want to scream that I am in pain, so much pain. The pain crushes my heart, as if caught in a white-hot iron vice. Like a madman, I flail about until I feel the sting of an injection and once again fall unconscious. What is the point in fighting? All this agony has made me weary. I want it all to stop, so I can let go and let the darkness in. Much later, as I come to, my entire body feels sore, and yet, I feel no pain, only a heavy weight on my chest.

Slowly I open my eyes, and it takes me a few minutes to realize what I am doing here. I have no clue what time it is, all I see is the daylight fading through the window. How long have I been here? Who found me and brought me in? They must have found Line then.

Line...

My heart breaks and the memory of her frail body, lifeless and pale, sprawled on the stockroom floor, hits me like a ton of bricks. My head spins violently; I feel nauseous. The sterile room around me is cold. I have trouble breathing. I try to sit up, to organize my thoughts, when a man wearing a white coat enters the room. "Mr. Miller, welcome back to Earth! How are you feeling?"

I have a hard time swallowing my saliva. My throat burns.

"Take your time. No sudden movements. You are in a hospital."

A splitting headache assails me unexpectedly threatening to make my head explode. I look straight at the doctor, feeling lost.

"You are still weak. Keep calm. The nurse will be in to give you some pain medicine."

What a joke! No medicine, no substance could possibly make my pain subside. There are no remedies for what I feel.

The doc sees my skeptical smirk and moves forward cautiously. "You gave us all a big scare, and when you arrived you were very agitated."

I hold my head in both hands, only just tolerating the throbbing radiating throughout my skull.

"I will let you rest now but will stop by again later."

Right! Or never.

My eyelids grow heavy once again. Probably the fluids in the IV.

I don't fight it. I no longer feel like doing anything anyway.

* * *

When I come to, my vision is blurry. Night has fallen and the room is plunged into darkness. Yet, I know I am not alone. I can make out a shape standing near the bed. It looks like her. But even before my vision even clears, I hear her voice. "Jordan..."

My nightmares are back, now taking Line's shape, to hurt me even more deeply than they already have. I snatch the glass of water resting on the nightstand and I throw it with rage at my ghost. "ENOUGH!" I scream.

The sound of shattered glass echoes throughout the room. Then there are screams, people running in and crowding the room. Suddenly, strong hands pin me to the mattress. I fight back but stop quickly when I recognize Timothy's deep voice.

"Damn it, Jordan! Calm down!"

Sonny is here too, holding my ghost by the shoulders. *What the heck is going on?* I stop fighting, out of breath, and I stare intently at one specific person.

Line. She is holding her head, her eyes filled with horror, she is scared. A thin line of blood rolls down her temple. *What did I do?* Everything is a jumble in my head. I can't speak. Whenever I open my mouth, nothing but a wail of pain comes out. Nurses come rushing into the room, ordering everyone out. Another shot and I fall fast asleep again.

I wake up much later to harsh looks from Sonny and Timothy. They are both glaring at me with folded arms, sitting at the foot of my bed.

"Here he is! His Majesty finally graces us with his waking presence!" Timothy shouts sarcastically.

"Do you even remember what happened, Jordan?" Sonny adds.

Their stiff posture is clear evidence that I screwed up, but my mind can't put the pieces back together. "If one of you could shed some light on the situation, I'd appreciate it."

Timothy paces around the room like a lion in a cage. "You were in an accident on the way back from Inverness, Jordan. You fell asleep at the wheel, and your car went off the road. Lucky enough, you ended up hitting a bale of hay. Still, you hit the dashboard and were unconscious when the emergency response team found you."

"What? No... I..."

Once more, pain throbs through my head and I hold it in my hands.

"What do you remember exactly?"

"I... I remember returning from Liverpool, parking the car, and going to visit Line at her shop. I—"

"You never made it to Liverpool, Jordan," Sonny interrupts softly.

Now I am staring at them both, one after the other, desperately trying to understand what they are saying and to reconnect what I think happened to me and what really happened. I gasp in confusion, I have a very hard time feeling my heart beat. It feels crushed. "What? Yes, I did. I made it. I saw her! She... damn it... she was in the stockroom, sprawled out in the middle of a bunch of boxes. I saw the syringe in her arm. And... and... she was so pale, so cold. She didn't have a pulse!"

Nervously, my hands start trembling at the painful memory of Line lying lifeless on the stockroom floor and my voice becomes shaken by spasms I can't control. I continue my story, nevertheless. "I screamed and yelled at the top of my lungs for help. But I think something happened to my heart. Yes. I felt a violent pain near my heart. Several of them. And then I passed out."

"Jordan. You were in an accident. None of that was real," Sonny reveals. "Your subconscious played tricks on you. The pain you felt in your chest was the emergency response team trying to bring you back to life. It was the cardiac massage you felt. On the way here, your heart stopped. You were gone, dude, but they fucking brought you back!"

My fists clench, attempting to control the spasms racking my body. I squint so hard I see little stars dancing on my eyelids. I was in an accident? "What? So, Line... she..."

Timothy, his face exhausted, his eyes marked with deep dark circles, looks up at me. "She is alive, dude. She is fine, well... sort of. You remember you threw a glass at her, right? You mistook her for a ghost. You hurt her, Jordan."

"No, no, no! I didn't mean to. Fuck, I need to see her!"

"Better stay away Jordan. Your little ghost episode cost her a few stitches on her head and cheek. Right now, she is in shock."

Again, I feel my heart beating out of control, starting to race frantically in my chest. The nightmare I have been living all these years trapped me in a phantasmagoric maze of fear. One where I am increasingly lost with every turn and completely isolated from reality. I live wrapped in an invisible shroud, in limbo between two worlds. And what I feared most came to pass. I hurt her when all I was trying to do was protect her from the demons within me. The very paradox of my life. We make mistakes trying too hard to do the right thing. "I have to see her, talk to her, I..."

Timothy comes near my bed, fixing his haggard gaze on me. "All in good time. First get better, then we will reconsider."

A nurse steps in to inform us that visiting hours are over. I watch them as they leave the room, and once alone with my thoughts, a multitude of unpleasant feelings battle among themselves in an effort to squash me. Self-hatred, despair, bitterness, anger... I was correct when I feared the worst would happen if I let her get close to me. Even knowing she is alive and well brings me no comfort. I caused her pain, not intentionally since I was delirious, but still the sad truth is, I harmed her physically and emotionally. I will never forgive myself. The burden of this guilt adds on to the one I already carry on my shoulders.

She lights up every room she enters, and I bring provide but darkness. I was so close! I had glimpsed a ray of hope. The mad hope that I could make a fresh start... with her. But I messed it all up. Once again, I dropped the ball. Will I ever learn?

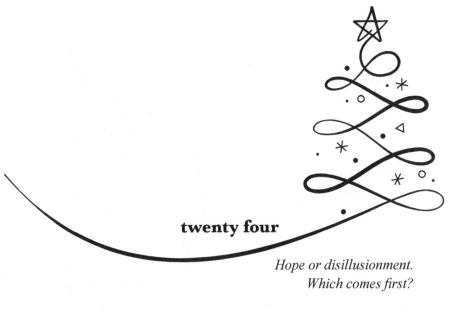

twenty four

Hope or disillusionment.
Which comes first?

Jean-Michel Ernewein

Line

It only took a few seconds for that moment I was ecstatic about finding Jordan safe for everything to smash to smithereens. Exactly like the drinking glass he threw in my face with such rage. The dark glow in his eyes at that precise moment chilled me to the bone. It replays in my head incessantly ever since. That look he shoot at me from his hospital bed, alight with anger, haunts me. What I saw in his eyes was way more than pain. He did everything in his power to keep me at bay, and I refused to listen. I insisted, I sought him out all the way to his shower. That's when I understood that he was nothing but darkness. But it was that fissure that drew me to him uncontrollably. That desire, to alleviate his troubles, to help him escape the pain, ran me straight to his arms.

On several occasions he advised me to run away. On several occasions, he pushed me away and, on several occasions, I ignored his warnings. Simply because I felt that he wanted me again. I thought he needed hope to get out of that nasty situation he was stuck in.

When Sonny came knocking at my door to tell me about the accident, I felt the floor collapsing from under me, as if swallowed by the pain pouring into me at hearing the bad news. The prognosis of the ER team was worrying. His heart stopped beating, they had to fight obstinately to bring him back. As if he was trying very hard to stay in limbo, between life and death. Thankfully, medicine prevailed against his stubbornness. I replay the scenes of these last hours in slow motion, becoming increasingly agitated. In the bathroom mirror, I observe my reflection and am afraid of what I see. The bandage that decorates the edge of my scalp expands all the way from my temple to the middle of my forehead. The deep cut on my cheek is also stitched up. But what strike me the most are the big dark circles around my red eyes.

A shadow of my former self, I neither ate nor slept, in agony over Jordan's condition. What am I supposed to do now? I thought I would succeed in catapulting him over the hurdles of his past, clearly, I was wrong. It's not possible to help someone against their will, and I am no match for Jordan's obstinance. The things I observed over the last few weeks were brutally laid out in front of me. Other than the fact that we spend precious moments in each other's arms, and that I caught a glimpse of his tender and caring side, what's hidden deep down can't be taken lightly. He revealed himself to be untruthful, aggressive, possessive, irritable, pugnacious, and now violent. Not to mention all those women cluttering his life or the secrets he keeps and carries around. I'm terrified. It's too much. I need to bring myself to let him lead his life as pleases. But there's one thing I know for sure, I will not stick around to witness his demise.

The days that follow seem surreal. I walk around in a daze, throwing myself into work at the shop, trying to keep my head above water. My days are interspersed with crying fits and my sorrow doesn't soften. Worst of all, my entire being seems to recite an elegy to my relationship with Jordan. The mark he left is eating away at my heart, it will be more difficult than I had planned to get rid of my feelings for him.

Capucine calls me daily, so does Victor. In vain, they both try to find the words to alleviate my suffering. Even Tim and Sonny stopped by to visit me at the shop, but I refuse to talk about Jordan. It's too painful. Besides they are in on their friend's secrets, and I am not. Therefore, I remain behind my wall.

I think back on the conversation I had with Tim and Sonny. I was not in great shape, so when the doorbell rang, I tried to appear cheerful. To no avail…

* * *

"Hey, Line, we're here to check on you," Sonny says, both hands in the back pockets of his jeans.

I feel the uneasiness that surrounds us. As I turn around to face them, I see the stupor in their eyes. It seems the makeup didn't do such a good job at hiding the cuts left by Jordan's outburst. "Things are going pretty well," I say with a touch of sarcasm.

"Shit. We are really sorry, Line. You know, what happened at the hospital, it's—"

"No need to smooth things over guys. The deed is done, and I no longer want to hear about it. I have neither the strength nor the courage for it."

They look at each other emphatically, understanding in this precise instant that my mind is made up.

"You know, his behavior was totally out of character. Don't hold it against him. He was lost and—"

At that moment, the levee breaks. A stream of words built up inside of me spews out uncontrollably. I explode, eyes reddened ready to burst into tears. "Stop! That's enough! I can't take it any longer! With him it's one step forward, two steps back. As soon as he comes close to me, he runs away. And then, there are all… all… all these fucking secrets between you guys. All the ghosts he has in tow. When I ask him questions, he changes the subject. You think I didn't see you see hand him something before he left Sonny?! When you saw me, you guys looked like three kids caught with your hands in the cookie jar. I am not naïve to the point of believing your cock and bull stories!"

Tim tries to calm me down without really knowing where to start or what to do. "Line, he is being above board with you. I swear to you that—"

"You swear? What do you swear, Timothy?" I say facing him with my hands planted on my hips. "That Jordan is not lying to me? Bullshit! That he respects me? Complete crap! Hanging out with Jordan is like playing *Royal Battle*, no one emerges unscathed. And then, there are all these women in the way. I can't take it anymore; it's too much trouble. He can have Elise, Jodie, Abigail and whoever else he wants to wine and dine."

Abigail. Just saying her name gives me goosebumps and a few tears slip out.

Sonny's hand runs through his hair nervously. "Jod—"

Timothy promptly interrupts him, slamming him in the chest with a sharp look. Then he takes one step forward and hugs me. In his arms I weep. When finally, I am able to regain my composure, Timothy looks at me with concern. "Are you sure you will be okay, Line?"

"Yes, yes. I… I'm sorry about all this and about your T-shirt."

Indeed, as he looks down at his shirt, he can't miss the smudged mascara on the fabric.

"No one cares about the damn T-shirt Line, alright?"

"Alright," I say my head hung low. "I'd like to be alone now if you don't mind. I have just one small favor to ask."

"Anything you want, Line. We'll always be here for you."

These simple words go straight to my heart and my eyes mist over as I look at him. How I would have wanted for Jordan to say them to me. "Could you take care of Stringer? It's too hard for me."

"Of course, Line."

"Thank you. And whatever you do, don't *ever* mention Jordan Miller's name in my presence again." I watch them walk away; their demeanor shows how deeply our conversation affected them.

* * *

Truly, it would have been too painful to keep his little companion at my place. That adorable ferret reminds me too much of Jordan and that last crazy night we spent before he left. At that time, I still believed that we had a chance at a future together. The disillusionment slaps me across the face and like a sponge it soaks up any feeling that could resemble pleasure. I am devoid of any positive emotion and wallow in my pain. I am exhausted and heartbroken.

They come and visit me at the shop every day, but we only make small talk about things like work and the preparation for the Christmas party at the children's hospital on December 23rd. That's only one week away and I still haven't found anyone to entertain the kids. Other than that, everything is ready. I feel guilty that I was not able to prepare a better party for them. But I must admit that preparing the Magic Cave for reopening was a lot more time-consuming and tiring than I expected. Not to mention my dealings with that annoying, bearded man.

Tomorrow, for reopening, the shop will be decked out with the prettiest of decorations. And after careful inspection of every minute detail, I sigh deeply, torn between the satisfaction of what I have accomplished here and severe exhaustion from the pain that ensnares my heart. I close the books, and as I look up, notice Jordan getting out of a vehicle parked across the street.

He's... out of the hospital.

Suddenly my heart goes berserk at the thought of seeing him again, but the pain caused by his behavior comes flooding back. The driver gets out and I discover the stunning Abigail Loxford. I get a bitter taste in my throat, and I feel nauseous. Like a conquistador, she moves towards Jordan, swaying seductively, and she slips her arm around his. I clench my fists and swallow my tears. This is too much! I shut down the shop, wishing for one thing only: to hole myself up at home, and lock the door tightly. Jordan suddenly realizes I am here, looks me straight in the eye, extracts himself from Abigail's grip, and starts heading my way looking determined.

I haven't answered any of his calls and, by his look, I doubt he is very happy about it. I rush into the building, run up the stairs, ignoring him as he shouts my name. I take refuge in my apartment, carefully locking the door behind me. I stand with my back against the door and the tears start to flow, overwhelming me. I don't even try to hold them back.

A moment later, banging so heavy that it makes my door shake clearly reveals Jordan's mood.

"Damn it, Line. Open the door!"

I don't answer. He keeps calling my name over and over.

"Line, for fuck's sake, open up! We have to talk! Liiiine!"

I sniffle loudly, my teeth clenched, well aware that he's not going to let this go.

"Line, open the fucking door or I will break it down."

Okay, I know what he is capable of. Might as well face him now and get it over with. I head to my bedroom and come right back as the incessant banging continues. I open it abruptly, stand firmly in front of him, and throw his sweater in his face. "Here! You forgot this at her place! Now, get lost and leave me be! I don't ever want to see you again!"

"What? But…"

He looks at his sweater dumbfounded and then looks straight at me speechlessly as he tries, and fails, to open his mouth again. "Line, we have to talk. I—"

I go ballistic, cut him right off and allow my anger to fill each and every word I hurl at him. "No! All of that… all that shit! It's over! I can't take any more! Keep your lies, your bros, and your bimbos to yourself. Abigail, Elise, Jodie… go back to *them*. I don't want to have anything more to do with you, Jordan Miller. Forget me, ignore me and most importantly, stop calling me!"

"Line! What can I do to—"

"Nothing. Please don't do anything! I fell for a man who refuses to move forward, but now, I'm done wasting my time. Keep all your unspoken words to yourself. Only they know the truth. You want to know something? You just can't stand living with yourself. And now that is your problem, not mine!" I turn around and forcefully slam the door in his face before yanking the lock. I burst into tears, run to the bedroom, and collapse on the bed sobbing. I lie there for hours, devastated with pain. I finally end up crying myself to sleep.

Early in the morning, as I wake up, I still feel trapped by grief. Deep inside my head, filled with images of Jordan, my thoughts are fighting amongst themselves. I replay the moments we shared over the past two months. How can someone go to such lengths to deny themselves the right to live and be loved? My phone rings and I look at it apprehensively, but it's only Capucine.

"What's going on? When were you planning on calling me?"

"Hello, Capucine. Can you be a little more specific?"

"You... Jordan... What happened? Timothy just called me."

"Wh... what? How can Timothy know about that?"

"Jordan spent the night at his place! Okay, I'm on my way and you'd better spit it all out!"

I hear the downstairs door and then Capucine's bouncy steps. No sooner do I open the door than I am buried in her arms crying profusely all over her sweater. She guides me inside and we settle in on the couch where I let it all out and explain the whole thing between sniffles.

She takes me in her arms and rocks me for the longest time. I let myself melt in her comforting embrace.

"You know what? Take the time to think things through, Line. Last night Jordan went to seek help from Timothy. Do you truly believe that if he doesn't give a damn about you, he would go straight to his friend in an attempt to find a solution? Line, Jordan's behavior might leave something to be desired, but I don't believe he is indifferent to what's happening. On the contrary. I am convinced he is mostly afraid."

"Afraid? Afraid of what damn it? What's so terrifying about me?"

"Not afraid of you, silly, afraid of the situation, of 'your' situation. You told me he refuses to think about the future, right? What if it is merely because he is caught in a crossfire? His head demands one thing, but his heart requires another. Do you understand what I am trying to tell you?"

"If he was not so stubborn, we could have a beautiful love story, Capucine."

I start crying even harder and my friend hands me a tissue compassionately.

"Hey, beautiful, who told you it was all over?"

"I did. I said it. I told him so last night."

"Those are only words, Line. Actions speak more loudly, as you very well know. At least give him a chance to prove he can change.

"I don't know if I can, Capucine. He has already caused me so much pain."

"It was not intentional, and remember he is at least in as much pain as you are."

I let my friend's words sink in and then go make some tea. Next, I will go open my shop and start my new life.

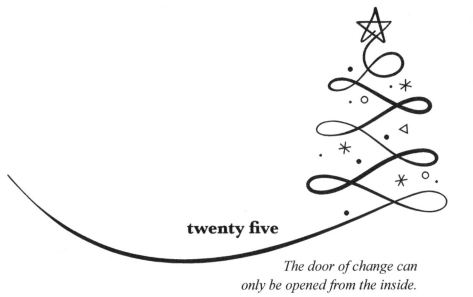

twenty five

*The door of change can
only be opened from the inside.*

Jacques Salomé

Jordan

Two knocks on my bedroom door snatch me out of my reverie.
For nearly four hours now, I have been lying down agonizing over
Line. How can I make her listen to reason?

If she would at least hear me out, it would be a great start.
When she opened the door to throw my sweater in my face, I
could clearly see the tears in her red puffy eyes and the gashes I
inflicted on her face as well as the anger and pain emanating from
the very pores of her skins. My shock only increased when I heard
her say the name Jodie.

Where did she hear that name? Who told her about it?

She was mad at me, and I can easily understand why. I
caused her pain, albeit inadvertently. Under no circumstances did
I want to cause her pain, but things got out of control and I was
powerless to stop it. Then everything kept coming at us like in a
cheesy movie where the main characters can't seem to find the
wherewithal to pull themselves together.

So here I am, crashing in Tim's guest room to keep myself
from banging on her door like a maniac. But will not give up.
Just as Line so aptly said, I will not let all the nonsense come
between us. Patiently, over many beers, I listen to Tim's counsel.

His assessment of the situation brings me for the days to come. She must listen to me. I will not back down, and I refuse to let her pull away.

The door cracks open and Tim cautiously peeks his head in. "Hey, dude, everything okay?"

I sit up on the bed and move to the edge rubbing my hair briskly. I need a good cup of coffee to help clear my head. "Yeah, sure. If you say so."

"I made breakfast. You coming?"

"Alright, Cinderella. I'll be right there."

He bursts out laughing and gives me a moment to get dressed. I open the windows wide and admire the immaculate white rooftops of Liverpool. The snow fell hard last night, and a thick layer stretches out, glistening in the sun. Dejectedly, I meet my friend who's busying himself in the kitchen pouring two steaming cups of coffee whose strong aroma floats all through his duplex apartment. My eyes land on a very small decorated Christmas tree sitting on a piece of furniture. "Did your tree shrink in the dryer?"

"Don't be sarcastic so early in the morning, Jordan. You know that every year I go to see my family for the holidays and their tree is huge. Since I live alone here, this is plenty big enough. At least, I have one!"

I perch myself on a stool at the counter when he looks up at me.

"Sleep well?"

"More or less, I slept like a log but to be honest I woke up pretty early."

"No wonder with all those beers you had! Nightmares?"

I look at him intently, pondering the worry engraved on his face. For years, they've been watching over me, he and Sonny, keeping me afloat; His tired-looking face bears witness to the bond of friendship that binds us. "Not this time. Actually, it's…"

"Line, right? You are spinning your wheels, trying to get out of this mess."

"Exactly. But, shit, why does she refuse to listen to me?"

"Why would she, Jordan? Seriously. Put yourself in her shoes for a second. Ever since she's known you, you have been untruthful, erratic, ill-tempered, and secretive. How do you expect her to react, damn it? And nevertheless, she has shown infinite patience, my friend."

Each of his words is like a burning blow to the chest, and collectively they shine a light on my propensity for destruction. I fuck things up. I fuck them up seriously. "Hey, I know that, Tim!"

"Alright then, shake a leg and go get her back! Prove to her that you are sincere. Tell her everything! Do it! She deserves for you to get your ass in gear, Jordan! That girl is the best thing that could ever happen to you. Take your shot before it's too late and you end up regretting it."

Our eyes meet briefly and in his I can see his determination to help me to get my life back. And I so badly want to do just that. She is the precipice into which I want to leap. The one that draws me to its depths. "I won't let her slip away from me!" I say while bringing the coffee to my lips.

There's a knock at the door, Sonny enters and sits with us. "Hey, guys. Well, what's going on? Timothy, were you able to get anything out of this knucklehead?"

I punch him amicably on the shoulder and he smirks. "That knucklehead is ready to go on the offensive."

Timothy pushes a coffee cup in front of Sonny and exclaims, "He has decided to fight for her."

Sonny gives me a sincere and friendly hug. "Fuck, it's about time! So, you got a plan? Tim, tell me he's got a plan."

The latter rummages through his thick mane before staring daggers at me. "If he doesn't, maybe I do."

Timothy presents his idea which perplexes me at first. But then I realize that this plan probably constitutes a step forward. Clearly, this is a last-ditch effort so I'd better not bitch about it, even though it does bring a smile to my lips. After all, I already took a giant leap in the right direction by driving to Inverness. In the end, it would just be another hurdle. I owe it her, to them, to myself. Whether or not she is ready will want it remains to be seen.

Then music fills the room, and the chords of Chris Daughtry's rock song "It's Not Over" resound around the room. As I turn around, I notice that Sonny and Timothy are standing defiantly, arms crossed. Alright, dudes, I hear you loud and clear.

"I'll try to do it right this time around
It's not over
'Cause a part of me is dead and in the ground
"This love is killing me,
but you're the only one
It's not over
We can't let this get away
Let it out, let it out
Don't get caught up in yourself
Let it out"

"Okay, I got it!"

Timothy walks my way with his head tilted to the side. "Today is her big day Jordan: the reopening of the Magic Cave. Don't you think it would be a good time to go congratulate her and try to start a conversation?"

"Really? You think?"

"Thinking is a waste of time dude. You need to take action instead of continually finding excuses to back down."

Sonny chimes in. "He's right! Show her that you want to move forward. But do it without pushing her, she is already upset enough with you. And one piece of advice: Don't fly off the handle if she snaps at you. She has very good reasons to be furious. So just shut your big mouth and bite the bullet."

I mumble to myself. I do know she'll probably let me have it, but like Sonny said, she has good reasons. I better keep my head down if I want to successfully make peace with her. I get off my stool and wave to my friends as I make my way out the door. Before I step outside, I turn around. "Thanks for being there."

They don't answer, they just nod in acknowledgement. Sometimes words are pointless.

Driving through heavy traffic, I tell myself the earlier the better. So, I decide to go home and shower. Next, I'll go see Line. I park and what see makes my heart sing: a long line of customers rushing into the store. I watch Line as she smiles at each of them. She did it! It's happening! The Magic Cave has reopened its doors, and it's a success. I feel proud. She deserves this.

I slip away before she can notice me and take refuge in my apartment, trying hard to channel the whirlpool of feelings inside me. Even though I am sure of my decision, I worry just thinking she might say no. Line has a very strong character. She may seem like a sweet, shy young lady, but inside her hides a fierce lioness who will not hesitate to roar when she feels threatened. But it's also her relentless fighting spirit that has allowed me to realize some important things. She shoved my face in my own shit and then helped me smell the sweet perfume of life again. A strange but extraordinarily effective course of action.

Now I want to heal and recover, taking Line along with me to face my fight. I want her by my side; I want to show her she was right. Beneath my thick skin, you can still see who I used to be. Who I was before. And that guy wants to come back for her.

What were the odds that a mere fender bender would prove to be such a life-changing event? What were the chances that this adorable Christmas-loving woman would make me so vulnerable that I would consider sorting my life out? What stroke of luck made this improbably encounter my lifeline back to the surface? Who would have thought it? I certainly did not. Not by a long shot! For six long years, my friends have tried to reason with me. Now she, with just a smile, a look, a few disarming words, she subtly succeeded when so many others failed.

After a long shower, it feels like I am finally ready to face her. I make myself look as good as possible, put on some jeans, an Irish sweater, and finish meticulously trimming my beard. I look into the living room and spot Stringer staring at me with his tiny beady eyes. He even seems to say: "You better nail this, dude!" I stretch out my arm and he climbs on happily. I pet him for a while, enjoying this bonding moment. It's soothing. As I set him down on the couch, I can't help but whisper to him: "It's on!"

When I push open the door to the shop, I discover that there is a real euphoria. Customers rave at the various pieces displayed here and there. I have to admit Line has a knack for layout. Never has the shop been so attractive. As charming as my cupcake. Buyers line up at the register and I get in line among them, awaiting my turn. Honestly, all I really want is to cut to the front of the line and snatch Line away to my place, but she probably wouldn't approve of that plan, so I grin and bear it. Suddenly I see her emerge from a group of people carrying a lamp. Chatting away with an elderly man, she smiles at him and seems to be firmly in her element. When she looks up though it's difficult for me to remain invisible. We exchange looks, and I know right away she is not excited to see me here. I think she is even about to turn me into a human lampshade. I fear the worst so I look down and make myself as small as a mouse, still hoping I will be able to talk to her.

It seems like I have been waiting for an eternity, I am hopping up and down with impatience. Finally, it's my turn and Line addresses the customer in line behind me, a mischievous-looking grandma.

"Ma'am, welcome to the Magic Cave, how can I help you?"

"Hello, my dear," the grandma answers, baffled. "I believe this young man was here long before me. I am in no hurry anyway. People my age, we have more time than we need."

Line smiles innocently, locks her eyes on mine, and casually addresses her client. "Well, you know, this man can wait, Ma'am. He doesn't know what he wants anyway."

I try to plead my case, but she ignores me pointedly. "Line—"

She walks around the counter, moves towards the old lady with confidence and continues her conversation. "I am all ears Ma'am. Did you find what you were looking for?"

"Yes, I will take the blue vase over there at the end of the room on the pedestal table. I know it's not the trendiest color, but I love its style."

She accompanies the customer all the way to the item she wants, and I can't help but follow her insistently.

"Such a pleasure to see someone take responsibility for their choices with so much conviction. Unlike others…" she says throwing me a meaningful look.

The customers witness our exchange, looking at both of us curiously.

"Damn it, Line. Listen to me for fuck's sake!"

"This is neither the time nor the place, Jordan," she replies testily. "Now, I suggest you go spend your energy somewhere else. Preferably, as far away from here as possible! Follow me Ma'am, I will ring you up. Would you like this gift wrapped?"

She turns around and walks away, carrying the vase. I grumble with exasperation.

What a fucking shitty temper!

I catch up with them while Line proceeds to check her customer out. I stand right in front of her in a final attempt to get her attention. "Alright! You refuse to listen to me? There's nothing I can do about it? I won't give up, Line. I just stopped by to congratulate you on the opening, but you are probably right. Now is not the best time."

The old lady smiles at this playful banter and pays for her purchase, then turns around to speak to me. "Good luck to you, young man. That is one tough young lady."

"Right you are. Talking sense into her is like swimming upstream."

"Then stop swimming, sailor. Get a motorboat!"

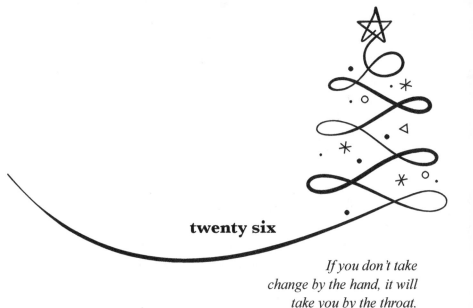

twenty six

*If you don't take
change by the hand, it will
take you by the throat.*

Winston Churchill

Line

After Jordan's visit to the shop, my feelings are fighting one another. I am caught between anger at everything I had to put up with, and affection when I see him trying to make it up to me. Yes, I am an incorrigible romantic. There is nothing I can do about that, despite the resentment I have felt through the weeks, this man turns me upside down. Prickly yet adorable. A bit like a hedgehog. Well, a lot sexier, I must say. Because thus far, to the best of knowledge, no one has ever heard of any woman screaming: "Oooooh, that hedgehog turns me on!" Nope. Not a one.

Jordan, he is more feline: powerful and unpredictable. The one that pounces when you least expect it. It was all I could do to contain myself when I saw him standing among my customers. But no way was I going to make it easy for him. No freaking way. For now, I try to focus on my customers, ignoring the storm raging inside me. All through the day the shop stays busy. I am filled with pride for this successful opening.

Grandpa Joe, I hope you are proud of me.

Time flies and it's around 7:30 PM, when I finally close the shop. Worn out, I head upstairs to my place, in a state of sheer satisfaction and extreme fatigue. The day was filled with emotions and all I want is to take a shower and go to bed. Unfortunately, I don't even make it to the bathroom before someone knocks at my door. I sincerely hope it's not Jordan. In my current state, I'm not up for a fight.

I open the door and find Timothy and Sonny standing there with their hands in their pockets. I squint and check to see if their friend is hidden in a corner somewhere, but they put my mind at rest right away. "Don't worry, Line. We are alone. We came to congratulate you on the inauguration."

I sigh at their sheepish attitude and invite them to come in. "Thanks, boys. I have to admit it was intense."

"It's so awesome! Really Line, we are thrilled for you. You had so many customers. We saw them filing past on the sidewalk."

"Oh yeah, indeed, even your buddy was there!"

There is a pregnant pause, neither dares look me in the eye. "Well…"

"Come on guys, don't act like you didn't know he was coming to pay me a visit. Please, don't take me for a fool."

"We didn't mean to," Timothy interrupts, "I swear. Yes, we knew he would visit. We even encouraged him to."

I sigh, exasperated, throwing my hands up as if imploring for some divine intervention. "In the future, do me a favor and spare me your harebrained ideas! Jordan wanted to toy with me, and he failed. His tough luck."

Sonny seems bothered by my words and takes a determined stance in front of me. "That is a bit harsh! Jordan is not a bad guy. Of course, he is clumsy, but you can't just write him off like that. At least give him a chance to talk things over."

"Oh yeah, well, he had plenty of time to explain himself and he did not see fit to do so."

"He wasn't ready," Timothy steps in softly but with assurance.

"What about me? I'm just supposed to be at his beck and call until his majesty is ready? That's what you guys are telling me? Alright, I know he is your friend and that you are standing up for him, but I have to think about myself guys. Don't forget that this relationship has been tough on me! Now I have an open shop to tend to, and I need to take care of it without a bunch of parasitic thoughts running around in my head."

Timothy approaches me and stares at me with intensity.

"You are lying to yourself, Line. You won't get him out of your head because you have feelings for him. Am I wrong? So, if you believe that burying your head in the sand will make things better, allow me to tell you that you are mistaken. It will eat you up."

"Alright now, listen. I'm exhausted. Although I do appreciate your effort trying to patch things up the only thing I really want right now is to go to bed."

"Very well, we will leave you be, Line. But don't forget that if you need anything, we are here for you, alright? And will you promise me you will think about it?"

"I will think about it, but I won't make any promises."

They both kiss me on the cheek affectionately and leave me with my thoughts.

I try in vain to get Jordan out of my head, but the fact is Timothy is right and that drives me wild with anger. I have the feeling Jordan lives in my head, that he has planted his tent in there and refuses to leave. I want to hate his guts, but every fiber of my being craves the touch of his warm, rough hands on my skin. Determined to take my mind off things, I make myself a cup of cinnamon-pear tea. Grandpa Joe used to brew some for me when I was feeling sick and it is always comforting. I am curled up on my couch in front of the TV when my phone rings. I check the caller ID and am disappointed that it is only Victor. "Hey, Victor."

"Hola, beautiful. So, I heard about your grand reopening. Seems like it was a big hit! I am so proud of you! You will accomplish beautiful things, there's a whole new life opening up before you."

"Thank you, Victor, I couldn't have done it without your support, and Capucine's."

"You only owe your success to your hard work, Line. You are a fighter and never shrink from a challenge."

"Not always…"

Suddenly my voice cracks and I can't hold back the tears.

"Hey, hey, Line, what's going on? Come on, calm down, beautiful. Don't forget, we are gremlins. Have you ever seen a gremlin cry? No, right?"

I burst out laughing at his attempt to cheer me up. He has the gift of bringing sunshine to a cloudy day. His tone shows that he is really worried. He is like a big brother to me. A shoulder to lean on and from which I can draw a bit of strength. It is probably his most prominent personality trait: protection. As the eldest of a family of four brothers and one sister, he plays the part of big brother part as best he can. And God only knows life has not been easy on him. The youngest caused him a lot of trouble, but he worked hard to ensure him a bright future despite his tendency to act up. With no father and their mother working all hours to make ends meet, he had to grow up very fast. Early on he assumed responsibilities and he spent his time and energy helping his mother out. I applaud his combativeness and self-sacrifice. Incidentally, it's part of the reason why he stopped playing music. All of his time was spent working and taking care of his family. "I'll be alright, Victor, don't worry. It's just a momentary setback. Today got the best of me."

"But you had a great turnout, so what's upsetting you like this? Let me guess. Your bearded neighbor! Of course."

"Well, I can't hide anything from you. Yes, he stopped by the shop today."

"For what?"

"He wanted to talk, to explain himself. But I don't see how that could possibly be helpful."

"Maybe you should give him a chance."

"Hey, I thought you were on my side! You're at it too, now?! Are you in cahoots with Timothy?"

"What? No! I'm just saying that if you knew what he has to say, it might shed some light on things."

"What are you hiding from me? I thought you didn't like him and now you are pushing me to talk to him?"

"I am not hiding anything, Line. Only sometimes you can make better decisions if you can see the whole playing field. If you don't hear him out, you might regret it for the rest of your life. I only want you to be happy. Don't let your preconceived notions keep you from finding happiness. It's too easy to judge someone on appearances. Believe me, I know what I'm talking about."

"What are you not telling me? You seem so confident."

"Just ask yourself the right questions, Line. Oh, by the way,

I found some people willing to perform at the kids' party, so that's taken care of. You don't need to worry about it anymore."

I am overcome with joy at the news. I was feeling bummed about it being only dinner and a few stories for the kiddos. Now, thanks to Victor, they will have an actual Christmas party. "Holy shit! That's amazing, Victor. I am so happy. How did you do it? We—"

"I gotta go, Line, just enjoy the good news and think about what I told you. Love ya!"

He hangs up and I find myself phone in hand, perplexed. That was an intriguing conversation, to say the least. However, I feel painfully tired, so I dash off to take a shower and then collapse onto my bed, drained by my conflicting emotions.

The following days fly by hectically. The shop is constantly busy, word of mouth having worked like a charm. Jordan makes himself scarce and I don't run into him. At the end of the week, I close the shop a little early so I can finish Christmas shopping. I end up picking a personalized gift for Sonny. I visit a local print shop to have a sweatshirt made, one that will do a good job of reflecting his personality. Capucine would totally agree with the words I decide to have printed on it! Now that I have most of the presents taken care of, I hesitate about Jordan's. Should I get him one? I feel so lost, and all of a sudden, I realize this will be my first Christmas on my own since I used to always spend it with Grandpa Joe. We always looked forward to it and he alone knew how to bring me the warmth and comfort of a loving family. From now on, I must learn to make do without him and I must admit the thought is terrifying. So far, I had only been faced with his absence, trying as best as I could to move forward. Now I realize I have subconsciously been hiding the fact that I am about to spend my first Christmas alone.

How will I be able to face this challenge and overcome the pain of your absence, Grandpa?

To avoid crying, we can busy our minds in a thousand ways. But when we are face to face with our heart, running away is no longer an option, only pain remains, and it holds us tight.

Even my friends will be gone. Capucine is going to go visit her family as are Timothy, Sonny, and Victor. As for my neighbor,

I suppose he will stay home like the Grinch since he loathes this time of the year. How dreadful.

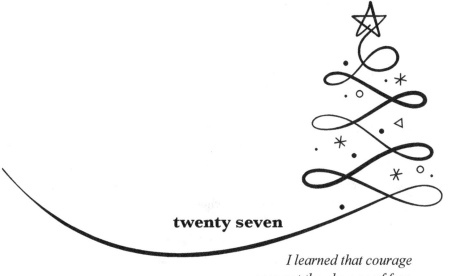

twenty seven

*I learned that courage
was not the absence of fear,
but the triumph over it.*

Nelson Mandela,
Long Walk to Freedom

Jordan

Saying that I am nervous is quite an understatement. I am totally
freaked out, but nothing could make me backtrack and change my
mind. I know someone up there that must be having an absolute
blast watching me, and I am sure that many people would pay top
dollar to see me right now and relish this unbelievable moment.
Yep, I am not proud, but I will own up to it as gracefully as
possible.

In the big white room, I am sitting on my chair waiting for
her. Timothy and Sonny are of no comfort whatsoever. Worse,
I am subjected to their whole barrage of jokes and incessant
laughter. How will she react? Will she accept my presence? I don't
have time to ask myself more questions before the door swings
open briskly, and Victor and Line enter. Everyone is holding their
breath. Dumbstruck, she eyes us one at a time and when she spots
me, the silent disapproval in her eyes is unbearable.

She swings around to address her friend and blurts out
menacingly, "You gotta be kidding me! Are you serious?!"

"Come on, Line. Look at them. Aren't they adorbs? They

are getting us out of a jam. Think about the kids, they'll love it!"

Timothy and Sonny come closer to her completely relaxed and start actively seconding Victor's idea. Grabbing his guitar from behind the table, Timothy announces proudly, "Line, I'll make a terrific singing elf!" he exclaims, shaking his head and sporting pointy ears and a hat with jingle bells. "Bet on it!"

Sonny falls into step right behind him, standing proudly in front of her. "And I am Santa's coolest reindeer. Look, I am the most handsome reindeer ever," he cheers on, pinching his red nose as it starts blinking colorfully.

Line bursts out laughing uncontrollably at the silly getups.

"I must admit, those are the most beautiful antlers I have ever seen!" she says unable to contain her amusement.

After Timothy and Sonny's little show, she stares at me attentively but has lost even the faintest trace of a smile. I almost feel like sinking into the ground. Cupcake is still mad at me.

"What about him?"

Chomping at the bit, I stand up and approach her, looking her straight in the eye.

Come on, stay strong dude, you can do it!

"Well, I am Santa," I reply pointing to my red and white costume jazzed up with a big black belt and a gold buckle.

"What the heck is going on with that beard! It's... it's silver!"

"Metallic gray, to be precise! I am a psychedelic Santa."

The reference to her mind-altering journey a couple days ago doesn't go unnoticed, I see it flash briefly in her eyes. She doesn't let it show though, instead she pretends to ignore me royally and turns to Victor. "Alright, Victor, but only because we have no other choice. But make my words, you will pay dearly for this."

He smiles brightly at her and for a moment I am jealous of the attention she pays him. He runs us through the afternoon program, and we all listen carefully. The kids' happiness depends on it, so we work on our parts diligently.

Victor recaps it all with great excitement. "Alright, we have one elf singing Christmas songs, one reindeer serving treats, Line reading Christmas stories, and Santa handing out the presents. It's going to be epic!"

I look at my cupcake attentively and try to find the chink in her armor that would afford me even the slightest smile.

"Okay, I can see that everything is in order, all I have left to do is change. Victor, meet me in the backyard."

Line leaves the room and I look at Victor questioningly. He winks at me before answering innocently. "Well, yeah. We also have Mrs. Claus…"

I fear the worst. To be close to Line all day bearing her anger is already challenging enough without having to see her in a Mrs. Claus outfit. It's more than I can bear. While all I dream about is touching her body, she doesn't seem the least bit interested and just looks me up and down with indifference. A friendly tap on my shoulder brings me back to Earth. Timothy looks at me compassionately and tries to cheer me up as best as he can. "It'll be fine Jordan. Don't worry about it. It's about making the kids so happy, right? Isn't it grand!"

"Yes, at least they will have a smile on their faces, that's a start."

Sullen, I get up to follow them mechanically. For crying out loud, I am dressed up as freaking Santa Claus! Who would have believed that a few months ago? We walk through a maze of corridors, and despite all the direction signs posted, it's still difficult to find our way around. About ten minutes later, we stand in front of a glass door that opens onto a small backyard. As I push it open, my heart bursts into flames. My God, this is inhuman! Clad in a perfectly irresistible little red outfit, Line eyes me angrily.

I must be out of my mind because, how can I put it? I have a huge hard-on for Ms. Claus. I will need a serious amount of self-control to keep Santa's equipment in his pants. I watch her move slowly towards me, taunting me in the most delectable way. Even though the cut is modest, that little dress makes her look particularly sexy. Cinched at the waist with a large black belt, a boat neckline, and topped with a cute matching bolero, it highlights the most attractive features of her slender silhouette. The thin trim, lined with white fur, sways against the edge of her thighs and hypnotizes me with every step she takes. Even her black leather zip-up boots, plain tough they may be, make me want to rip them off with my teeth. My thoughts come tumbling out, each new one more inappropriate than the last, leaving me dazed and confused. She has the confidence I have lost. She knows she won; I can read it in her eyes. At this very moment, it all becomes real. I no longer want to hide my emotions, all I want is for her to listen to me, but the timing couldn't be worse. A flock of kids starts to file in from the north corridor. Next, as per Victor's instructions, we will go around all of the rooms to visit the kids that are bed-bound.

My attention shifts back to Line who is standing right in front of me.

"Jordan, you got your part memorized, right?"

"Yes, I will hand them each a present and ask them if they are happy to see Santa Claus. Then, I will praise them for their courage."

"Correct. For once, you got something right!"

Stung by her scathing remark, I let it slide and let her enjoy the sweet taste of revenge.

We work non-stop, bombarded by a herd of excited kids, bursting with joy. The afternoon is emotionally intense. We give the kids our undivided attention to make this day a celebration they won't soon forget. In the backyard, under the huge Christmas tree trimmed in gold and white, an entire group surrounds Line. Sitting elegantly on the ground, she tells them a story. Another group snatches Timothy the Elf and his guitar, and together they launch into traditional carols.

As for us, Santa and Sonny the reindeer, we give away the remaining presents and snacks to the latecomers. Three hours go by. A few nurses give Victor a round of applause for the impressive efficiency with which he has coordinated this day.

Next, we treat ourselves to a short, well-deserved break, just enough time for a cup of coffee before we head out to visit the sickest of the kids in their rooms. I can't take my eyes off of Line. She smiles and laughs out loud. She is glowing and yet as soon as the children turn away from her, her face changes immediately, her pain resurfacing. The pain I am solely responsible for. I feel so miserable, filled with doubt. Should I really tell her everything, at the cost of losing her for good? As a steaming cup of coffee is placed in front of me, I look up and meet with Victor's dark look.

"Watch out, Jordan, you'll sprain your brain, and no one

here will be able to do anything to help you out."

He hands me the coffee, I grab it and thank him. I smile at his witty words designed to help me relax and take the opportunity to chat with him a bit. "Victor—"

"It's time for you and her to start living life to the fullest," he interrupts, as if able to read my mind. "Don't let doubts eat away at you. When the day is over, just go for it and tell her how you feel."

I look at him deeply and give him a quiet nod of thanks. These few words are enough to boost my spirits and as I turn my head, I catch Line watching me. Caught *in flagrante*, she feigns indifference and turns on her heels, to my great satisfaction.

At around four thirty in the afternoon, we start to make the rounds of each room. It is hard to come to terms with the fact that these kids are here suffering with horrible diseases. My heart is heavy with sadness. With each door we open it becomes increasingly harder to maintain that joyous, friendly smile. We are so insignificant on this Earth. Faced with that depressing thought, the idea that I shouldn't waste another second travels from my heart to my head. Really, what does the future have in store for us? If we don't make the most of the luck we have to be in good health, we miss out on the essence of our existence.

Life...

I can't stop watching Line furtively. I will never stop thanking the person, or the thing, that placed her in my bumpy path. Full of hope, I count the passing minutes. One hour left until I can finally talk to her, alone, just the two of us, without anyone eavesdropping. I must admit Timothy and Sonny impressed me today. I knew they had a big heart, but they actually postponed their vacation to be available for my cupcake. Proof that she has wormed her way into these bearded dudes' hearts. Once the last visit is done, we meet in the common room where Victor and Jeff, Line's supervisor, congratulate us warmly. In the corridor leading us to the hospital exit, I catch Line apart from the group. "Line! Wait! Please listen to me, I need to talk to you. Can I drive you home?"

Swinging around to face me, I can't help seeing the anger alight in her eyes. It breaks my heart.

"You seriously think I don't have better things to do than listen to you? You used me, Jordan. I'm driving home with Victor. He's going to drop me off before heading home to his family."

"Line... Please!"

Far from letting herself be moved, she looks at me one last time, just long enough time for me to see a tear glistening at the edge of her eyelashes. After that, she walks away confidently and disappears down that corridor that seems to suddenly close in on me. Fists clenched, I dash out of the place, cold air slapping my face vigorously. I get a mental slap as well. I am about ready to give up when I race to my car determined to have that conversation with her as soon as she makes it to our place!

Our place. It's odd to think about it.

This simple idea that came to me so naturally is living proof that I am not mistaken. She is the one I want in my life, no one else. The heavy snowfall slows traffic down substantially, but still, twenty minutes later, I am parked along the sidewalk in front of my shop. Since I didn't see them leave, I am convinced they're not here yet. I think hard, considering over and over how I will tell her, which words to use, and where to start, when the shining headlights of a vehicle meet mine and park across the street. The wait was not so bad after all. She climbs out of the car and waves goodbye as she watches it drive away.

Here we are. The time has come for me to walk into the lion's den.

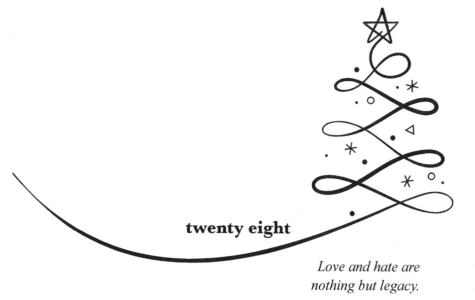

twenty eight

*Love and hate are
nothing but legacy.*

Idriss Mahamat Kosso

Line

What a day!

A hands-down success! I have to admit that I was a little leery of Victor's idea at first, but in the end, the day went much better than I expected. Still, my heart is heavy. So heavy. Crestfallen, I am about to push open the door to my building when a firm hand spins me around. Briefly I panic, but then find myself face to face with Jordan. He has also changed clothes and his black turtleneck highlights the fire in his amber eyes where his determination burns wild. "Let me go right now, Jordan! I mean it!"

"Not unless you listen to me! Stop copping out and face me!"

"Face you? That's all I've done since I met you! Look where that led us! What a waste of time!"

Towering above me, he doesn't blink and gathers his courage. "Line, you're entitled to be mad at me. But running away from the problem, won't solve it! At least hear me out."

"Why? You'll just end up ruining everything again anyway. You're too dense!"

"No, to be honest, denseness is overrated. It's much worse

than that! If you have more things to get off your chest, go for it! Let it out, Line."

Shaking with rage, my anger bursts in tandem with my voice. To hell with the neighbors! I scream until my vocal cords are raw. "I fucking HATE you! Alright? I hate your lies; I hate your silences. I hate that the chicks you banged throw your clothes in my face. I hate when you tell me everything's fine when you don't even believe it yourself. I hate when you scream another woman's name at night, and I feel like the most miserable person on Earth. I hate what you have awoken in me. I hate that I hate you. I hate the emptiness I feel when you are not around. I hate when you look at me the way you do and make my world stand still!"

As I spill my guts, Jordan's eyes narrow. It seems he has finally realized all the pain he caused me. Then, all of a sudden, he stiffens. His muscles tense and it's his turn to shout. "Oh, *you* hate *me*? Well, I hate you too! I hate when your stubbornness prevents you from listening to reason. I hate how you put up Christmas decorations everywhere. I hate how your perfume permeates the stairwell and inebriates me. I hate how your nose wrinkles up when you get mad because then all I want to do is take you in my arms and comfort you. I hate when other men look at you with lust because I want to be the only one. I hate when your eyes glisten the way they do right now because I can see in them the tears I'm responsible for! And everything I see in them confirms only one thing: I love that I hate to love you! Line, you brought me back to life."

Dumbstruck by his belated confession, I feel bitter tears burning my eyes. Standing on the sidewalk, we stare at each other as a thick layer of snow covers us. Nothing else matters. Neither the cold, the snow, nor the wind. We are all alone in the universe. Lowering my eyes, the tears begin to flow, and I start in again. "We are like day and night, Jordan! I was wrong to believe this could work. I see that clearly now. Just look at yourself. You hate Christmas and it's my favorite time of the year!"

"You're wrong, Line! I don't hate Christmas. I hate the memories it rekindles. That's not the same thing!"

"What on earth are you talking about?"

"Come, and let me explain."

He holds his hand out to me hoping I will accept it, and after several minutes of hesitation, I give in. Without further ado, maybe concerned I might change my mind, he gently pulls me against him and starts whispering in my ear, "Line, I am terrible with words so I will quote a man who wisely wrote. 'As for the future, your task is not to foresee it, but to enable it. Of course I'll hurt you. Of course you'll hurt me. Of course we will hurt each other. But this is the very condition of existence. To become spring, means accepting the risk of winter. To become present, means accepting the risk of absence. So, you see, I must risk the pain for the joy.'[5]"

I immediately recognize those words. I have read them so many times. I breathe my answer, my voice filled with emotion, "Antoine de Saint-Exupéry. Jordan, you read his letters?"

"I did everything I could to try to understand you, to bridge the gap between us. He has the perfect words to illuminate all that is bubbling inside me. I have so much to tell you! I know what brings me joy, Line, and it's you! The joy of getting to know you a bit more each day. Watching you sleep, seeing you smile. Casting my ghosts away at night. Some people say that love requires courage, but it's really much more than that. But first, you have to agree to hear me out."

"Jordan, you have just opened up your heart to me. That's already a lot."

"True, but that's only one part of the issue. The crux of the matter is something else altogether. I'm not even sure you will still be able to look at me the same way you hear what I have to reveal."

"Jordan, you're scaring me! What—"

"Not out here on the sidewalk, Line. Let's go inside and get something warm to drink. Then I will tell you everything."

Hand in hand, we climb the stairs to his apartment.

Entering his place, it all comes back to me: the aromas of wood and leather and the masculine decor that suits him so well. The tears, and of course, the pleasure.

The red ambers of the fire crackle, and the warmth envelops

---

[5] from a letter that Antoine Saint-Exupéry wrote to Nathalie Paley

us like a soft cocoon. An army of emotions march through me forcefully. That is simply the "Jordan effect." I watch him as he silently prepares some coffee for us and I am on pins and needles, unsure of what to expect. Silently, we down our drinks, letting them warm us, and after a brief pause, he finally breaks the silence. "Come," he says taking my hand.

He guides me slowly to his bedroom, makes me sit me on the bed and takes a spot next to me. Inhaling deeply, he turns to face me looking very serious. "I don't really know where to start."

Placing my hand on his for support, I tell him softly, "I am listening, Jordan."

With his other hand he reaches between the bedframe and the mattress and extracts a delicately chiseled wooden box. I'm ready to bet it is Timothy's handiwork. I watch as he opens it feebly, all the while holding his breath. His tense face discloses how painful it is for him to look inside, and my stomach clenches. As if in slow motion, he takes out a photo of an incredibly beautiful young woman with delicate features. My heart almost stops when I notice a single tear rolling down his face.

"This is Jodie," he announces, his voice broken with sadness.

The name he screamed in the middle of that first night we slept together. The woman he is obsessed with every night. Holding back tears, I continue as valiantly as possible, despite the pain tearing me apart. "Jodie... You loved her, didn't you?"

"More than anything. We were kindred spirits, and I killed her."

Covering my mouth with both hands, my eyes bulge with fear at this revelation that crushes me like an anvil. *No... no! It can't be! Not Jordan. He could never commit such an evil act. I refuse to believe it!*

Suddenly, I feel like I've been transported to a parallel universe, one where everything I thought I knew is obsolete. "What do you mean you killed her?"

"It's the truth, Line. I am responsible for her death. And it has been haunting me for the last six years."

"Your nightmares..."

"Yes, every single night for the last six years."

"Had you been together for a long time when..."

"Since forever. Jodie was my twin sister."

Hell, how could I have missed the resemblance? The same amber colored eyes, the same highlights in their hair. Jordan had a sister. Yet there is not one photo in his apartment that could have led me to believe that. Actually, there are no photos connected to his past life at all. Even Timothy and Sonny never mentioned it. I feel completely disoriented. In response to all these revelations, my body starts shaking violently.

"Line, you're freezing! Wait here, I'll get you a sweater," he says suddenly panicked as he rushes to his solid oak dresser. He is absolutely right. My clothes are soaking wet due to our prolonged stay on the sidewalk. He hands me a black sweater which I put on right away. His somber, tortured look weighs me down. He seems so worried "Thank you. And don't worry. I won't melt, Jordan."

"She used to say that too."

A moment of silence passes.

"Tell me, Jordan. You need it, I need it. Even if we are here until dawn, you have to let it all out. I need to understand, to understand *you*."

"I'm afraid, Line. Afraid of how you will look at me afterwards."

"I am ready to hear all of it, Jordan. Keeping everything bottled up inside makes you your own worst enemy."

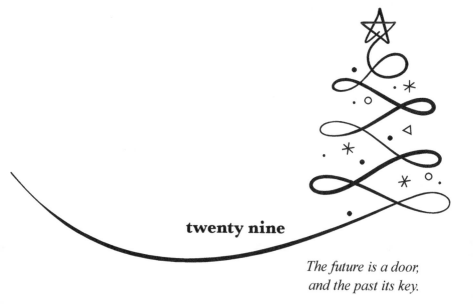

twenty nine

The future is a door,
and the past its key.

Victor Hugo,
Les Contemplations

Jordan

How does she do that? I just told her I killed my sister, and she is still here, encouraging me to continue despite it all. She somehow knows exactly what to say. The era of silence is over. I let go and dive into my past, no matter how painful. I take a deep breath, once, twice, three times, and let the memories wash over me.

* * *

Six years earlier

"Jodie, when will you finally understand that this shit is killing you gradually? This is your fourth trip to rehab!"

"I will pull through this time. I promise you, Jordan."

"How many times have I heard that story, Jodie? How many? Do you even think about us? The pain you cause us? We do everything for you, and you destroy it all. Shit, what are you trying to prove for heaven's sake?"

"I don't know. I feel so bad sometimes, so I tell myself just a little bit to—"

"To what? To actually overdose? Because that's what's in store for you if you keep this up."

Her complexion pale and her eyes rimmed with dark circles, my sister is nothing but the shadow of her former self. She had a brilliant future ahead of her before she started hanging out with that group of young folks on her college campus. For three years now, she has been digging her own grave at breakneck speed. Every attempt to extricate her from this hell has failed. I spend my days and nights trying to reason with her, trying to show her everything life has to offer. I come running at the slightest call for help. We were as thick as thieves, inseparable, as is often the case with twins. But now, I don't even recognize her. Emaciated, weakened, shivering even when the weather is at its warmest, talking nonsense. This is our last resort. She will be admitted into the strictest rehabilitation center in the region. We are all hoping that this nightmare will finally come to an end.

Two months later, she finally gets out and seems to be doing much better. She has gained some weight back, and even manages to smile now and then. My mother and I agree, she will stay with me for a while so I can keep an eye on her. So, weeks go by, punctuated by calls from my panic-stricken sister, mostly over bagatelles. No sugar, chocolate cravings, out of fruit… And every time, I leave work and come running, imagining the worst. I've already been written up twice. Next time, I'll be fired. I try to keep it all together, but I am growing weary. How long will I be able to handle Jodie's whims? Because even though my sister is my entire universe, she takes undue advantage of the situation. Yes, I coddle and overprotect her, but only to help her hang on.

That Thursday, at the end of the evening, my boss asks me to work two extra hours to make up the times I left early over the last few days. Of course, I get it. He has a business to run. I glance at my phone. But one missed call from my sister doesn't surprise me. Just another voicemail, identical to all the others. "Jordan, it's urgent. I need you."

One more whimsical demand to add to the list. Well, tonight, no can do. She will have to deal with whatever it is on her own. I continue working as attentively as I can even though my mind is distracted by Jodie's unread voicemail. At the end of my shift, I decide to surprise my sister. Tomorrow is Christmas, and we had planned to go spend the holidays with Mom. She is a big fan of the Beatles and I want to find her a small gift, so I head to the museum dedicated to the legendary band. The snow falls so heavily that it is almost impossible to see the edge of the road. As soon as I park, I notice a crowd of people gathering nearby. As I get closer, I feel oddly ill. I can see flashing red and blue lights. Cops are moving about. The snowflakes dancing before my eyes start to get in the way, obscuring my view. I rush through until my world shatters to pieces.

My footsteps crunch in the snow as I run towards her, but I get stopped, held back. I can't get any closer.

"You can't go through, young man!"

"Jodie!"

I thrash about, screaming, as my anger explodes accompanied by pain so brutal that I want to die. I cannot tear my eyes away from her weakened body lying in the snow, a syringe dangling from her arm. Blood stains the white snow. Her blood. I am overcome with grief at what I see. Her eyes are wide open, glassy, dark and it seems they are telling me "It is your fault. You did not come when I needed you." My brain refuses to compute. I wail. I cannot stop wailing. I drop to my knees in the snow, my fists pounding the pavement hidden beneath it. I wish someone would rip my heart and bowels out with their bare hands. It would be less painful!

* * *

Slowly, my mind wanders back to the present moment, but I still don't dare to look Line in the eye. I am so ashamed. I was supposed to protect Jodie, watch over her, and now she is gone. What will Line think of me? Tears roll down my cheeks, ending up buried in my now-wet beard. To my great surprise, Line carefully kneels between my legs and holds my face tightly in her cold hands. Her look, filled with tenderness, disarms me.

"Jordan. It's not your fault. There is no need to hold yourself responsible. You did everything in your power to help her. You are not to blame. The group of kids she hung out with and the guy who sold to her are. She couldn't have dreamed of a better brother than you. And from where she rests, I am sure she is proud of you."

"I let her down, Line. I…"

"No, you were there until the end. We are not machines, Jordan. Everyone gets tired when pushed to their limits. It's normal. You have nothing to feel guilty about."

Stunned by her unwavering support, I reach out and caress her face. "She would have loved you, you know."

"And I am sure I would have loved her too. She got caught in an extremely difficult spiral, but you helped her as best as you could."

I nod silently, weary from the wealth of emotions. Line picks up on it.

"We still have a lot more to clarify, Jordan, but I think that it's enough for tonight. What say we pick this up again tomorrow?"

Just the thought of her leaving me causes my body to tense like a drawn bow in opposition to the sheer idea that she could even consider it.

"You… you want to go? I—"

"No! I want to stay here, with you, tonight. We will sleep and then resume tomorrow."

I immediately nod in agreement. I am happy to have her by my side for the night or I should say, totally overjoyed. Just being able to hold her against me is a giant step forward for our future. "Do you mind if I call out for a snack?"

"Oh, I wouldn't say no to that."

"Alright, and if you'd like to take a shower, make yourself at home. Turkish food?"

"That would be wonderful. The delicacies at Faruk's are to die for!"

After a quick call, I start setting the table for the food we are about to receive when my phone rings. I notice that Line is heading to the bathroom and pick up right away. "Hello?"

"Hi, Jordan! So, how's everything going?"

"Tim, you're a real busybody. Couldn't wait until tomorrow for me to call you?"

"Well actually no, after the scene you guys made out in the

street, we were worried and wanted to check to make sure you guys were still alive."

"What? You guys were there?"

"Well, yeah, we were right behind Line. But, to tell the truth, when you two started screaming at the top of your lungs, we hugged the walls."

"It was pretty rough, but you know what? I was able to open up to her. Well, to talk to her about Jodie and about what happened."

"How did she take it?"

"Well, a lot better than I expected. She amazes me, dude. She is attentive and non-judgmental, even when it comes to the things that I blame myself for. That said, we're not out of the woods yet. I still have lots of things to tell her. There's the situation with Styx, Abigail, and Inverness."

"You got this, Jordan. Be honest, tell her everything and all will be well. She is a smart girl."

His wise words comfort me, and I feel bolstered, ready to fight for Line's affections. "You can say that again. When are you leaving to go see your family?"

"I'm flying out tonight, and Sonny's leaving too. But dude, if you need us for anything at all, we'll turn around pronto, got it? Don't hesitate to call. And whatever you do, keep us posted, alright?"

"Sure. And… thank you. You guys are like brothers to me."

Filled with hope for the upcoming days that seem much brighter ever, my thoughts are weightless as they wander to my one and only. The very same person that is currently naked in my shower. I want the rest of the night to be drama-free and as peaceful as possible for the both of us, so I put on some music to cozy up the atmosphere.

When I turn around, I find my cupcake looking sublime in a T-shirt with my shop's logo on it. Timothy, Sonny and I are very proud of that logo. We wanted it to have a trendy, rock vibe to set the tone for our barbershop. And we nailed it! The shirt looks great, and no one wears it better than she does. Yes, I know. Obviously, I am biased. Watching her, standing in the middle of the living room, her damp hair still dripping onto her slender neck, I would be lying if I were to deny that she turns me on like crazy. I know it would be completely inappropriate for me to move forward to hug and kiss her, among other things. She doesn't seem angry, but she does seem somewhat baffled by my confession and remains cautious. Now, it's up to me to put her mind to rest.

"I borrowed this one."

"It looks lovely on you."

The intercom buzzes, announcing dinner and giving me a chance to recuperate from the dizzying sight of her. "I'll get it," I say heading out the door.

I run down the stairs in a flash. It only takes me about three minutes to get the bag, pay, and go back up. When I get back, she is settled comfortably on the living room sofa, her legs crossed underneath her. Lord, what a sight for sore eyes! Oh, how I would love to see it every day for the rest of my life. Her. Here. In a home that would be ours.

We pig out on Turkish food, while carefully avoiding any reference to our previous conversation. We make small talk to try and keep things light while we eat. The tune of "What Am I To You" by Norah Jones envelops us, accompanied by the crackling of the red-hot fire.

The moment is so soothing it seems unreal. I catch Line's looking at the sentence tattooed on my forearm "My memory is my purgatory." Like a prior condemnation that I can't seem to shake, it troubled her deeply during our first meal together. "Do you understand it better now?"

Looking serious and saddened, she smiles shyly at me. "Yes, it is much clearer. Your guilt haunts you so badly that you felt compelled to engrave it on your skin. As if you didn't want to forget and let go of this tragedy. But you have to move on Jordan, nothing will erase the past."

"Dance with me, Line."

First taken aback by my unexpected request, she then nods and stands up gracefully. I feel a profound desire to hold her in my arms, to prove to myself that this moment is real. I need to breathe her in, to feel her heartbeat against my chest. I dim the lights and move close to her without breaking eye contact. Our eyes lock as we hold and tame each other.

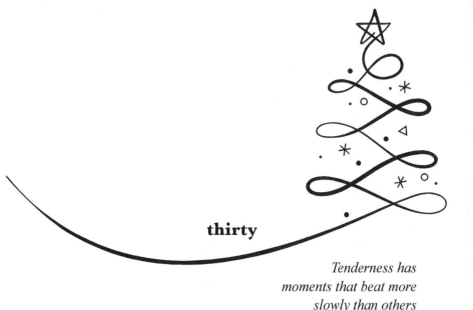

thirty

*Tenderness has
moments that beat more
slowly than others*

Romain Gary, *Gros-Câlin*

Line

Emotion, caution, doubt, desire… So many things now transpire
deep in his amber eyes. My favorite song by the same artist, "Turn
Me On," lulls us as we nestle against each other, savoring these
precious minutes. The title, seemingly written specifically for us,
mirrors our internal struggle. Like a message we wanted to share
but never dared to say out loud.

> *"Like a flower*
> *Waiting to bloom*
> *Like a lightbulb*
> *In a dark room*
> *I'm just sitting here waiting for you*
> *To come on home and turn me on."*

My body responds simply to this call, snuggling up even
closer as he holds me in his arms tighter and tighter. We let
ourselves be carried away by this magical moment. Softly, he
cradles me in the middle of the living room, burying his face in
my hair, breathing me in eagerly as if to fill himself up with my
presence. My head spins, caught in a subtle, voluptuous moment
of lightheadedness. It rests on his chest and his heartbeat is like

a melody that soothes every single part of my body. Through the window I see snow falling heavily in the ice-cold night while we are safe inside in a cocoon of tenderness.

I close my eyes and imagine Grandpa Joe and Jodie watching over us, both sitting on a star, smiling at our embrace. I let myself be rocked gently, enjoying the warmth of his body pressed against mine. I don't even try to think anymore. I feel so good, so safe in his tattooed arms. His hand reaches up to caress my hair delicately and tenderly as if he feared I would break. When the music ends, Jordan doesn't let me go. Instead, he tilts my head up so that my eyes can meet his and looks at me attentively. There is a mysterious spark in his eyes.

"Thank you. Thank you for this dance. Thank you for being here, and thank you for entering my life."

I stare at him intently, endeavoring to divine his thoughts. But all I perceive in this precise moment is profound sincerity. The wounded man within him already seems to be fading away, being replaced with a man eager to bounce back and enjoy life. I nod timidly, accepting his thank-you and responding with a faint smile. These last few days have been exhausting, and I feel a crushing fatigue weighing down on my shoulders. Jordan picks up on it.

"How about we get some sleep, Cupcake?"

Anxious and biting my lips, I nod and follow him to the bedroom.

"Hey! What's going on, Line?"

"Nothing. It's just that…"

"We are just going to sleep. We are both exhausted and there is still so much to say. And nothing can happen until I have laid out all my cards on the table. Then, it'll be up to you to make a decision. Until then, just let me hold you close."

"OK."

Without waiting any longer, we both slide under the covers, infused with his spicy, manly smell. He instinctively takes me in his arms and nestles his beard in the crook of my neck. We snuggle up against each other as if our bodies were destined to find each other again. "Jordan…"

"Hmm?"

"You never told me. Why the nickname 'Cupcake'?"

"Because the first time I saw you in your car, I fell for you and wanted to eat you up. You can be pretty crunchy when you get mad, but you also can melt deliciously well. You are perfect for me. Now get some sleep."

At these last words my eyes close and all I can hear is his slow, steady breathing. Throughout the night, he squeezes me tightly as if to reassure himself that I really am here by his side. Regularly, his mouth brushes my neck with soft kisses in his half-sleep. I feel alive in his arms: strong, and filled with hope.

Early in the morning, still foggy with sleep, I open my eyes but remain motionless. My thoughts take over and are in perfect harmony. I evidently love this man. For his strong fragility, for his comical arrogance, for the broken soul he wants to piece together again. Yes, I love him. I love him to death. I am still waiting for the remaining secrets, but my instincts tell me that Jordan is "the one." What people call the love of their lives. The one that barges in without warning and makes you love as profoundly as they make you suffer. The door creaks slightly and interrupts my train of thought, two small shiny black eyes shine stare at me. *Stringer*...

Carefully, so as to not disturb Jordan's peaceful sleep, I climb out of bed noiselessly and leave the room discreetly, scooping his companion up in my hands. "Hey, little thing! Are you hungry?"

Climbing up to nest on my shoulder, the ferret starts to pay me some attention in answer to my question. *Alright, that's a no-brainer!* I head to the kitchen, find a little bit of meat, and prepare it for him with a few chunks of vegetables. I pour myself a cup of coffee and settle in the living room with Stringer. I don't have time to emerge completely before Jordan barges in, panicked.

"Fuck!" He exclaims wiping a hand over his eyes.

I set the cup down on the coffee table, stand up, and try to console him. "I'm still here!"

"I thought that..."

"Stringer was hungry. I took the liberty of fixing him a small plate and grabbed myself a cup of coffee while I was at it."

Coming close to take me in his arms, he hugs me deliberately, then places a long kiss on my temple exhaling in relief. I nestle against him, fully relishing in this rush of tenderness.

"Good thinking. Make yourself at home, Line, you—"

"You thought I was going to leave without getting all the answers? Are you sure you are truly awake?"

Holding my face in his hands, he addresses to me softly, his eyes never leaving mine.

"You'll get all your answers, I promise. Let me just grab some coffee and take a shower. Then, I'll fill you in on all the rest."

"Sounds good to me. Go ahead and take your shower while I fix breakfast."

"Great, thanks. I'll be quick."

He heads straight for the shower while I get busy pouring him a cup of coffee. Then I head to the fridge and readily find the orange juice and some eggs. I am beating them when I hear someone knocking at the door. Since I can still hear the shower running, I decide to go get the door. Maybe it's Tim or Sonny stopping by to check on us. I continue beating the eggs as I open the door and find myself face to face with my worst nightmare. Abigail is standing in front of me, staring at me with a devious and disdainful look.

"Don't you live across the hall?" She says to me scornfully.

"What do you want?"

"Calm down, sweetie. If I want to see Jordan, the nitwit neighbor cannot stop me."

As soon as she finishes her sentence, the contents of my bowl end up all over her porcelain face. "The nitwit neighbor would like for you to know that eggs are excellent for one's complexion. Bitch!"

Squealing, she starts yelling like a total shrew: "You slut! What do you think? I already told you: Jordan always comes back to me. You think acting like a perfect little housewife and cooking him comfort food will be enough make him stay? Forget it! Jordan is mine!"

We are interrupted by a stern, deep voice coming from behind me. "What's going on here, damn it! Abigail, what the fuck are you doing here?"

My nerves get the better of me. Tears burn my eyelids, and

I can't contain them. The worldly princess covered in eggs starts yelling again, trying to get Jordan to defend her. "Look at what she did to me! I was just stopping by to check on you. Look at the state I am in!"

My anger comes bursting forth and I immediately say to Jordan, "She cussed me out! And it's not the first time! She is the one who threw your sweater in my face telling me you were hers and that you would always come back to her!"

Tears roll down my cheeks, I am about to take off when Jordan grabs me by the shoulders. "You are not going anywhere, Cupcake. As for you Abigail, get the hell out of here and I'd better not see you again. Got it? If there's one person here I belong to, it sure as hell ain't you, but her. You have no fucking business being at my place! Now, leave this building and don't ever come back."

He slams the door in her face and rushes back to my side holding me and whispering to me softly, "Shhh, calm down. I'm so sorry, Line. I never dreamed she would come here."

"Who the hell is that wack job? I must say, some of the company you keep is pretty shady."

"Come on. Let's sit down, Line."

Settling on the couch and pulling me toward him so I can sit on his lap, he goes on with his explanations. "She is my therapist, or should I say she was my hypnotherapist."

"Jordan, why... Are you... are you sick? What do you—"

"No, no, I'm fine, Line. Don't worry. But, after Jodie passed away, I was so devastated, I couldn't move past the grief. You know, twins have really tight-knit relationships. I missed Jodie terribly, and the guilt..."

A muffled sob comes out at the end of his sentence. I effortlessly wrap my arms around his neck and rest my head on his shoulder, showing him that I'm not going anywhere.

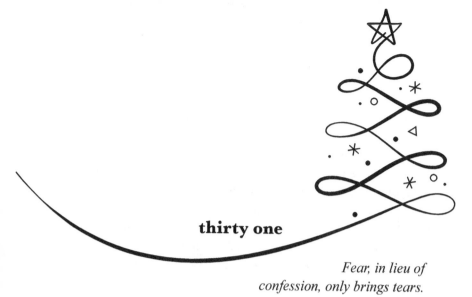

thirty one

*Fear, in lieu of
confession, only brings tears.*

Népomucène Lemercier,
Clovis

Jordan

I inhale deeply and resume my tale, drawing a bit of strength from
Line's body, cuddled up against mine. "I couldn't handle it. So, I
went to her for sessions during which I would relive moments of
our childhood. Not the final years when my sister had passed the
point of no return. No. Happy moments, carefree moments of joy.
It was as if I were going back in time. As if I could rewind my life
to erase what had happened."

"Jordan, all you were doing was destroying yourself even
more. You were stuck in the limbo of your past. All you did was
take a cue from your own sister. She gave in to drugs; you gave in
to guilt. She allowed drugs to destroy her mind, and you allowed
your pain to destroy your inner beauty. She succumbed to her
addiction, and you gave way to your psychosis. Your remorse is
slowly killing you. But beyond your pain, Jordan, there is a world
out there that is waiting for you with open arms. If you close your
eyes with cowardly disregard, no one will ever be able to help you
out. The past belongs in the past, Jordan. There is nothing you can
do to change it, you just have to accept it and move on."

"Yes, I know that, but it allowed me to limit the number of

gruesome images popping up in my mind. I was trying to fight the darkness with lighthearted moments spent during our childhood. I knew it wasn't an actual solution, it was more like a stopgap measure. But it would work for a while, then the images would come rushing back again. Then I would go back to see Abigail. I was powerless. I couldn't stay away, Line."

There is a moment of silence, then I address the elephant in the room. "What happened between the two of you?"

"Nothing. She always hoped it would, though. She always tried to wear me down, but I never saw her as anything other than my therapist. She became obsessed with me. I tried to limit the number of sessions to a bare minimum. But if I wanted to keep my head above water, I needed her. And she knew it. Sometimes, I told myself that as a hypnotherapist she must have conditioned me to return to her. It was like a drug. In pain when you are jonesing and relieved when you get your fix. It's pathetic, I know. I was doing precisely the same thing to myself that I would ride Jodie about. In a less intense way, admittedly, but still, I was strung out.

"Jordan, you tried. Nobody is entitled to pass judgment on another person's pain. There is usually much more to it than meets the eye. Fighting doesn't only mean hitting back! Fighting means struggling against yourself, finding the strength to get up again, moving forward, and allowing yourself to continue trying. Fighting means accepting assistance, welcoming a helping hand to regain your strength. Every little step forward is a victory. Why on earth did you hide all that from me?"

Caressing my face gently, Line knows just what to say as she reassures and encourages me. She is my beacon, the one I am drawn to, the one I want to follow. "Because I was convinced I didn't deserve happiness, I failed at being a brother despite my promise to always be there for her. Losing someone is too painful, so I wouldn't allow myself to get close to anyone. I was in enough pain as it was. More would have been impossible to handle. Besides which, who would have stayed if I had confessed to killing my sister? My head was in complete disarray. Then, you entered my life."

"You mean I wrecked your car!"

"No, Line. You wrecked my heart. You woke it up. On the staircase, you told me, 'One day this heart will awaken, and I will be there.' You were right."

She runs her hand through my hair, probing me with her sparkling eyes. We are both overwhelmed with emotions. Deciding to take a break, she tells me softly, "I also promised you breakfast, but the eggs never made it to the pan."

How not to smile at her effort to lighten the mood? "They ended up in exactly the right place! I approve! I'll go get you another cup of coffee and bring mine while I'm at it."

She follows me to the kitchen, sits on a stool, and watches me fill up the cups. I'd be lying if I said I was not distressed. So many emotions make my hands a little unsteady, and my heart too because I am still uncertain about the decision she will make. I hand her the steaming mug, and she thanks me with a smile.

"So, this guy Styx. Was he your sister's dealer?"

Taking a piping hot swig, I grip my mug until my knuckles turn white. Just hearing the name infuriates me. "Yes. He was part of the gang she hung out with on campus. He was the one that pushed her downhill. When she came to live with me, I had no idea where he was. But apparently Jodie knew and kept it to herself. He was dealing on Albert Dock, which was where we ultimately found her. Then he was off the grid for a while. He moved his dealings elsewhere. I ran into him several times in clubs like LK1. It always ended up in fistfights."

"But do the police know? I mean, do they know he's guilty?"

"Of course, but they didn't have any evidence to hold him. This guy is really slick. But now they are closing in."

"How so?"

"I spotted Styx when I was leaving Abigail's place, and I followed him. He was headed to the Docks. And when Styx talked to you at the Beatles museum, he showed his hand. If he was there, it means he has resumed his business in that area. Victor notified me right away."

With eyes wide open, Line's mind seems totally boggled by everything I just revealed.

"What? Victor?! But how?"

"He stopped by the shop. He knows all about Styx. His little brother used to hang out with him for a while. You must know he got tangled up with the justice system, right?"

"Yes. He did indeed tell me about that. So, Victor knew about Jodie?"

"No, not about Jodie. Did you know he even threatened me? Victor tried to protect you by ordering me, and my infinite baggage, to stay away from you. But, after we explained that we were trying to bring Styx down, Victor agreed to help us."

"How?"

"Styx is the one who trashed our shop. In doing so, he allowed me to set a trap to catch him red-handed. While he was trashing everything like a deranged lunatic, he dropped a bag of dope with his initials on it."

"Was that what the guys gave you the other morning?"

"Correct! Victor went to borrow a car from Devon, my mechanic, and parked it near Albert Dock. Tim's cousin who works with the police lent us a video camera, that we placed inside the car so we could observe Styx's movements and bring him down for drug trafficking. Then, of course, we turned the bag over to the authorities. It shouldn't be long before this piece of trash ends up behind bars and rots in jail."

Line turns pale and starts shaking like a leaf. "Hey, Line, are you alright?"

"I thought you were mixed up in some shady dealings. When you left town, I even thought you were doing drugs when in fact you were just trying to avenge your sister and bring this bastard down. And that woman, that Abigail, there's something about her that troubles me. I… you… have to remain levelheaded. I know that this… this…"

"Calm down, please."

"Jordan, I understand that she kept you afloat, but something is off! Her behavior today only confirms my concern. It's outrageous! Do you realize that coming to your house goes against all codes of ethics?! It's sick. She completely overstepped her bounds. Have you ever even considered that? Last time, when she threw your sweater in my face, she made herself out to be your partner, not your doctor. Had she been to your place before? Did you invite her over? Did you insinuate that you would like for her to come over?"

"No, no. Never! I have always kept my distance. I realize

now that the woman is toxic. If she behaves that way with me, she probably does likewise with others. Until now I've been in denial, only thinking about how she helped me. But now it's clear that I can't allow her noxious behavior to continue. I was under her spell for way too long. Thank goodness it's over."

"You have got to report her if you want to prevent other patients from falling into her clutches."

"You're right, Line. We can't let her keep that up. I won't see her anymore, but I'll let Tim's cousin know about her professional transgressions. From now on, it will just be you and me."

"Why did you go to Inverness?"

"Because it was time for me to make peace with my past so I would be able to build a future with you."

"I... I don't understand."

"While the guys were setting up everything to bring down Styx, I was busy facing up to something else. My entire past is located in Inverness, Line."

"So, if I understand correctly, you grew up over there? Is that what you're telling me?"

"Yes. And I had not seen my mother since Jodie passed away. I was so ashamed of my failure that I cut all ties. I was unable to look her in the eye, to bear the depth of her sadness. Yes, it was selfish because her pain was even greater than mine. Even so, I refused all contact for six years. But you made me realize that I had the right to move on, to lead a happy life. Thanks to you I found the strength to go back there and face her."

"How did she react, Jordan? Please tell me you guys made up. You can't continue being alienated. You have both suffered so much. It's—"

"She is expecting us tomorrow at her place for Christmas dinner if you are up for it, Line. I know I hurt you by trying to keep you away from me. I also realize that I'm not the easiest person to live with. But will you ever be able to forgive me?"

I stand there with bated breath, awaiting her answer as one would those of a prophet. The kiss she gives me speaks louder than a thousand words and seals my love for her indelibly. I return it softly, while holding her tightly, tears of happiness and relief raining down upon my cheeks. This space in time, the one that marks the moment when your life turns on a dime thanks to love, is the gift of a lifetime. For the rest of my life, I will cherish this moment of deliverance from my demons with Line by my side. "You are my Christmas miracle, Line."

"I believe I love you. It's as simple as that."

My heart leaps out of my chest so much do these simple, honest words intoxicate me. The poison that was flowing through my veins is replaced by a sea of love and tenderness for this lovely little woman with dazzling eyes. It feels like I am waking up from a long sleep to rays of sun caressing my skin. I feel myself coming back to life, and damn, it feels wonderful! "I believe I do too. Is love contagious?"

"Sometimes."

"So, then it's official: I'm freaking crazy. Crazy about you!"

* * *

The next morning, we wake up arms and legs entwined, attached to one another for fear all this was but a dream. I am delighted to realize it's indeed very real. And all good. Here she is, in my arms, in my bed, and in my heart. Last night was short, intense, sweet, and passionate. I made love to her like never before, determined to fulfill her every expectation, desire, and wish. This is the most beautiful relationship I have ever had, the kind that allows you to open yourself up. Sure, it got off to a rocky start, but it was all worth it. And if I had to, I would do it over and over again to feel the joy of finally finding each other again. I turn and look at her at length in the dark as she sleeps languorously with the hint of a smile on her lips. I look up at the clock and see that it's already four in the morning. It's still pitch dark outside, and I must curb my craving for her body. We agreed to leave at 5 AM, so we could arrive at my mother's by noon. Instinctively, my finger caresses the skin that I feasted on endlessly the night before. Eventually, she opens her eyes slowly. "Hey! Merry Christmas!"

"Merry Christmas to you too!"

"It's time, Cupcake."

"Mmm, just a little longer."

I kiss her softly and can't help whispering in her ear. "If

I stay in this bed with you one more minute, you will have to call my mother with some excuse as to why we aren't coming. Because if I start, I won't be able to stop."

"Mmm, but you drained me dry."

"Just wait until we get back then you will really know what drained means," I tell her teasingly. "I'll go make some coffee. Strong coffee."

"Right. Make fun of me."

Stretching languidly like a kitten, she finally gets up, naked, spectacular, swaying her hips gracefully as she walks to the bathroom. I am under her spell. She is so scrumptious that I can't take my eyes off of her. My manhood stands at attention. Fuck, she excites me!

"I can tease you too," she says playfully with a mischievous smile.

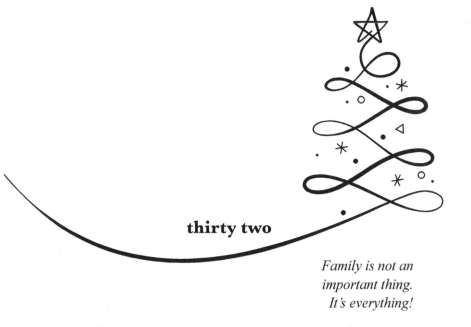

thirty two

*Family is not an
important thing.
It's everything!*

Michael J. Fox

Line

In life, there are essential things that can't be ignored. Such as the
heart. You must listen to your crying heart in order to learn to love
it. Whisper its pain to alleviate it, murmur truths that only it could
understand, and watch it come back to life. Yesterday, our hearts
conversed, they loved each other, and today our souls are one.

On the road to Inverness, in northern Scotland, I can't
help but admire the man sitting by my side. He is handsome, in a
raw and wild way, he is strong and proud, but above all he looks
unshackled. Of course, the past will always exist, and Jordan will
need all my attention to get over it and turn over a new leaf. Every
day will be a victory to be won over the darkness that took him
over.

"Are you doing okay, Line?"

"Doing wonderfully."

He takes my hand in his, brings it to his mouth and kisses
it gently. Oh, the sweet sensation of being loved! I let myself
be carried away by happiness as I gaze out the window at the
falling snow. Culloden Moor is so beautiful, it seems chimerical,
and the vast plains stretching around us appear to be floating as if

suspended in religious silence. These grounds that once witnessed horrible wars, today are peacefully covered in a thick white blanket. "It's… magnificent!"

"Yes. Jodie was passionate about these places, about their history. When we were kids, she used to tell me countless stories about the tragic and victorious things that happened here, sparing no detail. I'm certain she would have loved you!"

"Introduce me to her, Jordan. Help me get to know her better."

"What do you mean?"

"Talk to me about her every day. Tell me how much she loved to laugh at your shenanigans, what her favorite food was, who would win when you raced each other, or who took off the training wheels first. Let these glorious, sequestered memories resurface Jordan. Let's keep her among us. Let her shine in your heart to appease it."

Pulling over skillfully despite the snow, Jordan stops the car before taking my face in his hands and placing a fiery kiss on my lips.

"You. Are. My. Angel. I. Am. Head. Over. Heels. In. Love. With. You."

Then, just as quickly as he stopped, he starts driving again, leaving me to celebrate this spellbinding new step towards better days. It's a little after noon when we turn on to a winding stone driveway that leads to a picture-perfect house. The beauty of the place is stunning with its meticulously trimmed heather shrubs. And the stone façade adds undeniable charm to this home where he grew up. We get out of the car right away, a little stiff from the long trip. My contemplation of the grounds is interrupted when the door opens, revealing an elegant woman whose amber eyes are filled with kindness.

I hang back, watching Jordan reunite with his mother in a lingering hug that is filled with love and sadness at the long, lost time. Both rendered speechless by overwhelming emotion, they seem to communicate with implicit looks alone. His mother still in his arms, Jordan turns around towards me and tells her, his eyes filled with tears, "Here she is, Mom. This is Line. Line, this is my mother, Rose."

I move forward and blush a little under Jordan's piercing gaze. "Mrs. Miller, it's a real pleasure to meet you."

"Please call me Rose. 'Mrs.' is too formal, don't you think? Line, I don't have the words to thank you."

She hugs me warmly, and I can feel the wealth of emotions this moment symbolizes. For us all, a new life begins.

"Alright, come on in quickly. Let's go warm up. Jordan, I prepared your room."

"Thanks, Mom. You ladies go on in, I'll get the bags."

His mom's arm over my shoulder, I enter to find the interior of the house decorated in Rose's image. Sweet, welcoming, and cozy. As we go into the dining room, I become aware of just how much thought Jordan's mom put into preparing this meal. A gorgeous table is set in our honor. The bright, white tablecloth is covered in gold embroideries that sparkle under the light of the crystal chandelier. Plates, silverware, glasses. Everything is tastefully laid out in a very refined manner without being gaudy or flashy. The result is just perfect. I wore that gray skater skirt that Jordan loves so much, and I am glad I did because Rose is also dressed to the nines.

Then we sit down at the table and, to start things off, Jordan proposes a toast. As he stands there awkwardly raising his glass, my heart melts for this man who is trying so hard to reconnect with his former life. "I would like to propose a toast to the future. But, also to both of you, the loves of my life. You never stopped believing in me despite the pain I caused you. I'm sorry. Deeply. I promise that, from now on, every one of my days will be dedicated to loving you. Mom, Line, Merry Christmas."

He kisses us in turn, comes back to my side, and then we dig into the delicious feast his mother prepared. We talk about everything: my shop, Jordan's, what I like, how we met. I tell Rose how my grandfather took care of me after my parents passed away. She explains how she lost her husband when Jordan and Jodie were only children. But mostly, we share the happy memories. We laugh. In short, we become a family.

Often, I catch Rose looking at her son in awe. Her adoring look speaks volumes about the love she has for him and the relief she feels that he has finally come back after all these years. We linger at the table until mid-afternoon, topping the mouth-watering meal off with ice cream yule log. Suddenly, I notice Jordan's eyes and seem to be unsuccessfully looking around for something. "Jordan, is everything alright?" I ask, placing my hand on his thigh.

"Yes, everything's fine. It's just that… Mom, you don't have a Christmas tree?"

Lowering her eyes to conceal her sadness, Rose shrugs her shoulders sheepishly. "All alone, I didn't really see the point in brightening up the house. The three of us used to decorate the tree. I don't have the energy to do it by myself."

"You still have the decorations, Mom?"

"Yes, of course. They are all boxed up in the attic, but why do you ask?"

"Because today, there are three of us again. So, I was thinking that if you're okay with it, I'd go cut a fir tree so we can decorate it together."

At hearing this idea, my heart is overwhelmed with love for this man who has so much of it to give. Jordan has gone all-in, and every new step forward is a giant leap. And the more I see this side of him, the more the truth about my feelings become self-evident. He is the one I was waiting for, the one I wanted, the one I will love forevermore.

"Oh, what a wonderful idea, my boy!"

"Is the ax still in the shed?"

"Yes, yes, it's still in the same spot."

"Great! Come on, Line, we are going to cut our first fir tree together!"

Excited, I put on my coat while his mother hands him a set of keys.

"Here! It's cold outside, you might need them. Everything has remained exactly as it was. I went by there every day to check."

Hugging his mother warmly, Jordan thanks her and grabs me by the hand leading me outside. We walk happily in the snow, hand in hand, for ten minutes until we arrive at the edge of a forest lined with fir trees. My cheeks are pink from the cold, I look at the immaculate white scenery with fascination.

"Come on, the shed is this way."

Finally, we arrive in front of a big red wooden structure that looks like the exact replica of a movie set. As we enter, we see an entire lifetime of labor. Tractors, tools, a workbench. I'm looking around when Jordan says to me plainly, "It's my father's shed. He was a lumberjack, like Tim's father. That's probably where he got his passion for woodwork. Jodie and I were still young when he had his accident. A bad fall. It was important for us to keep this place intact. Everything here breathes of him."

Curling up close against him to shield him from those painful memories, I answer tenderly, "He would be proud of you today."

"Thanks. Come on, let's go find that fir tree!"

One hour later, we admire the fir tree resting on the ground. It is perfect! Neither too big nor too small.

"You know, Line, I have a present for you, but you'll have to wait until we get back home."

"Me too. I have one for you, but you'll have to wait as well."

"We have what we need, Line, 'us.' It's the most beautiful gift of all."

"You got that right, my bearded hipster!"

He mumbles with pleasure, catches me by the hips, and pulls me close to him possessively. Kissing me all over my neck, he murmurs in my ear as he pushes me against a tree, "Mmm, I love it when you say that. I love everything about you. I want to love you right now, Line. Right here."

"Here? Now? It's a little cold for that, don't you think?"

"Follow me," he says guiding me towards the back of the shed. "Are you afraid of heights?"

"Uh, no. Why?"

He points to the top of a tree and I look up. Through the foliage I spot a treehouse perched on high.

"It was Jodie's and my hideout. Come on, climb up!"

Once at the top, I'm at a loss for words. It looks like a wooden studio apartment, furnished, cozy, with a bed, a dresser, and a coffee table. Behind me, Jordan wraps his arms around my waist and pushes me all the way to the bed kissing me incessantly. Voracious, our bodies seem to be searching for one another, desiring each other more and more. His hands caress me with an almost bestial desire. My whole body is on fire when his fingers slip under the delicate lace of my underwear. Teasing me until I go wild, he strokes my clitoris enthusiastically. My back arches with pleasure, I hold on to him tightly, massaging his toned butt through his dark jeans. His expert, ardent caresses continue, and then he goes down on me with abandon. Fire courses through my veins, I am dizzy with pleasure. His soft beard in conjunction with his tongue, warm and moist, have me screaming with pleasure. I am pushed to the limit, shuddering with pleasure, when he slips two fingers inside me while sucking on the sensitive tip of my intimacy. He comes and goes, tantalizing every single one of my nerve endings, and then slips in a third finger, going deep with agility. I can't breathe. I gasp as my orgasm comes quickly, making me scream even louder.

While I attempt to catch my breath, he looks straight at me and whips out his thick member engorged with desire.

"I want us skin to skin, with no barrier. Nothing will come between us anymore. I am clean, Line. I get tested regularly."

"So do I. And I'm on the pill."

With a dazzling smile, I pull him onto me. Not being able to contain himself any longer, he penetrates me vigorously and then withdraws slowly savoring the thrill of this very first contact. The passion of his thrust can only be compared to the love I feel for him. Powerful, he comes and goes with more strength, taking us all the way to the bursting point where we share an orgasm of unparalleled intensity. It is as if our bodies had merged together. Our panting is the only thing disrupting the calm that reigns around us. As we catch our breath, I can see fluffs of floating snow through the skylight. They seem to surround us protectively, like a barrier.

Today, on this 25th day of December, I am a very happy woman.

Jordan made love to me in the clouds, and my eyes are filled with stars.

***

Later, back at the house, after we decorated the tree, we gather around it. Our eyes sparkle with joy. This scene brings about feelings that make my heart sing. Our families were destroyed, and now, from those ashes, we are building a new one. It is hard not to let emotions take us by surprise. Each one of us has suffered, cried, and loved. In a corner of our heart, there will always be traces of the past. But today, life resumes his course. We look towards a promising future. Rose speaks warmly, in her hands she holds a wooden star rimmed with gold. "In the past, when my husband was alive, we used to hang the star together at the top of the tree. Would you join us and perpetuate this tradition?"

"It would be an honor, Rose."

And thus, our hands place the ornament at the top of the tree, symbolizing the unity of this family.

"Mom, these last six years have been a nightmare, but I promise that you will never again be alone for Christmas."

"Nothing would make me happier. Except maybe becoming a grandmother," she says winking mischievously at him.

He fiddles with his beard; I believe I see him blushing. But he looks at me bravely and answers without breaking eye contact, "It might be a little early for that, Mom. But I assure you that as soon as Line is on board, I'll get right on it. Maybe we'll even outdo you and dad. Who knows? Triplets?" he says beaming. "What do you say, Cupcake?"

My cheeks burst into flames at his enthusiasm about our future together. I let his words course through me softly, and a single tear slips out and rolls down my cheek. "I... uh... I didn't know you wanted to have children."

Caressing my cheek to wipe away the teardrop, Jordan makes then the most beautiful declaration of love. "I didn't either, until you came along."

Laughing and crying at the same time, I answer looking him straight in the eye as Rose looks on fondly. "Sign me up for a whole tribe of little bearded spies!"

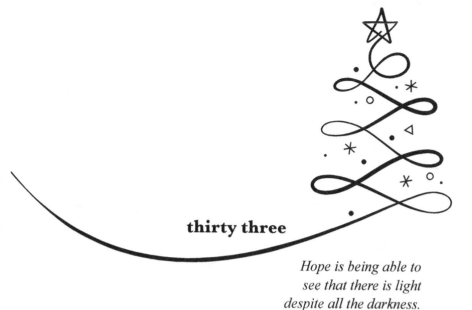

thirty three

Hope is being able to
see that there is light
despite all the darkness.

Desmond Tutu

Jordan

The next morning, on the road back to Liverpool, Line and I are closer than ever. We reach for each other's hands constantly as if fearful to see this growing happiness disappear. I know I still have a long way to go. But with Line by my side, I am ready for anything. By the time we get home, we are exhausted from the drive. Stringer is happy to see us again, and we go to bed early. Well, more or less. I lose myself in her body over and over again. We quench each other's thirst with matching intensity. Her sighs are like a breath of fresh air, always bringing me a bit closer to the light.

At daybreak, we are worn out but satisfied from our lovemaking; we look at each other in wonder. My phone rouses me from my contemplation, I pick up, absentmindedly, without checking caller ID. "Hello?"

"Jordan, this is Elliot, Tim's cousin."

Suddenly, the caller has my undivided attention. I get up, turn my back to Line, and stand in front of the window.

"Listen, I've got news. You need to come by the station. It's urgent."

"Tell me what's going on, Elliot."

"I can't tell you over the phone. Come as fast as you can."

"Tell me you got something to lock up that piece of shit, Elliot!"

My fists are clenched as I wait for the answer.

"Yes, we got him. But we need you here. We found something else."

I hang up and no sooner do I turn around than Line is right behind me, wrapped up in our sheets. She places her hand on my shoulder to soothe me. I am no longer alone. I can do this. I'll bring down Styx, that scumbag. I turn around and hold her tightly in my arms. "I have to go to the police station for Styx's investigation. It shouldn't take long."

"I'm coming along, Jordan."

"Are you sure?"

She looks me straight in the eye, slides her small hands behind my stiff neck, and plants a soft kiss on my lips. "You are no longer alone. We are going together."

As we drive to the station, a wave of anxiety makes it hard for me to breathe.

"Are you alright, Jordan?"

"Yeah, well, it's a weird feeling. I have been waiting so long to see this guy get taken down! I'm worried about what they are going to say. What if they can't lock him up?"

"But you did tell me Elliott assured you it was all good, right?"

"Yes but... What he said after that..."

"I can't imagine what else he would have to announce. Maybe he just wants to prepare you for the possibility that the procedure might take some time?"

"Like that creep hasn't caused enough trouble as it is. You are probably right."

We park in front of the white building and push open the door together, hand in hand. It is bustling inside. People typing, some talking loudly, others rushing around. It is as frantic as I feel. Line's hand squeezes mine, giving me courage, so I smile at her and draw her near. "Alright, let's do this."

I look around for Elliott when I spot a silhouette, from the back. "He's over there. Let's go!"

We hurry to him, and he greets us with a worried look on his face.

"Elliott, I came as fast as I could. This is Line," I say, looking at her lovingly.

He nods hello to her and asks us to follow him into a private office. Elliott's demeanor is making me uneasy. He places a file in front of him.

"Jordan, we watched the videos we got from the car. We clearly see Styx dealing and even threatening some girls."

I wipe my sweaty hands on my jeans and let out the breath I had been holding.

"Great, you can book him then, right?"

"Yes, yes, Jordan. Consider that a done deal. However, we found something else. It's… it's a bit tricky to talk about so…"

"What is it?"

He opens the file and grabs a photo that he slides over to me. "Jordan, do you know the person there with Styx?"

I grab the photo and see Abigail chatting away with that bastard. I frown, swallow with difficulty, and try to connect the dots. What possible explanation could there be for her presence in that photo? I notice Line turning pale when she sees it, so I squeeze her hand to comfort her. "Well, yes. That is Abigail Loxford, my therapist. I… I don't understand why the heck she is with him. It doesn't make any sense."

"Listen, Jordan, what I'm about to tell you is not easy. It seems that your therapist knows Styx very well. In the videos, we see them meeting regularly. That's why we started investigating her. There was something fishy about that woman, so we got a warrant to go search her place."

"A search warrant? But why? I have never seen Abigail take drugs."

With one hand he rubs the back of his neck. He seems suddenly seems embarrassed and the tension in the room is so thick I could choke. He grabs a remote, and warns me cautiously, "We found videos, Jordan. At her place. Recordings of her hypnotherapy sessions."

"She was recording her sessions, so what? Lots of

practitioners do it. What are you not telling me, Elliott? Just play the fucking video!"

"Jordan…"

The video starts and I feel nauseous. I can be seen arriving at Abigail's place for my last session. I take off my sweater, sit down on the couch. Then she brings me a glass of water which I drink, as usual, and she lights up some of those damned incense sticks. Then she starts talking to me and gradually I close my eyes. I am afraid of what I will hear when it is in fact what I see that paralyzes me. I watch her lift her tight skirt, straddle me, and rub against me like an animal in heat. Her hands slide along my chest and unbutton my shirt as she continues rubbing herself against my penis. She starts kissing me, scratching my pecs with the tips of her nails, leaving that mysterious mark.

This time, I'm going to puke for sure. I jump out of my chair, run my hands through my hair, and howl with rage. Line is flabbergasted at the sight of me being straddled by Abigail the wack job. Her hands are covering her mouth and her eyes wide open in shock. I look at her horrified, I don't know what to say. Here I am on this fucking video being manipulated like a puppet by a woman with no scruples whatsoever. I punch the wall. I feel sick to my stomach. My ears are buzzing, and I'm trying to control my breathing when Line takes my hand in hers. She makes me look at her, only her, not the screen. Our eyes meet as tears roll down my face.

"She will pay for that Jordan. Just like Styx, she will pay for that."

"How could I be so stupid that—"

"She tried to take advantage of your distress. But she failed, Jordan. Her life is over, her career too. We, on the other hand, have our whole lives ahead of us. This too shall pass."

Elliott chimes in tactfully, "She's right, Jordan. Both of them are done for. The glass of water you had at the start of each session was very likely laced with GHB. We found some in one of her drawers. How did you know Abigail?"

"I happened upon her business card while sorting through Jodie's stuff after her death. It read: 'Relive your happiest memories with the help of hypnotherapy.' I was missing Jodie.

Fuck, what an idiot!"

Elliott nods apologetically, confirming my doubts. "We think they set up a very profitable business together. Styx probably supplied drugs to Abigail, who in turn, scammed her clients. We found a stash of credit cards, jewelry, and cash. They were probably splitting the profits. That is our current theory. Now, your story is a bit different in that she became obsessed with you. Right now, they are both under arrest, Jordan."

"She manipulated me from the start. She…"

"They won't get away with it, believe me. The list of charges against them are as long as your arm. I'll keep you posted about the case."

We all leave the office still engaged in conversation when a commotion at the other end of the room distracts me. I look up and meet Abigail's eyes, her hands handcuffed behind her back. Rage courses through me. The scenes from the video replay in my head and my rage doubles.

She calls out to me, shamelessly. "I love you, Jordan. I did all this because I love you. But you, you don't get it. You—"

I don't have a chance to answer before Line storms over in her direction, slapping her forcefully in the face, her eyes brimming with tears. The remarkable blow came so fast that even the cop escorting Abigail wasn't able to pull her away in time.

"That isn't love! It's manipulation! Your life is over bitch, but ours is just starting. You'll get a taste of your own medicine in your shithole. You make me sick."

I get to Line and take her in my arms to hold her tight. This little wisp of a woman is a real warrior, and she definitely doesn't hesitate to show her claws. I feel so proud of her, my heart soars. "Come on, Line. Let's get out of here."

I slide my hand in hers, and we leave without looking back under Elliott's satisfied gaze. Once outside, Line looks at me with concern.

"Are you going to be alright, Jordan? Would you like to talk about it?"

"No, I want to forget all this shit. I want us to move forward and never look back. But…"

"Tell me."

"Jodie. Will I always see her that way? Pale and broken?"

"No, but it will take time for you to get rid of that image. You will have to be patient and make it a point each day to remember that your sister was a good person initially. To remember much you loved her."

"Summoning her back every day from deep inside me so that you can get to know her better, correct?"

She nods quietly, her hand closes more tightly around mine, proof that I no longer am alone. She picked me, no matter how broken I am. The whole package. The nightmares, the angst... But I will show her I can do it. From now on, she can count on me despite those wretched videos. I don't want to waste a single minute. I've already wasted too much time. "Well, if that's the case, we might as well start now. Follow me!"

I take her to the car without revealing where we are going. I drive to Albert Dock when Line seems to realize where we are headed. Suddenly uncomfortable, she squirms in her seat and looks worried. "Jordan. Where are we going? Isn't here that—"

"Yes, it is, Line. This is where I found her. But I have beautiful memories with her here too."

I park and caress Line's face tenderly. While the discovery of those videos should have left me in a state of profound disarray, instead, they gave me a fierce desire to succeed. I want to move forward with Line by my side. I want to show her that with her help, I am ready to move mountains. I no longer want to get sidetracked. I have found my guiding star, the one that motivates me to plan for the future I want with my cupcake.

I point at the Ferris wheel standing in front of us and lead her towards the ride. Her eyes are filled with wonder and childlike joy. It warms my heart. That is what I want for her, for us. As we walk towards the ride, I lay the first foundation stone for our future. I open up to her and explain why we are here. "Every year during the holidays, Jodie and I would come here. It was a moment when we would come together again. She was always so excited, every time was like the first time. And I would see that light in her eyes again. The light the drugs had dimmed. My sister was such a passionate woman."

Line's eyes fill with tears, but I know she is not sad. Those are tears of joy at this emotionally charged moment. One day, one memory to bring Jodie back to life. This is the first of many more to come.

The festive lighting reminds us how special this Christmas is. It's our first Christmas together. The beginning of a promise I will never stop fulfilling. To make her happy. We slide onto the seat and slowly, the pod takes us up, way up, away from the world. Away from the past. Towards our future.

And under the clouds, I give her a blazingly passionate kiss.

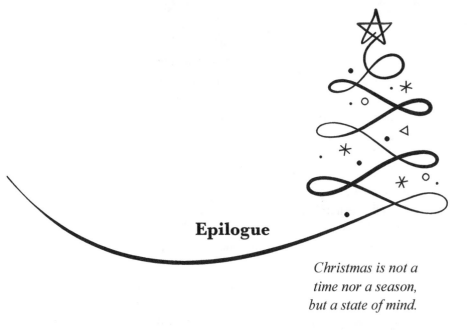

Epilogue

*Christmas is not a
time nor a season,
but a state of mind.*

John Calvin Coolidge

Line

On the way home, words are superfluous. We were blindsided by Styx and Abigail's appalling actions, but even though they left us speechless, we are also greatly relieved. That chapter is closed, and a new one begins as we set upon our path of living and loving together.

After a night spent desperately chasing away the vision of that video with shamefully passionate lovemaking, we wake up early in each other's arms, our legs intermingled amidst the crumpled sheets. Lazily, with the tip of his finger adorned with a steel skull ring, Jordan caresses my bare shoulder softly. "Good morning, Cupcake," he whispers in a voice husky with desire.

I turn to face him and caress his soft beard which love with every fiber of my being. "Good morning, you."

He covers me with warm kisses, and the wet trail his tongue leaves on my neck elicit a moan that he immediately captures with his lips.

"Mmm. Whatever your desires may be, I will try my best to fulfill them."

"You've already fulfilled them. All night long."

Eyes smoldering, he grabs my butt and makes me straddle him as his eyes devour my naked body before him. My legs, still shaky from the previous night's lovemaking, get goosebumps when I feel his morning energy grow. "You really let me have it last night; I'm still sore with pleasure."

"In that case…"

Jordan flashes a hungry smile, his rough hands take an even firmer hold of my butt, and he pulls me forwards until I am on his face. His insatiable mouth makes me explode with pleasure as the first rays of sun slowly peek through the curtains.

It is almost ten in the morning when his ringing phone rouses us from bed. A first call followed by another. Very quickly my phone seems to take over, informing us that each of our friends has returned to Liverpool. We rush to organize a get-together dinner so we can bring them up to speed and tell them about the recent events that we've been keeping to ourselves so as not to spoil their family time.

That is how we end up that very same evening all together at the Shiraz, Faruk's restaurant, reunited around an assortment of Turkish delicacies.

"What the fuck?!" Timothy exclaims smacking the palm of his hand on the table by his plate.

Our friends' serious looks are filled with anger when we tell them about our visit to the police station. In turn, they each offer their unfailing support.

Jordan takes my hand and kisses it tenderly before addressing us. "I'm a lucky man to have you all as friends. Tonight, there is much cause for celebration. Those two shitheads are out of commission, and they will rot in jail. And then, my path crossed that of the sweetest woman ever. Victor, Capucine, thank you for being there for Line. Timothy, Sonny, thank you for standing by me through it all. I know it wasn't easy but look at us now. What a beautiful family we are! Don't you think?"

Sonny raises his glass and takes a long sip. "Totally, dude! It freaking sucks that we didn't get to spend Christmas together, though. Speaking of which, I got presents for you guys."

Capucine springs up suddenly with childlike enthusiasm. "Hey! I know! We can work it out! Why don't we celebrate Christmas again? I mean really, Jordan is right. Friends, close friends, are like a second family. They support one another and stick together through thick and thin. So why shouldn't we do a second celebration if we feel like it? And I have presents for you guys too!"

Won over by Capucine's idea, Sonny cracks a giant smile. "You, beautiful lady, are simply a genius!" he answers winking at her and making her blush.

Jordan hugs me even tighter and kisses me on the head delicately.

"I love that idea! I have lots of Christmas parties to catch up on, don't I?"

Timothy taps him on the shoulder with pride. "That's right, buddy! It is so good to see you happy! When should we do it? The day after tomorrow? That should give us enough time to get organized, right?"

Victor rubs his necks looking embarrassed. "Shit! The day after tomorrow my little sister, Adelina, is coming to stay with me for a while. I don't want to leave her alone on the day she arrives. Count me out, sorry."

"What? There is no way you're getting out of this! Bring the sister, dude, and you can both celebrate Christmas with us. It's non-negotiable," Sonny shouts out decisively.

"Well, in that case, I'm in for December 29th! From now on, that date will be the official date of the Friends' Christmas Party!"

We all raise our glasses and toast joyfully. Faruk buys us another round while outside snow starts falling again.

$$* * *$$

Jordan

December 29

Taking center stage in my living room is a fabulous spruce. We prepared everything with care. Sparkling ornaments in silver and white transform the room spectacularly. The table, set by my cupcake, reflects exactly what Christmas is supposed to be. A festive time of sharing, of joy, and of gladness. The doorbell rings, and Line rushes to open it. At the doorstep, Timothy, Sonny and Capucine are all dressed up and laden with bags of gifts. Methodically, they all place the shiny packages under the tree. I take care of starting putting music on to perfect this atmosphere that continues to fill me with emotion. I choose a Fifth Harmony cover of the Christmas classic, "All I Want for Christmas Is You."

The first few notes start when the doorbell rings again. Timothy goes to open it and greets Victor who is accompanied by a sultry, young brunette.

"Hi friends, this is Adelina, my little sister. She is moving in with me for a little while."

I go greet them to invite them in, surprised by Tim's behavior. He seems to have completely zoned out. Introductions are made and we get the party started.

After a memorable dinner filled with joy and happiness, we exchange gifts.

Sonny immediately put on the sweatshirt Line gifted him, it reads: "The bearded man, try it, you'll like it."

Victor promises to start playing the guitar again, and suggests that he and Tim schedule a few jam sessions. He agrees but I can see he is uneasy. Adelina keeps staring at him and I can see that it's making him uneasy. As for the gift my cupcake got me, it is rather surprising. A second ferret that runs to meet Stringer right away, the latter proudly wearing an elegant black bow tie for the party.

As for me? Well, I got Line a carved wooden box, crafted by Tim at my request. I suggest that we keep note cards of every happy moment, every day. We will read them together, every year on Christmas Eve, to relive the year that just went by. New memories for a new life. Christmas is extraordinary but I want our life together to be magical.

Our tradition. Line is radiant, standing by the tree with a box in her hands. I feel as though my heart might burst.

A new song starts, Sonny inconspicuously dims the lights and invites Capucine to dance to "Oh Holy Night" remarkably covered by the band HomeTown.

The string lights are reflected in Line's eyes, and I realize I never want them to extinguish. I want her eyes to hold that spark of delight every minute of her life. When she wakes up, when she eats, when she thinks, when she looks at me.

I no longer want to live without her.

I can no longer live without her.

I want the joy of each day to shine in her eyes like it is doing at this very moment.

She is my Christmas miracle, my personal guardian angel.

She cut through the darkness and rekindled the light inside of me. Her smile chased my demons away, replacing them with clouds of kindness that have embraced my wounded heart. The past can't be forgotten, but it can be tamed. Line has conquered my pain thus affording me a glimpse of the splendor within.

I am a broken-hearted man in recovery.

And Line…

Well, Line is my healing.

* * *

One year later

Snuggled against each other in front of the magnificent tree dominating our living room, we await our friends. Our living room? Well, yes, two months after our last Christmas, we decided to take the plunge and move in together. We tore down a few walls and here we are in a magnificent, sprawling apartment.

Stringer and Boxer both seem fascinated by the ornaments and Christmas knick-knacks merrily adorning our tree.

Boxer? That's the name we picked for the ferret Line gifted me last year. I'll let you guess why. My little friend adopted him right away. I'll let you guess how he got his name.

Today I know I have fully recovered when I look at her and place my hands on her round belly. It brings me strength, and I can hardly wait to meet "our three little princes from the clouds," as she likes to call them. They weren't conceived on that first visit to the treehouse, but a few months later when we went back there, as we regularly do.

I will never be able to thank her enough for saving me from myself. But one thing is for sure:

I will forever love her, and them, with all my heart and soul.

Acknowledgments

Here we are, turning final the page. It is always with mixed emotions that we stamp the words "the end" on a story. Especially this story, since at the time it was completed, two chapters of my life came to a close as well. Writing this story was complicated and unsettling but also allowed me to keep my head above water. As I was writing this novel, I lost my father at Christmas time. One month later, my grandmother passed away as well. Two painful losses. Twice the sorrow. But as I lived through the grief, I called upon the pain to build this story. I was able to rely on the unwavering support of my man, who did everything he could to ease my sorrow. He lifted me up in the most beautiful way at a time when I was completely drowning. He is my happiest encounter, my happiest tale.

I also received powerful and touching acts of kindness from my friends and beta readers.

I think about Marie, my little angel who knows that when I become quiet, I need constant support. You were there to keep me afloat when I was silent. I cherished your comforting words when my heart was overwhelmed with pain. You didn't expect answers, you were just there, by my side, every day. Thank you.

Nadège, our friendship keeps on growing. Your presence, your words, your support are like a breath of fresh air. You can make me laugh through the ears, you get my singular sensitivity, and you show tremendous tact whenever I retreat into my writing bubble. Thank you.

Pauline, your words, your encouragement, and your steadfast support gave me the strength to deal with it all. You are one of the strongest people I know. An extraordinary mom, a brave hearted lioness. Always in my corner, you believe in me completely. Thank you.

Claude, how could I not mention you when your words are so impactful? Beta reader from the very beginning, you have been there, outspokenly honest, quelling my doubts. I always impatiently await your feedback because your unique commentaries often bring tears to my eyes. Thank you.

Thank you as well to all the bloggers, readers, and friends on social media. You are always there, following me, encouraging me, and your kind posts are real twinkles of happiness. They bring me strength. You motivate me to work even harder to bring you stories in which love meets courage, where anger often conceals heartbreak, and where friendship is a fundamental pillar of life.

A huge thank you to the entire publishing team that never ceases to bear with me. You guys rock!

And to each and every one of you I want to say, *"Je t'aime"*!

You have turned this simple adventure into an amazing love story.

Merci beaucoup!

Other novels from
WARM PUBLISHING

Falling for the Voice
by *Mag Maury*

The sexiest of surprises... and the most unbearable!

My plan was simple: Find a job quickly in order to make rent. And I found one. A waitressing job at the hottest pub in town!

Everything was going smoothly until he arrived: Matt. Sexy. Arrogant. Six feet three of muscles that drive women into a hysterical frenzy at every single one of his concerts.

This guy is really comfortable on stage and oh, so enticing. We girls can try to put him out of our minds but we end up wanting him anyway. And he knows it.

Except me, Charlotte. I say no!

Well... Maybe! After all, I have never really been good at resisting temptation...

My Stepbrother: A Sexual Revelation
by *Sophie S. Pierucci*

Cassie is a highly intelligent young woman... Too much so for her own good! And she is as daunting as she is intriguing. Carl, the son of his father's second wife, would hardly say otherwise!

Carl is the exact opposite of his steady father. He is a player and a slayer. Afraid of nothing and no one. Except for Cassie when she asks him to introduce her to the pleasures of the flesh.

And when the situation gets out of control, it is too late to turn back, and the two lovers find themselves ensnared in forbidden passion. Forbidden by everyone: society, their parents, their friends.

But how to resist the desire that consumes them?

The Amicable Pact
by *Ana K. Anderson*

She is about to get married. But not to him.

Quinn MacFayden, an accomplished expat businessman in New York, is set to return to Scotland in extremis to protect the precious family legacy. His 91-year-old grandfather is about to marry a perfect stranger sixty-six years his junior... And that is out of the question! Quinn swears it. Over his dead body will Dawn Fleming ever be part of the family!

But Dawn is not a future bride like the others. She is nowhere near the gold digger he imagined and, above all, she knows just how to stand up to him. And so a game of cat and mouse begins between them. A war with no holds barred and where surrender has never been so tempting...

About the Author

 Budding French author, Mag Maury, was showcased at the Paris Book fair in 2018 and is a rapidly rising star on the French literary scene.

Before becoming an author, she trained as a medical secretary then and decided to change careers and went into infographics. She actually started writing on a dare while she was bedridden after a serious operation. Once her first novel was complete, a friend encouraged her to submit it to a publisher and she did. Her career went uphill very quickly thereafter owing to her very charismatic novels that are as energetic as they are entertaining.

Mag is a self-professed compulsive reader who likes a wide variety of literature especially dark romanticism, urban fantasy and new adult fiction. She also likes country music, long walks and fine cooking. In addition, her creative spirit has led her into the world of visual art where her work has won awards.

Originally from Nîmes, she currently lives in a quaint river-adjacent cottage at the foot of the Cevennes with her significant other—an accomplished athlete who is her own personal superhero—and her Yorkie, Fanou. In the summer you can often find her down by the river and in the winter, at home, in front of a roaring fire.

CPSIA information can be obtained
at www.ICGtesting.com
Printed in the USA
BVHW031007041021
618090BV00008B/335

9 781734 596175